also by David Littlejohn

Dr. Johnson: His Life in Letters
Black on White: A Critical Survey of Writing by
    American Negroes
Interruptions: Essays, Reviews, Reflections
Gide: A Collection of Critical Essays
The André Gide Reader
Dr. Johnson and Noah Webster: Two Men and
    Their Dictionaries
Three California Families

THE
MAN
WHO
KILLED
MICK JAGGER

THE
MAN
WHO
KILLED
MICK JAGGER

a novel by David Littlejohn, 1937-

Little, Brown and Company   Boston/Toronto

FIRST EDITION

T/05/77

LIBRARY OF CONGRESS CATALOGING IN PUBLICATION DATA

Littlejohn, David, 1937–
  The man who killed Mick Jagger.

  I. Title.
PZ4.L78115Man [PS3562.I785]   813'.5'4   76–56752
ISBN 0–316–52782–3

The author is grateful to the following publishers for permission to quote
from previously copyrighted materials:
  Alfred A. Knopf, Inc., for "Tonio Kröger" from *Stories of Three Decades*
by Thomas Mann, translated by H. T. Lowe-Porter. Copyright 1936, renewed
© 1964 by Alfred A. Knopf, Inc.
  Chappell Music Company, for "I Don't Hurt Anymore" by Don Robertson
and Jack Rollins. Copyright © 1953 by Anne-Rachel Music Corporation.
Copyright and all rights assigned to Chappell & Co., Inc. International Copy-
right Secured. All rights reserved.
  United Artists Music Publishing Group, Inc., for "I Wish I Had A Girl" by
Gus Kahn and Grace Le Boy Kahn. Copyright © 1908, 1951, renewed 1936
Robbins Music Corporation, New York, N.Y.
  ABKCO Music, Inc., for the following songs by Mick Jagger and Keith
Richard: "Get Off My Cloud," © 1965 ABKCO Music, Inc.; "I'm Free," ©
1965 ABKCO Music, Inc.; "Jigsaw Puzzle," © 1968 ABKCO Music, Inc.; "The
Last Time," © 1965 ABKCO Music, Inc.; "Live With Me," © 1969 ABKCO
Music, Inc.; "Midnight Rambler," © 1969 ABKCO Music, Inc.; "(I Can't
Get No) Satisfaction," © 1965 ABKCO Music, Inc.; "Stray Cat Blues," ©
1968 ABKCO Music, Inc.; "Street Fighting Man," © 1968 ABKCO Music,
Inc.; "Stupid Girl," © 1966 ABKCO Music, Inc. All Songs All Rights Re-
served; International Copyright Secured.

Designed by Janis Capone

Published simultaneously in Canada
by Little, Brown & Company (Canada) Limited

PRINTED IN THE UNITED STATES OF AMERICA

We had fed the heart on fantasies,
The heart's grown brutal from the fare;
More substance in our enmities
Than in our loves; O honey-bees,
Come build in the empty nest of the stare.

—W. B. Yeats

... j'étais comme ces hommes mutilés
qui rêvent des béatitudes pour eux
insaisissables, et qui se créent un
songe dont les plaisirs égalent les
tortures de l'enfer.

—F.-R. de Chateaubriand

THE
MAN
WHO
KILLED
MICK JAGGER

# one.

Yellow. Yellow signs. Big yellow letters stenciled on concrete walls, walls that seem to run on and on for hundreds of yards. Funny that was what stuck in his mind, that out of everything else. That and the parking lot.

He knows he doesn't belong here, even from the parking lot. The very image of the place gives him the cultural shudders. Separated from him now by matched rows of sodium-vapor reflections off the roofs of three thousand cars, it looks like an obscene glass bandbox glowing off in the distance. Ronald watches through his windshield as the darkening shapes of his fellow pilgrims diminish into small black silhouettes, then converge into an army of ants moving up the ramps and into the region of icy, unnatural light.

He was scared, too. He couldn't pretend that he wasn't, or explain why he was.

He gets out of the car; shuts, locks the door; stands still. Then he sets one row of teeth tight atop the other, fixes his eyes on the cylinder of light, and marches toward it along with everyone else.

As he draws near the crowd thickens, the pairs and groups clot into a mob that moves very slowly up the ramp. Thousands of other people are moving up the sister arc that rises to meet it from the south parking acres, and these two monumental approaches, curving and ascending in air, give to the whole spectacle the quality of a pilgrimage. Le Puy; Vézelay; Mont-Saint-Michel. No: Saintes-Maries-de-la-Mer. The gypsies: from all points of the compass they come, converging out of the darkness into the region of light.

And such people. For five and a half years he had ordered himself, day after day, to accept the fact that they were harmless, they were human, they were people like himself. But it never worked. He could not argue himself into any sense of kinship with these creatures. He could feel himself contracting, physically and emotionally, feel as if he were made of something hard sleek and slippery like glass, as these fluid bands of gypsies poured past him like water, all lean bouncing boneless limbs streaming with hair and fringe and soft fabrics blowing in the wind.

As the procession of soft easy people pushes higher up the ramp, further into the yellow-white light, it is diverted here and there by immobile creatures, boulders in a stream. Last-minute buyers and sellers of tickets. Ranting political types, trying to melt down the mob. People with bells. People with posters. People with torches. Hare Krishna monkeys harassing everyone within reach to buy their foul-smelling sticks. Creeps in huddles (selling dope?). Before each new obstacle Ronald Harrington winces, shifts, feels his face shiver and then stiffen as he tries to avoid contact of body or eye: lepers.

At the top of the ramp, they are all herded through a dozen turnstiles by men in red blazers. Once past the chutes, Ronald finds himself (twenty thousand people find themselves) inside mindless, concrete-walled spaces, spaces of a dull cubic hugeness that have nothing to do with people. The arena was one of those barren, brutal buildings that reminded him of Antonioni movies, buildings that always seemed to be making some big social point, except that no one else even looked at them anymore, let alone took offense. He found himself hating such buildings with a hard, fixed hate. It was hard to believe they had not been designed to elicit precisely this response, designed as great hate symbols out of *Alphaville* or *1984.*

But everyone else seemed to take them for granted. People he admired lived half their lives in L.A. airports. His mother adored brand new muzaky shopping centers better than anything else.

A curving lobby corridor fifty feet wide went round the circumference of the building. To one side of it was fixed the glass sheathing of the cylinder, acres of thick glass divided by gigantic steel X's. On the other side were red and blue and yellow doors, each numbered and lettered for its particular function or plot of seats. In between were souvenirs, programs,

four

hot dogs, Cokes, the musty Victorian smell of all those Hare Krishna sticks, the happy pilgrims in faded Levi's and flapping fabrics and worn leather fringe, all somehow naked and at home in this monstrous tomb, flowing, knotting, meeting, parting as smoothly as the slip-slap handshake of blacks. For a moment Ronald thought of promenading around the circle himself. But he didn't like the idea of walking through all these people, so he went off in search of his number instead.

The wide center aisle of the arena floor: a great crush of flower people, teenyboppers, Hell's Angels, and lean loping bands of black boys hoping to slip unnoticed into the seven-dollar seats. Ronald finds a seat bearing the same number as his ticket, and sits down. The stage is set up perhaps a hundred feet away. He has a clear line of sight down the center aisle. No one will be pressing against his left side.

Knowing his base, feeling a bit more secure, he goes back and stands in the middle of the center aisle, and lets the funky, funny people crowd by. Already after seven: the show nowhere near starting.

A girl pushes past him, naked under a long, loose, raggedy gown, and for an instant he imagines himself lifting the raggedy cloth, feeling her (pinching her) there in the aisle, but the vision passes so quickly his mind scarcely realizes it has even gone by. To anyone who might have looked, he was just a stiff, serious, out-of-place man beginning to sweat, twenty-seven years old, straight and overweight, caught up in an endless stream of soft young coming and going bodies. (Inside his head is a spiderweb — dead bugs of dreams, taut strands of needs. But no one can see that.)

He gazes into yawping distances, tries to distinguish pin-size faces in the blackness a thousand feet away. Overhead, a giant circle of orange lights is dimming and rising; practicing; waiting. From far off behind in the building, tunnels of light play around the stage, chasing each other ponderously like anti-aircraft beams.

During the next three hours, the man in Row P feels more and more acutely what an alien celebration he has come to. During the next three hours, he comes to sense how different are his notions of time and order from theirs, these calf-like, incredibly patient people. Fifteen, twenty, twenty-five minute waits take place without a word of explanation, during which a kind of amiable electronic chaos maintains. Boy technicians in bluejeans drag off one group's gear and drag on the next's, push things back and forth, chat, change their minds: housewives trying to decide how to rearrange their living rooms, except that here the furniture is made up of gigantic gray boxes standing like so many refrigerators across the back of the stage, long black coils of cable, control panels, electric organs, drums. Ronald is disoriented by the freakish mix of primitivism and technology, by the unconcern for tidiness or schedule. It is all so unlike anything he has been through before.

Perhaps a quarter of the downstairs folk wander up and down the aisles the whole time. They are obviously accustomed to this sort of desultory nonevent, live their lives by different sundials and sandglasses than his. Ronald finally gives in and acknowledges that this casual stretching out of intervals into great recesses of time is to be the rule, and not the exception, and tries to ease away his impatience by wandering with the rest.

But there is nowhere to wander to. Police, or people dressed like police, keep shut every door out of the arena floor except two at the rear, and those, he finds, lead only to rest rooms and to long institutional corridors stenciled with yellow signs. Many boys seemed to be using one cavernous men's room as a place of refuge, a kind of club. Urinating alongside them, Ronald feels himself stared at as an intruder, but that may be only the suspicion of a spider's imagination.

He would have liked to stare at *them*, in any case. These skinny, long-haired youths are somehow of a different sex from his, and though he distrusts them absolutely, he wouldn't mind the chance to examine them unbuttoned. Of course he dares not, keeps eyes and fingers on his own affairs.

Washing his hands before the long mirror, he observes himself as part of the frieze of faces. Pale-faced and moonfaced, an ugly scar down his right cheek; a moustache that fooled nobody; overweight, overage, anomalous; everything about him unlike everybody else. His reflected eyes dart glances here and there at the reflections of his fellows. Every other toilet had no door, so every other toilet went unused.

Still, the vastness of the cold arena twanged on his nerves when there was nothing happening onstage. Uninviting though it was, the men's room was at least better than that valley full of death.

So he returned to the toilet twice more. On the third visit he was shocked to see two short-haired young men in red blazers leaning against the walls. On guard, it would appear; watching.

Watching for what? Homosexual acts? Vandals smashing up the plumbing? Pot? But surely half the people outside are already smoking it.

Whatever their function, the two ushers destroy the smoky camaraderie he himself had been disturbing, kill whatever escape appeal the men's room might have held. From then on he confines his promenading to the cold arena floor.

But by that time the three hours' wait is almost over. What they have come for is about to begin.

He had stayed in his seat through two and a half of the three preliminary acts, but they only confirmed his convictions about this sort of music. Thin as water, as skim milk, no more complex or intellectually resonant than a TV commercial. He could have come at ten o'clock and missed nothing. He could have stayed *home* and missed nothing. It was so absurd, the cultural pretension of the advocates of rock music. Why, there was *nothing* here — nothing. Talentless children magnifying their ineptness with electronics.

A British foursome had come on first, in spatter-dyed undershirts and great Brillo pads of hair, armpit or crotch hair growing wild on the head. A voice on the loudspeaker pleads *Let's give the boys a welcome,* but no one does, as one of them begins to burble some phrase over and over, striking great whiney plangs on his electric guitar. His mates pound and grunt away, all of it amplified into jet-exhaust volume, to a murderous, mind-aching noise.

As if it meant anything. As if it mattered. As if a giant enlargement of a pea made it something more than a pea. A large movie screen had been hung above the stage to reflect magnified closeup images of the performers out to the faraway seats. But in the case of this feeble lot, the effect struck Ronald as simply inane, like the Brobdingnagian amplification of their noises. Such a pitiable fraud. He glowers at the stage, trying to irradiate scorn. Such punky little faces, such a runtish surly crew trying to mask its inadequacy under filthy fat tangles of hair all of this blown up on the screen to twenty feet across great juicy blackheads the size of plates; take away the enlarging devices the amplifiers the TV cameras, the whole witless sham would gape like a naked asshole.

Ronald tastes his reaction; unfair. But no matter. He has come to enjoy feeling himself fill up with hate.

The next act confuses more than annoys him — a vulgar, sleek set of blacks. The lead plays a sky-blue guitar, and keeps rearranging his sonic effects by twisting the dials on a silver control box alongside his microphone. The harmony group behind him, in electric-blue and silver suits, croons a stylized series of doo-doo-woo-woo effects, and dip-sways in unison from side to side. The few blacks in the crowd become noisy and happy: one of ours. Whites applaud with dutiful respect: one of theirs. Ronald passes.

Another long wait, another shuffling of gear, and on leaps a twitching, moaning little creep, bare-bellied and spastic, dressed in filthy white pants cut to below the pubic hairline. With him at the front is a fat lady in a muumuu, shaking her breasts. The two of them start into an elaborately programmed fake-erotic routine. Ronald leaves before the act is half over, to make his third and last trip to the john.

I should never have come.

He lived his life by *means* of escapes like this, used them to keep himself in balance. He didn't even pretend otherwise anymore.

And the ticket had all but fallen into his hands.

But this was absurd.

eight

I was wretched enough before, he thought, now I feel worse, more nervous, more high frenzied, more at odds . . .

They had picked him up late at night, hitchhiking home from the garage. The one on the right, the one not driving, had pulled out a gun. He could see his face now, smell the steel and the sweat, the dusty inside of an old car. A Chevy.

But then there were only two of them. Now there are thousands.

The last wait is the longest of all. The voice on the loudspeaker breaks promise after promise. "The boys are on their way now," it lies. Ten minutes. "They're waiting back here, folks, but you'll have to clear the aisles before they can come on." Fifteen minutes. "They're backstage now!" it shouts, electronic, excited. *Liar,* Ronald thinks.

The tension in the arena mounts rapidly, unpleasantly. At one point, in fact, a proletarian takeover of the floor appears imminent, as more and more of the upstairs people try to move into downstairs seats.

The six- and seven-dollar people (outnumbered ten to one) begin to get scared. Hell's Angels swagger about, drinking wine from gallon jugs. Shouts spurt up from the upstairs ranks, here a *shit,* there a *fuck,* obscenity answering obscenity. Black bullyboys in white sweaters appear from behind the police and begin ordering people back into their seats. The tension climbs, spreads: electric. Unavoidable. Ronald fights against its power, but there is little he can do; dissolving as an individual, he feels himself transmuting into one twenty-thousandth of some irrational undefinable thing, a web of shrilly humming nerves.

When? When. Twenty, twenty minutes they have waited. He stares at his watch. 20. Thirty. 35. 36. 37. 38. 39. 39½. 39:45. Forty.

Are they doing this on purpose, he asks himself, *trying* to generate this tortured mass response?

"Are they doing this on purpose?" he asks again, out loud to his neighbor this time. "Huh?"

Soon.

nine

Soon.

It must be soon.

It was.

It is.

"Ladies and gentlemen, The
ROLLING STONES."

An all-engulfing wave breaks up the walls of the arena, the internal pressures of twenty thousand people exploding, standing up and screaming, because the boys are *here*, real and alive; they are really *here*

two.

As a rule, Ronald Harrington avoided mob scenes, particularly when the mobs were made up of people with whom he had nothing in common. As an undergraduate, he had stayed away from the campus most Saturday afternoons in autumn, so as never to have to *see* the sort of people who went to football games, all ruddy cheeks and pom-poms and superficial passion. He went to movies in the city at midweek matinees; that way he could sometimes have almost a whole theater to himself. Other people pressed in so terribly, forced one to feel and smell their clothes, to look at their faces, to think about their lives. And he didn't want to.

Early in his junior year at Berkeley he had discovered scholarship and art, simultaneously. He changed his major from business administration, the family choice, to art history, a choice all his own, and decided that for the rest of his life he would remain there, in the protected, cogent, and civilized world that combined scholarship and art.

From the family's point of view, even his being at Berkeley was cause for concern. They had moved out west when he was fourteen, from Granger, Indiana, to San Salvador, California. But in many respects San Salvador was closer to Granger than it was to Berkeley, the morally suspect university town fifteen miles to the north.

San Salvador was one of a flat, sunbright sprawl of new lower-middle-class suburbs that had burgeoned since the war along the Eldorado Freeway, conservative all-white towns populated with southern and midwestern families like the Harringtons. Until 1940, they had been little more than a scattering of bungalows and crossroads stores between flat open acres of farms. By 1957, when the Harringtons came, San Salvador and its neighbors were coalescing into the classic California landscape: little white or pastel one-family, one-story stucco blocks plonked down like toy Monopoly houses on fifty-foot lots, row after row, street after street. East to the ocher-brown hills they stretched, west to the freeway, north almost to the factories and the black jungle of Oakland, south as far as the land speculators could reach. Along empty sidewalks they ran, identical front lawns divided by almost identical hedges, here and there a scraggly new palm or an old walnut or cherry tree left over from the orchards and farms they had long since displaced. The only accent in the pattern was created by the boulevards: occasional lines in the grid twice as wide as the others (two lanes for parking, four lanes for traffic), lines that ran straight on for miles, along which were set the used car lots and new car showrooms, Grand Auto Supply, Kar Kover Kings, the A & W and Kibby's and Foster's Freeze and real estate offices and western bars, each with its own parking lot (for patrons only). Each Thanksgiving, different-colored Christmas lights were looped across the boulevards. Giant plastic foam candy canes and vacuum-formed Madonnas were wired to the date palms and the streetlights. They were taken down again each January, to be stored away for another ten months.

In five years, the population of San Salvador had doubled, in eight, quadrupled, in ten, octupled. By 1969 it was eighteen times the size of Granger (which had shrunk in the meanwhile), and three times the size of Fort Wayne, Indiana, the big city with tall buildings where Ronald and his parents were born.

Ronald's parents quickly discovered their own kind of people — at church, in the shopping center, in the big Ford dealer's in Hayward where his father worked. For his older brother, Hank, California was like coming home. Out on the prairie, he had dreamed of a cut down, glo-maroon Mercury convertible all his own, of cruising down eight-lane freeways at eighty miles an hour; of having money and freedom and

twelve

sharp haircuts and clothes; of wild, do-anything California girls; of getting quit of school and joining the navy. Now, within scarcely more than a year, he had it all. And his parents didn't even seem to mind.

But Ronald Harrington hated California.

In Indiana, first in Fort Wayne, then in Granger, they had lived in solid two-story wooden houses, houses with high ceilings and attics and big screened porches, surrounded by plenty of trees. The porch of the Fort Wayne house, which had once been his grandfather's, went around all four sides of the house. Here the family sat on summer evenings. Here, on hot nights, the boys slept in their underwear on a pair of creaky iron cots, talking in low voices of a million things, watching fireflies burst into light and then disappear.

In 1954 they had moved to Granger, a farmer's market town forty miles to the north, because Ronald's father had made the big decision to go into business for himself. He leased a showroom on Detroit Street in Granger, a showroom that had been abandoned when Studebaker gave up making cars. There he started his own Ford agency, Harrington's Ford of Granger, Indiana.

Unfortunately Ronald's father was a terrible businessman. He wasn't sharp enough to deal with his own mechanics, let alone Lorenzo County farmers or the Ford people up in Dearborn. Within three years he was sixty thousand dollars in debt. He had developed a duodenal ulcer, gained twenty-five pounds from his ulcer diet, and begun to go soft and gray, like a seal. The bank manager in Granger, the people in Dearborn, his own father-in-law advised him to quit. Ronald's mother *begged* him to quit, to give up and move out to California. Her sister Kate had been out in California since the war. Kate and her husband had a trailer and a speedboat and their own summer house at a place called Russian River.

So one Sunday after church, Henry Harrington drove out to his father's farm, fourteen miles south of Fort Wayne. It had not been an easy thing to do. His ulcer gave him no peace that whole day. When he came back home, well after dark — Grandma Harrington had insisted he stay for supper — he had signed over to his father his equity in the house and the Ford garage in Granger, along with most of the furnishings and stock. He had also put his name to a paper acknowledging that he had, as of this date, received his fair share in the family estate, and would make no claim on it in the future. In return, old Mr. Harrington had assumed responsibility for his son's debts. He also gave him a check for ten thousand dollars, with which he was to start over again in California.

It was all very hard, for Ronald no less than for his father. Ronald liked Granger even better than Ford Wayne. Here, he had decided (when he was twelve years old), was where he wanted to live out the rest of his life.

Granger, Indiana, was a self-sufficient little town of about four thousand people, the county seat of Lorenzo County. It had a solid brick courthouse with a cornerstone inscribed 1878, set back in the middle of a grassy square. There were a movie house and a bank and about two dozen stores (including Harrington's Ford) along Detroit Street, which stretched out north and south on either side of Courthouse Square, forming a part of Highway 89 between South Bend to the northwest and Fort Wayne to the south. The Victorian brick library and fire station stood up a gentle rise near the rear of the courthouse, where Amish farmers from a nearby settlement still tethered the horses that pulled their handmade black carriages. Five cross streets turned off east from Detroit Street downhill to the creek, the railroad tracks, the two rival grain and feed mills — Hennessy's and the Co-op — and beyond, to Central School, the high school, and the big tree-girdled open space of Lorenzo County Park.

The house his father had bought stood on one of these quiet downhill streets. It was a tall wooden house of the 1880s, its white paint faded and peeled. With it came a small apple orchard and vegetable garden, a disused barn, a summer house, and a woodshed, all scattered about two weed-overgrown acres alongside the creek. Ronald grew his own corn and beets and carrots, marigolds and zinnias. He picked apples, played in the creek, read library books lying on his back on the wooden benches of the summer house. In the woodshed, a previous owner had stored and left all manner of things, including a red-bound set of *Woman's Home Companion* from the 1920s, which Ronald used to pore through in the cobwebs, like some wonderful treasure book from a faraway world.

The ache of Henry Harrington's failure generally spread to the rest of the household, as the months in Granger wore on. At mealtimes, his father fussed at what he could and couldn't eat. His mother sighed and frowned at his fussing. His brother bolted his food and slammed out of the house. Ronald sat eating in miserable silence.

His brother had been bitterly unhappy at first, since he hadn't been able to go to high school in Fort Wayne with all his friends. But he had his learner's permit now, and was allowed to drive secondhand cars from Harrington's Ford, which did wonders for his status at Lorenzo High. He argued with his parents, told Ronald all he knew about sex, and stayed out of the house as much as he could.

Despite the family's difficulties, Ronald had been more happy than not in the house, in the town. The house was full of old-fashioned nooks and crannies. There were window seats along the stair landings, and a cellar for his mother's canned fruits. There was even a tiny square tower room you entered by stooping through a low door off the attic.

Ronald made very few friends in Granger, but he didn't mind, much. He had begun, by the seventh grade, to live most of his life in imaginary worlds. The old house with its dark woodwork, its busy wallpapers, its strange lights and noises; the rambling, weedgrown garden, and dank and pebbly creek composed into a perfect seed ground for dreams.

Dreams of what? Of travel, of power, of olden times. Lately of sex. Daydreams spun out of the piles of books he carried home on his bike each week from the library up the hill, books on knighthood and clipper ships and World War II, *A King's Story* and *Annapurna*, Sabatini and A. J. Cronin. If he had no library books on hand, an old Book of Knowledge set Grandma Hemann had given them would serve just as well. He loved to take two or three volumes to the window seat, or the tower, or the summer house, or his own room, choosing his spot according to his mood. There he would read of Oliver

Cromwell, or how to make puppets, stare at gray illustrations of the old *Mauretania* sliced in half lengthwise, or of Greek and Roman statues without any clothes on.

Even school he was able to incorporate into his private world. He was in junior high now, and, though much of the day was still the same drone, he found the stories in the new readers grown-up and enchanting. "The Pit and the Pendulum." "The Sire de Malétroit's Door." They were reading poems too, and Ronald tried to memorize the ones he liked best. "The Raven." "The Highwayman." Even James Whitcomb Riley, the great Indiana poet. If the teachers were strict, and wanted nothing but silence, the history and geography books in junior high were as fascinating as library books or encyclopedias. In ninth grade they started biology, and for weeks Ronald dragged the creek, hiked miles out into the country with an empty mason jar hunting for insects and frogs and odd plants. He sent away five dollars to Chicago for a collection of fossils.

The school was too small, the teachers too tired for there to be much pressure to do anything — to get A's, to put on plays, to play football, to go to college. So Ronald was free to dream and read and wander, as brother Hank was free to go to hell.

With six of Grandpa Harrington's ten thousand dollars, Ronald's father had made the down payment on a brand new home in San Salvador. It was located in a twenty-block tract called Rancho del Oro. The place had been recommended by his brother-in-law, who sold real estate in Oakland, at the Rancho del Oro developer's office. Henry Harrington had no trouble finding a job at Val Bigger Ford in Hayward, even if it was something of a comedown to be one of a dozen salesmen on the floor after having owned your own shop. But the pay was good (everyone here seemed to need a new car, or a second new car), and credit came almost frighteningly easy. After the grim struggle of the last three years in Granger, California seemed like heaven. Within two months of his arrival, Ronald's father had not only a brand-new ranch-style home and a job, but also a console TV, six new charge accounts, and a houseful of new furniture. He also had the one car he had held onto out of the showroom stock in Granger, a new 1957 tan and cream Montclair station wagon.

They had left most of their old furniture in Indiana, but it hardly mattered. The new house had come with lime green wall-to-wall carpets (even in the bathrooms) and matching nylon draperies, so they had no need for any of the old curtains or rugs. The kitchen was fully equipped: electric stove with *two* window ovens, dishwasher, garbage disposal in the sink, marbled green formica counter tops. The vinyl-asphalt flooring was tinted and ridged to look almost exactly like tile. All they kept from the old house were the pots and pans, the dishes and glasses and silver. And as soon as all the new charge accounts were opened, Mrs. Harrington started replacing her old kitchenware with aluminum pans, and plastic TV trays, and pottery mugs in bright California colors more in keeping with her marvelous new kitchen.

It was smaller than the kitchen in Granger, she would grant you that. There, they had eaten breakfast and lunch around a big oak table with carved lion's-foot legs that stood in the middle of the room. Two hand-hooked rugs of her mother's nearly covered the floor. There, she had had a separate pantry, and a gigantic glass-front cabinet for best china and glassware. The morning sun, there, made its way in first through the apple leaves, then through the fragile greenery of herbs she grew in little pots above her sink.

But this new kitchen was *so* much easier to work in and clean, she wrote and told her mother. She loved it. She missed nothing. She wished she had had it all along.

But Ronald found it a desert, all of it, his room, the house, the backyard, the street, the neighborhood, the town. To him the barren newness of California seemed a shabby exchange for the clutter and density, the weeds and woods and dream stuff of Indiana. Here there was nothing to make dreams out of, nowhere to curl up in or escape to. His room was a low-ceilinged, beige-painted plaster cube, exactly like the other rooms, with green carpeting exactly like theirs, a constant nubby nylon softness underfoot that gave him the creeps. There were floor-length green "drapes," as his mother called them, on his one small window, but all the window looked out on was an identical small window (with blue drapes) in the house next door, scarcely eight feet away. He had put his ship models and his fossils and his schoolbooks on the new shelf under the window. The old Books of Knowledge were there, too, in their own oak case. Thumbtacked over his bed were two travel posters of Paris. He had bought them with his own money to brighten up the room.

But still the room felt like a cell, like a barren, alien, dreamless cell, and he hated it. He spent hours lying on his back on the bed, trying to make out maps of foreign countries in the beige plaster trowel work of the ceiling.

His brother's room was next to his: a pile of dirty clothes and car magazines his mother picked up once a week. Then a bathroom. His parents' room. Their bathroom. Kitchen, living room, dining room. Except for the kitchen, they were *all* beige plaster cubes with green carpeting and drapes and little punched-in windows that looked nowhere. No stairs, no window seats or crannies, no attic or cellar, no tower or woodshed, no creek or orchard — no trees *at all* yet, though two wisps had been duly planted and staked in the backyard. A flat, white-painted, lath-and-plaster box divided into smaller boxes, one of a hundred, one of ten thousand, on a fifty by one hundred foot lot. The patch in front of the house was gradually turning into a lawn. Tending it was Henry Harrington's big weekend occupation, along with going to church and making waffles and fiddling with the horizontal control during football games. And of course washing the car. Hank and his father both washed their cars in the driveway on Sunday afternoons. It was the only common interest they had left.

The backyard was a flat rectangle of dirt (or, in December, mud) with its two skinny treelets. Since Mom had a new washer and dryer in the garage, there was no need for a clothesline, even. She talked about planting some more shrubs, maybe some bulbs. But Dad had decided to have a patio laid instead, the way the Lees had, sometime next year, so they just left it bare for now — except to buy an aluminum and plastic web folding chaise longue, three basket chairs, a redwood table and benches, and one of those $12.95 metal barbecue grilles on wheels from Sears, which they used twice and then put away in the garage, along with everything else.

Since they were all lined up and exposed, each identical to the next, no one in Rancho del Oro ever used his front yard, except to mow and weed and clip in. The only change came at Christmas, when a few Rancho del Orans put up cardboard Santas on their roofs and plaster Nativities on their lawns, lit by blinking colored lights. No one sat on his porch, either — it would have looked lazy and midwestern. Besides, the porches were all about six by four feet, with scarcely room for a door-mat (embossed "Welcome," or "The Harringtons"), a bicycle or two, and the metal shopping carts that housewives wheeled home from El Rancho Shopping Plaza and often neglected to wheel back.

Like the Harringtons, most of the families on the 700 block of Coronado had two cars. One was kept in the driveway, the other parked out in front. Garages in California were for stor-ing things, or doing woodwork, or for the dog's bed, or Cub Pack meetings, or simply for keeping clean. And just as people were rarely to be seen in their front yards (except on week-ends, when they were either gardening or washing their cars), so rarely were they to be found on their sidewalks. Everyone in California seemed to drive or be driven everywhere, or else stay indoors. Ronald found no more charm, or human content, or food for imagination outside the house than in.

He tried very hard to discover the resources he craved. His parents had joined Trinity Methodist in San Salvador because Fred and Kate belonged, and because it looked like such a well-to-do church. But it meant nothing to Ronald. If he still went to church with them on Sundays, it was only out of a dim sense of filial duty, a sense his brother had lost somewhere on the journey west. Trinity Methodist was a modern, two-hundred-fifty-thousand-dollar triangular affair of ocher brick and redwood set in two acres of parking lot, with a gigantic stained glass window at its prow. Rows of comfortable beech-wood pews set at obtuse angles to each other converged on a cylindrical, stainless steel pulpit. The floors, of course, were carpeted. The inside walls were teak.

The city park in San Salvador was mostly paved, for tennis

courts and parking lots and playgrounds. The only grass there grew on the football and baseball fields, which browned out in the hotter months. There was a community swimming pool, but no creek, no pond, no natural water anywhere. San Francisco Bay (or at least an estuary of it) lay across an eight-lane freeway, its scummy shoreline taken up by industry and army docks except for a tiny patch of beach on the western side of Alameda Island, six miles away.

In a year he would be sixteen. Then he could drive a car. But in the meantime he had to walk, or ride his bicycle, or be driven wherever he wanted to go — usually by his parents. Hank rarely had the time. During the first summer, Ronald tried to share a few of his brother's new pleasures, when he was tolerated: rolling a few lines at the bowling alley, cruising the drive-ins on San Jacinto, hanging around customizing shops. But it was hopeless, they both realized, and so Ronald stopped trying. They had moved unbelievably far apart since Fort Wayne, Ronald and his brother. Their days of talking late into summer nights on cots side by side had been left back in Indiana with Grandma Hemann's old rugs. There had been one terrible double date to the Alameda Drive-In, where Hank and Julie tried to tease Ronald (and Julie's thirteen-year-old sister Helen) into doing things neither of them wanted or knew how to do.

That took place late in the summer before school started, a month after his fifteenth birthday, and pretty well marked the end of Ronald's efforts to join the California way of life.

High school days in California were not something Ronald looked back on with much affection, later on. He didn't have to go through the indignities of "initiation," since he entered San Salvador High as a sophomore, not a freshman. But that was about the only torment he was spared in the three years he spent there.

At fifteen, he was heavier and shorter than most of his classmates. White, pudgy, bodyhairless, and genitally underdeveloped, he undressed and dressed as quickly as he could in the boys' locker room for P.E. Some of the lean, mean athletic types in the class — the Tidwell-Brady-Korzeniewski crowd —

loved to make fun of his shape, or snap wet towels at his bottom, or sneak up behind him to pinch the soft roll of fat at his middle. He was once brought to tears when Ted Korzeniewski walked up to him in the shower and squeezed the pink flab around his nipples as if he were a girl.

He grew so ashamed of being overweight that he stopped taking off his shirt or going swimming, and hence stayed unnaturally white in a country where great-grandmothers work desperately to keep themselves bronzed. Beach parties at Alameda, Stinson Beach, even Half Moon Bay were all the rage, but Ronald rarely went along. At the sophomore class picnic at Stinson he stayed dressed the whole day, and nasty-minded kids made jokes about "that time of the month." He was narrow across the shoulders, thin in the arms, and he walked in a kind of shuffling waddle. He usually stood slightly stooped (*Stand up straight, Ronald*) with his hands in his pockets (*and take your hands out of your pockets*).

His face was round, almost moon-shaped. The chin was small and weak, the ears stuck too far out. His keen eyes, eyes of a bright sky blue, were as nervous as a rabbit's and set close together under whitish blond, almost invisible brows. His cheeks were so pink they looked rouged in so pale and round a face, touched with the faintest baby down. His nose (he had been a very cute baby) turned up slightly at the end. He wore his whitish yellow hair in a half-inch crew cut, as almost all the kids had in Indiana. In California now, crew cuts were less common. In any case, the style did nothing for Ronald. It heightened his babyish aspect, his soft round vulnerability. In almost every photograph taken of him during his high school years — even those in which he is smiling for the camera, or caught off guard — there is a glint of frightened defensiveness, even a kind of terror in the close-set eyes: small, bright, beautiful blue eyes unprotected by visible lashes or brows.

Teenage fashions for boys had become very important in northern California during the late 1950s. Pegged pants, elaborate D.A.'s, off-white cashmere sweaters, a whole new set of styles came in with each school term. Boys took after-school jobs to get money for deep purple shirts with giant collars, fruit boots, huge copper belt buckles, Japanese motorcycle jackets embroidered with dragons. Ronald did spend some money on a pair of low reddish brown boots and a couple of heliotrope shirts, and he got an orange angora sweater for Christmas. But such gear only drew more attention to his shape, and he reverted to the anonymous costume of gray cotton workpants and white or blue cotton shirts, which he wore with the sleeves rolled up. In winter, such as there was of it in San Salvador, he switched to one of his fourteen-dollar Pendletons, or the maroon and yellow school jacket Aunt Kate had given him for his fifteenth birthday, just before he started school. School-color jackets had gone out of fashion by 1957, but she could hardly have known that.

Ronald did well enough in class at San Salvador. By his junior year, in fact, he was getting almost all A's and A−'s, except in physics. He was called on to explain math problems at the board. More than once Mrs. O'Neill read his sophomore English themes aloud: his "Description of My Room," for example (a small classic of its kind); or the very clever "Why Is an Orange?"

But such attentions, however satisfying to one's *amour propre*, can end up being very burdensome to a boy of fifteen. At San Salvador High, brains were not popular. And popularity was terribly important.

Two teachers in his junior year, Mr. Creighton in history and Miss Golubin in French, seemed to understand this, and tended to praise his work privately, in late afternoon conferences, rather than in front of a class. Miss Golubin, a civilized French-Canadian lady of forty, was delighted at Ronald's efforts to learn her native tongue. She talked to him of Paris and Quebec, let him take home the copies of *Paris-Match* that piled up in the school library. He was one of two boys in her French Club. She appreciated his hardiness in going against the norm by enrolling in a "girls'" class, and saw to it that he was chosen vice president of the club.

It was she who first put seriously to him the idea of going to college, and if possible to Cal, where she had received her M.A. years before. Students at San Salvador thought of going on to college far more than those at Granger, if only because that was what one *did* in California. But (although all new seniors were ritually taken on a tour of the campus) very few thought in terms of the huge state university nearby. They regarded it as an oversized, inaccessible kingdom, society blondes at fraternity football parties, a lot of commie intellectuals. But Miss Golubin made it sound a wonderful place to be, and Ronald entered it on his register of dreams.

Mr. Creighton, who taught auto shop and history, persuaded Ronald to enter a competition in American citizenship sponsored by a local newspaper. He lent him college-level textbooks to prepare for it, and quizzed him privately after school on things like cabinet members' names and the bases of America's moral superiority. At home, on his own, Ronald virtually memorized the two Barnes & Noble U.S. history outlines, and in the end he won third local prize: a check for two hundred dollars. The school received a new set of the Encyclopedia Americana for his victory. Mr. Creighton got fifty dollars just for being his teacher. And Mrs. Sibbel, the principal, called him into her office for an embarrassing few minutes of congratulations. (*And what do you plan to do with all that money, Ronny? I don't know for sure, ma'am. Maybe buy a car. Oh dear: even you. I hoped perhaps you'd want to save it for college.*)

His small triumph was announced at assembly, where the principal handed him a giant gilded trophy and his check in front of the entire school. A picture of him accepting the trophy (and looking even more terrified than usual, more a fat, newborn puppy) appeared on page three of the Sunday *People,* and page one of both the San Salvador *Shopper* and the Hayward *Star-Advertiser.* His mother got no end of calls.

He did, in fact, buy a car with the money, his first car, a 1950 Chevy Tudor in two-tone green. But aside from that (and his father wouldn't even let him drive it until he could pay for the insurance), winning the contest brought him little satisfaction. If anything, it pushed him all the farther outside the wild and racy high school world he longed to be a part of.

He still read great armloads of library books. Clipper ships and Books of Knowledge yielded place to more serious works of history and biography. Mrs. O'Neill had tried to elevate him from A. J. Cronin and C. S. Forester to Steinbeck and early

Conrad, from "The Highwayman" to Shelley. But his reading was for the most part still voracious and undiscriminating. He plowed through every selection in the Reader's Digest Condensed Books, new volumes of which his parents received in little cardboard boxes every three months. *Time* magazine he thought the very pinnacle of sophistication, and he tried very hard to imitate its wit. Lost inside the world of a book, almost any book, almost any *magazine,* he could forget how much he wished he were different from what he was.

But it was getting harder all the time. The reality of the world of Tommy Tidwell and Korzeniewski, of beer busts and night football pressed in so hard.

There were others like him at school. Albert Grossman, Ron Leitner, bright girls like Carla Stanton and Jo Crosby got even better grades than he did. But (except for Carla, who managed to pull off the trick of getting A's *and* being popular, because she was beautiful, and a girl) the other brains in his class were all total creeps — weedy, pale, pimply creatures with glasses — and he couldn't bring himself to claim kinship with them.

One man might have helped: Mr. Zack. Both his junior and senior year English classes were taught by Adrian Zack, a Stanford graduate with a red beard, who had once written a pornographic novel under another name, or so went the rumor. No one had ever tracked it down. Ronald wanted desperately to please him, so that Zack would invite him to his office after class, read his papers aloud. He stayed up past midnight agonizing over book reports and themes for his classes. He chose books, subjects, styles of writing he thought surely would impress this dapper young cynic, the youngest and cleverest teacher he had ever had. He fantasized private sessions with Zack in which the older man gave him praise and assistance, offered him sherry and cigarettes. He constructed little playlets at night, before going to sleep, of himself and Zack reading or taking long walks together.

But none of it ever happened. Zack gave him A's (or A−'s) regularly enough, but his written comments rarely went beyond a few petty corrections, the word "Good." He called on Ronald to answer only when no other hand was raised — and then often with a kind of half sigh, half sneer, as if he were winking a warning to Tidwell and his crowd: watch this smartass sounding off.

Despite his obvious taste and intelligence, Mr. Zack *did* seem to prefer the neckless, noisy jocks, the C−/D+ characters from the football and basketball teams, the boorish track stars and swimmers. He called on them first. He laughed good-naturedly at their mistakes, even at their inattention and horseplay. He directed his jokes in their direction, especially his double entendres. One day they snickered for ten minutes over all the dirty jokes he had found in *Macbeth*. He sometimes ate with them in the cafeteria, or borrowed cigarettes from them after school. He gave them lifts in his MG, smacked them matily on the backside.

It all left Ronald feeling cheated and confused. The one teacher he most respected, the one adult he might have expected to appreciate his ideas, the one he would have done *anything* for, seemed determined to ignore and insult him, and to consort with his enemies instead.

In almost nothing did Ronald's real interests coincide with those of his classmates. Oh, there were bound to be other loners, other freaks in a class of two hundred and forty-seven — others who couldn't force themselves, deep in their hearts, really to *care* about twin pipes and the Everly Brothers and beating San Leandro.

But there were certain qualities possessed by most members of the Class of 1960 at San Salvador High that Ronald Harrington did not share. If you look through the senior pictures and profiles in the 1960 *Golden Oak* — a thick volume, bound in soft gold and maroon imitation leather, with an oak tree embossed on the front — you will see pages of little faces in rectangles, faces of girls, pretty girls, perky girls, pimply girls, pudgy girls, girls in flips and beehives and kisscurls, all smiling and lipsticked, their eyes and lashes touched up for Senior Picture Day, all but a few in the sweater and pearls the photographer had asked them to wear. And pictures of boys, in *their* little rectangles, all posed in a costume of white dress shirts (without ties) and V-neck sweaters most of them wouldn't have been caught dead in except on Picture Day. D.A.'s, modified D.A.'s, Presley cuts, flat top and fenders, a few rococo L.A. greaser styles, classic crew cuts, shaven heads, Roman emperor bangs — all the things California boys did with their hair, in the years before hair came to matter so much. The boys had soft American potato faces, bright-eyed and characterless, faces that looked as if sixteen interesting racial strains had been superimposed to create one dull set of Identikit features: too thin or too fat, freckled or zitz-ridden, glasses or big ears, no-necks or giant Adam's apples. Here and there was the self-conscious lad who *knew* he looked like R. J. Wagner (because all the girls said so), and who therefore puffed out his lower lip and combed his hair with greater than ordinary care.

Loves the Shondells and Jumpin George, but goes to bed with a modified V-8 named Bobbie Jo—named after who, Fred? And plans to be an auto mechanic.

Has eyes only for R. L., keen on Rocky Roads and Ricky Nelson. Pom Pom Girl 58–59, Cheerleader 60. Senior Play, Drama Club. Ever to be seen at Kibby's after DeMolay dances, Beverly may go to Cal State and study drama. Hollywood, here we come!

Football manager for two years, J.V. baseball, Auto Club. Works after school for Grand Auto. Digs Little Richard and M. M. (or was it M & M's, Chuck?) the most. Ambition: to take over Grand Auto, and then the world.

How could Ronald Harrington hope to fit among the likes of these?

Ronald Harrington, 4-B. French Club Vice President 58–59. *People*'s Americanism Contest 3rd Prize, 1959. Life member, C.S.F. Pretends he likes to read and listen to KBAK (wherezat?) and also driving along the ocean. (Who with, Ronald?) Works at Old Vienna Bookstore, will study Bus. Ad. at U.C.

He was not yet so emotionally independent that he could look into the others' world from outside without yearning to join it. Some Saturday nights (once he had managed to afford the insurance) he would drive his car to school, park outside the gym, and listen to their music. For an hour or so, he would just sit there in the dark and watch them, laughing and shoving, coming and going in couples and gangs. Then he would drive away, car radio tuned at full volume to his classical music station, flushing out the din of Elvis and Ricky. Sometimes he drove across the bridge to the city, then the full length of Geary Boulevard, just to stare at the waves of the ocean.

Or he would go to night football games and spend the time under the bleachers or out by the cars, trying to catch the musty, drunken thrill of it even from there. In the stands, he knew, kids were huddling close under car coats and blankets, handing back and forth pints of whiskey in paper bags, cheering for maroon and gold players out under the lights, the boys hoping for a fuck or at least a good feel before the night was through. He caught glimpses of them in cars or behind the grandstands, tripped over them on the ground, kept as far clear as he could of the knots of chuckling, menacing males who came without dates, who came looking for trouble and always found it. Once he had been trapped by a gang of black kids from Hudson High. ("Hey fat boy. Whatcha looking at?") The memory of what they had done left him sick to his stomach for weeks.

Of such memories were created his San Salvador years.

He kept walking at the football games, partly to keep warm, partly to look as if he were going somewhere, meeting someone, as if he had something to do except hang around lonely and bored on the sidelines of other people's sports. When the game was over, the cars all revved up in a great happy din and barreled out of the parking lot, barreled out to Kibby's or the Mountain House, to Grizzly Peak or the beach, to nude parties with lots of booze at the house of somebody whose parents weren't home or didn't care, to all sorts of wonderful things Ronald vividly imagined as he drove home alone on a cold, clear, clean November night.

"Nice game, Ronny?"

"Yes, Mom."

"Who won?"

"We did. Twenty-one to six."

"That's nice. Go anywhere after?"

"No. I didn't feel like it."

"Oh, well, dear. Another time. Leave the porch light on. Your brother's still out. Good night, sweetheart. Give mother a kiss."

"Night."

"Good night, dear. Quietly, now. Your father's asleep."

Yeah, I can hear him. The fat slob.

Ronald had been working in the Old Vienna Bookstore, after school and on Saturdays, since the beginning of his senior year. After school he opened cartons, shelved books, wrapped parcels, made deliveries, and swept out the store. Saturdays he waited on customers, along with Mr. Koerner. And every day he was there he walked up and down the shelves, looking at the books, sometimes touching them, opening a few of them, curious to know what was inside every one. Mr. Koerner let him buy books at a twenty percent discount, and he did buy them, one or two a week, out of his wages. In time his private library came to take up the whole length of a four-foot shelf that hung over his desk. He used to lie back on his pillow and look at his books, gloat over their heft, their different colored covers. Imagining the richness of their contents, he smiled to himself with proprietary satisfaction.

Some he never read, like the Modern Library philosophers he had longed to own, and then found impenetrable or tedious. He tried a few pages of most poets and then quit. Dostoevsky had been impossible. But he was still pleased to own them all.

He *would* read them, all of them, one day. And meanwhile they were his.

Otto Koerner was an Austrian-American homosexual in his early sixties who lived for two things: his books — those he sold in his shop in the El Rancho Shopping Plaza, which actually made more money from greeting cards and stationery than from books, *and* a few fine editions of his own — and the high school and college boys he could occasionally pick up hitchhiking and persuade to earn a few dollars by taking off their pants. He had given Ronald a job for wholly practical motives, however, tinged by no sentiment whatever, save perhaps a touch of pity. He had watched the boy mooning about the store for two years, rarely buying, mostly looking, the way others look at toys or clothing or jewels. The boy obviously loved books, and had few apparent friends or other interests. He needed a job, as it turned out (to pay for gas, mostly, and the insurance on his car). He had wrapped parcels all last summer at Montgomery Ward's. He worked hard, and was willing to work cheap. And Otto Koerner needed a boy.

As the months wore on, the gray-haired bookseller grew fond of Ronald, in an uncle-ish sort of way. The boy was so weak in many ways, so ready to be hurt, so much a clumsy dreamer. He drew Ronald out about his reading, suggested books and authors.

Over Easter vacation of his senior year, Ronald had burned himself badly in an accident and had to spend three weeks in the hospital. His right arm and the right side of his face were wrapped in bandages. His mother had called Mr. Koerner to let him know. "Tell the boy not to worry," he had told her. He could manage by himself for a few weeks. The job would be waiting when Ronald came out.

But when Ronald was gone, he found himself missing the lad, thinking about him a good deal of the time. After a week, Otto Koerner went to visit Ronald in the hospital.

He talked to him for a few minutes, reassured him about the job, asked him how it happened, how much it hurt. He found himself looking fixedly at the pale, damaged face, bright sky-blue eyes set close together, growing perhaps too warmly aware of the form beneath the sheets. So he grasped Ronald's good arm tightly and left his little gift — a collection of short stories by his own favorite author.

And so Ronald lay in his high hospital bed, where the sun shone in through dry eucalyptus, and read of Mario and the magician, of Siegmund and Sieglinde, of Gustav von Aschenbach and the beautiful Polish boy, and was troubled and confused by them all. But what stopped his heart was the story of Tonio Kröger.

Tonio, according to the story, was the son of a stiff, prosperous German father and a beautiful mother named Consuelo, who had come from somewhere like Italy or Spain. He lived in a cold old city in northern Germany. Tonio was dark and fragile, unlike his schoolmates. He felt things deeply and wrote poetry. But he longed all the while to be like healthier, happier people, the blond and blue-eyed ones who didn't write poetry or feel things deeply.

At fourteen he fell in love with a classmate, a handsome, athletic, instinctual boy named Hans Hansen, and he suffered torments from his unreturned adoration. At sixteen, he agonized over a second infatuation, for a girl named Ingeborg Holm. Like Hans Hansen, Ingeborg was beautiful, blue-eyed and blond, laughing and unthinking and forever at ease.

Tonio's father dies; his mother remarries. Tonio goes away to Italy, then Bavaria, becomes a moderately famous writer. After thirteen years' absence, he goes back to his native town. The family house is now a library. Nobody recognizes him. He is nearly arrested, mistaken for somebody else. He sails across the Baltic to a seaside resort in Denmark, where everything is lonely and gloomy until a large party of guests arrives one day for a kind of family celebration.

That night, Tonio Kröger stands outside on the veranda looking in at their dance, and stares with envy and longing at a handsome blond couple who look like Ingeborg and Hans.

He goes up alone to his room.

He undressed, lay down, put out the light. Two names he whispered into his pillow, the few chaste northern syllables that meant for him his true and native way of love, of longing and happiness; that meant to him life and home, meant simple and heartfelt feeling. He looked back on the years that had passed. He thought of the dreamy adventures of the senses, nerves, and mind in which he had been involved; saw himself eaten up with intellect and introspection, ravaged and paralyzed by insight, half worn out by the fevers and frosts of creation, helpless and in anguish of conscience between two extremes, flung to and fro between austerity and lust; *raffiné*, impoverished, exhausted by frigid and artificially heightened ecstasies; erring, forsaken, martyred, and ill—and sobbed with nostalgia and remorse.

Much of the story was hard going for Ronald. About half-way in, the author had written a philosophical conversation about life and art that the boy found very difficult to follow. He had to keep stopping and reading lines over. Much of it was uncomfortably foreign — the way people talked, the things they did, the things they worried about. He was embarrassed by the silly man Tonio Kröger met on the boat, who went into raptures over the stars. He was embarrassed by the dancing master, with his chubby hips and French phrases. He was embarrassed, above all, by Tonio's passion for Hans Hansen.

But never in his life had Ronald read anything that affected him so much. Here, through gauzy screens of foreignness and strangeness and philosophical talk, was *his story,* the story of his life, written out by a great writer for anyone to read. In a book, a famous book, a story that had been in print (he checked) for fifty-three years! If before he had felt a freak, a runt, something mistaken and alone, he did so no more. Or if he did, at least he felt *justified* in feeling so, exonerated, transfigured into something serious and defensible by a great German writer's fifty-three-year-old tale. To how many lines, how many paragraphs did he not feel himself nodding a passionate assent, reading them aloud in his own voice. *Yes.* That was how it was!

> It begins by your feeling yourself set apart, in a curious sort of opposition to the nice, regular people; there is a gulf of ironic sensibility, of knowledge, scepticism, disagreement between you and the others; it grows deeper and deeper, you realize that you are alone . . .

God, wasn't that true?

The words in books, and the worlds they evoked, had for several years been for Ronald Harrington more illuminate, more glowing and hard-edged than the tangled, troublous world other people thought of as "real." But here, suddenly, in a paperback book with a blue and yellow cover, Outside and Inside fused, flashed together with a light of truth that was almost more than he could bear. *His story,* he kept telling himself: in a book.

thirty-one

Three times he read Tonio's story, lying in a white, backless hospital gown between starched white hospital sheets; or sitting up in his robe, face and arm bandaged, a leaf-filtered sunlight shining in the window onto his page. After the third time, the story lost its existence as something whole and outside of him, and he felt a great need to make absolute and private his possession — particularly his possession of certain passages he knew almost by heart, in the fullest sense of the word.

So he took a spiral notebook with a soft, dark brown cover — one of several he had brought to the hospital in order to keep up with his classes—and wrote the passages down in ink.

Why is it I am different, why do I fight everything, why am I at odds with the masters and like a stranger among the other boys? The good scholars, and the solid majority—they don't find the masters funny, they don't write verses, their thoughts are all about things that people do think about and can talk about out loud. How regular and comfortable they must feel, knowing that everybody knows just where they stand! It must be nice! But what is the matter with me, and what will be the end of it all?

The veranda was empty and dim, but the glass door stood open into the hall, where shone two large oil lamps, furnished with bright reflectors. Thither he stole on soft feet; and his skin prickled with the thievish pleasure of standing unseen in the dark and spying on the dancers there in the brightly lighted room. . . .

He was exhausted with jealousy, worn out with the gaiety in which he had no part. . . . Always with burning cheeks he had stood in his dark corner and suffered for you, you blond, you living, you happy ones!

To be like you! To begin again, to grow up like you, regular like you, simple and normal and cheerful, in conformity and understanding with God and man, beloved of the innocent and happy.

Things were a little different in the few weeks of high school left him after his release from the hospital. He had been admitted to the University with a small scholarship. That, together with the gauze bandage he still wore on the right side of his face, gave him a certain mysterious new status in the eyes of classmates, teachers, and family alike.

Many of the old high school rules were breaking down, these last few weeks, as the Class of 1960 found itself moving nearer and nearer to freedom. Many of the power brokers and style setters of the last few years were finding themselves displaced in the heat of new expectations. The team captain or cheerleader who had nothing better in view than a selling job in San Salvador began to seem a smaller figure than the boy or girl heading for college and (it went without saying) prosperity, position, a safe harbor in the adult world.

The parties went on, the picnics, the spring dances; the senior play, the last baseball games and track meets. But there was about them, for the seniors, at once a greater frenzy — more noise, more passion, more people drunk, more things broken — and a timorous sense of withdrawal. As soon as the seventeen- or eighteen-year-old girl or boy reflected that this bright, busy game was soon to end, the game itself began to seem childish, hard to take as seriously as one might have before. By May, the graduating senior looked at sophomores and juniors trying to ape his own antics with a new sense of distance and near-adult condescension — and with regret, as well, regret that his own high school days were coming so rapidly to an end.

The scarred face and scholarship came opportunely to prop up Ronald's new sense of self-respect. His letter of admission to Cal was at once a passport to new freedoms, new possibilities, and a seal of the great world's acknowledgment of his merit, a seal even people like Tommy Tidwell and his brother and Uncle Fred were obliged to respect. Mr. Zack had come to visit him in the hospital, where he showed himself genuinely impressed to find Ronald reading Thomas Mann.

The fire had burned a large patch of his face, from the right cheekbone down over the chin onto the neck, a patch that was to stay whitish and puckered, hairless and moist-looking for the rest of his life. Each morning, as he replaced the old bandage, he inspected the scar closely. It became for him a symbol, a vivid physical manifestation of the lesson of Tonio Kröger. He *was* different. Now, he was visibly, grotesquely different. Everyone could see it.

Well, so be it. Already other people were affording him a new respect, since his unhealthy difference had made itself manifest in his face.

It cannot be said that he moved any more equably among his fellows, or felt any more at home in their company. Nor that he gave up his longings to be one of them (though he was already blond, and blue-eyed), any more than Tonio had.

No: the active difference, those last frantic weeks, was that Ronald began to indulge his baser, one-of-the-gang impulses more freely than he ever had before. He got drunk at the Senior Class picnic on a six-pack of Country Club stout, then sang dirty songs and passed out and had to be carried back to the bus. After that, he began to get invited to parties by people who had never paid him any attention before. And at each of their parties, he drank enough to enable him to act insulting and obscene, which was exactly what they had invited him to do.

His mother was worried half to death at the sudden change, but Ronald knew very well what he was doing and why. He even planned his performances in advance, knew just how much of what he would have to drink in order to release the New Self. To have Block S lettermen pouring him drinks, Beverly Polestri herself sitting on his knee, laughing at his songs!

Of course it was a farce, a charade. But he had longed for it for three years, and he wasn't going to let moral scruples or clucking self-awareness spoil it now.

The weekend before graduation he rode down to Tijuana with five classmates in Walt DuBois's truck, drank himself sick on tequila, and, for five dollars, saw a live-action stag show (with animals) in a barn out of town. On graduation night he went to three parties in a row, drank more than ever, smoked his first marijuana, and ended up getting laid (also for the first time) by Liz Reilly, a wealthy doctor's daughter who wanted to touch his scar, upstairs at Don Guttierez's parents' house on Dartmoor Road.

Dealing with the opposite sex was rarely easy for any American adolescent of Ronald Harrington's day. It was an intricate, uncertain, brambly sort of game, with an endless succession of hurdles and traps. How to ask for a date, how to accept (or refuse); the agony of acne, or too small breasts, or bad breath, or being short, or parents, or your older sister needing her aqua cashmere on the very same night you do. What to talk about. What to do. When to make the first move; how to respond; how to act; how far to go. That above all. How Far To Go. And every boy and girl who played the game had to work out all the answers for himself, as if no one had ever played before.

But the millions who have played it, with whatever success, can have very little comprehension of what life was like for all those who wanted to play it and could not. Boys who wanted girls, girls who wanted boys; teenagers who saw everyone dancing the dance, and could do no more than stand outside on the veranda and press their noses to the glass.

What did one do? they wondered. *And what was it like?* They read about it, spied on others doing it, watched movies that mimed it, lay awake in bed imagining it, and ended up making love to their pillows, which whispered back flattering and sensuous things.

All through high school, Ronald had been one of these. And now he knew.

In the summer after graduation, Ronald worked full time for Mr. Koerner. Hank was away with the navy in Okinawa. His parents had rented their usual cabin near the Lees' place at Russian River, this time for the full month of August. But Ronald convinced them (over his mother's worst fears) to let him stay behind. His first year at college would cost them that much less if he could work the extra month and save up what he made.

So Ronald lived alone, for the first time in his life, during the whole month of August 1960, in the family house at 726 Coronado Road, San Salvador, California.

His mother's worst fears were not entirely unfounded. Once he talked Liz Reilly into coming over to the house for a repeat of graduation night. He was pleased to find he could do it sober, but the encounter was not a great success. Both these homely, inexpert children were anxious to seem at once passionate and wise, which they were not. They ended by quarreling and insults, and that was the end of that.

Ronald reverted to the solitary's game. In fact, it had become a near mania during this month by himself. It was as if the empty house demanded of him something corrupt and unspeakable, some willful desecration of his parents' bed (which was where he usually performed). He saw lots of movies that August, including one grainy skin flick in Oakland. He spent a whole Sunday afternoon studying photographs of naked men and women he discovered in the back of a drawer of Otto Koerner's desk.

Many evenings he kept the television on for company, no matter what it was. He found himself reading every word in the dull, middle-class magazines that came in the mail. Again and again he would go to the refrigerator, more for something to do than for something to eat. Or else he drove out, to model racing tracks, pizza parlors, twenty-four-hour drugstores. Two nights, and one Sunday afternoon, he found himself sinking into a causeless, unidentifiable melancholy: all three times he drank himself into a witless stupor with his father's whiskey — and suffered three abominable mornings after.

But on the whole, he enjoyed the month of freedom. These were just the lettings-go, the occasional dips of disequilibrium in a sensitive young constitution unused to total independence. He paid the price, pulled himself more or less together, and began to learn to live alone physically, as he had done so long already in spirit.

He read a great deal, sometimes a book a day. Oddly enough, the silence of an empty house turned out to be more distracting than the noise and interruptions of his family. The slightest wind outside; a car passing in the street; even the faint hum of the refrigerator motor beginning its new circuit, and he would jerk his eyes up from the page, at once craving and hating the distraction. A ringing telephone, one especially empty evening, jarred him to near insensibility.

But books were still the surest way he knew of becoming

someone else — books, and night dreams, and the near-dreams of his wish-fulfilling fantasy world.

Music helped, too. He turned his father's stereo or his car radio to KBAK and let somebody's symphonies wash over him. But such music was never really enough, he found; a sedative, a mind deadener, at best, a great wave one tried to catch, an invitation to escape rather than escape itself. Corny hit tunes had a far greater impact on him than any Wagner or Beethoven. He could bring himself to the point of free-flowing tears by putting on a particular Frank Sinatra LP; or by trying to remember last summer's hits at the River; or by saying over to himself the words of an old Ames Brothers tune he had adopted as his own, when he first heard it in his sophomore year.

> Gee, I wish that I had a girl
> Like the other fellows do —
> Someone to make a fuss over me,
> To cheer me up when I feel blue.
> On Wednesday nights I'm all alone
> When I oughta be up at some sweetheart's home,
> And I'm lonesome, so awfully lonesome —
> Gee, I wish I had a girl.

One night so hot he had left doors and windows open, he was reading stretched out on the living room couch. He had just got to the place in *The Fountainhead* where the hero learns that his life is shot, his career is wiped out, and suddenly decides that nothing on earth matters.

Ronald put the book down on the coffee table and sat up, took a sip of his cream soda. Then he stared at the wall and started thinking.

What matters?

What matters to me.

Books.   Reading.   Thinking.   The life of the mind.

Religion? No.

School? School *work*, most of it. I like doing it. Writing well, getting to understand French. Making equations work out. Doing chemistry experiments. I like my success in it. Getting A's, winning prizes, getting into Cal.

Sports, no. Music? Sometimes. Movies, TV as an escape. Clothes? Not especially. (Maybe if I looked better.) My car? Yes. It lets me get away, be free, go anywhere I want. Money? Not money just because it's money, just to have in the bank, like Dad and Uncle Fred, that's just gross. But money to buy things, yes. Things I want.

What sort of things? Oh — books, things to eat, gas for the car. Travel, one day. A trip to Europe.

Things. All my things, my collections, fossils, shells, stamps, autographs, matchbooks, ship models, travel folders: drawers, shelves, boxes full of them. All the things I've saved, one after another. Do they matter?

Yes. I don't know why, but they do. I don't ever want to lose them; I want to keep them forever.

Other people? Oh, I suppose so. Some of them. Mom, Dad, Hank: I don't want to hurt them, anyway. I'd like to make them happy, make them pleased with me. But I don't suppose I ever will. Mr. Koerner . . . Zack, I guess. A few kids at school I can talk to, Albert, Carla.

But nobody very much. Not those assholes in Tijuana. Not Liz.

At this point he stopped talking out loud, because he didn't want to ask the next question, and he didn't know the answer. He abandoned his conscious self-assessment, let his mind soften into the fantasies of a confused, sensitive seventeen-year-old American boy, left alone in a house on a hot summer night.

Sex *did* matter to him, obviously, but in a diffused, unlocatable way. It mattered insofar as he wanted it, or at least wanted to want it. Curiosity about other people's bodies, male and female, could torment him to distraction. He found himself staring at, imagining, even dreaming about them — kids in his class, teachers even, movie stars, Hank, his own parents, people on the street. What were their bodies like? All over, up close, what were they like to touch?

But doing the deed with Liz he found himself plagued with a dispassionate self-consciousness, the presence of another self that stared down and analyzed everything he did — as if he were fated to be a voyeur even of his own achievements, as he had been of Walt DuBois's and Jack Brady's at the whorehouse in Tijuana. He longed to be carried away on waves of animal urgency, to let his mind be submerged by his blood; but it wouldn't happen. He kept *telling* himself what to do next, pretending to brutal needs and sudden impulses, to upspurts and downswoops of emotion that he didn't feel at all, but felt he *ought* to be feeling.

And yet when he was alone, by himself, wonderfully erotic things could occur. The sight of swelling flesh under clothes, the nape of a girl's neck in front of him in class could set tingling a million tiny pinpricks of delight. So a breeze blowing across his stomach, as he lay on the beach at night. So the tiniest shift in the temperature of his skin. A bleeding cut; the sound of thunder or waves; the feel of certain fabrics all warmed his blood as no real-life woman could.

He tried, that hot, solitary month, to face up to his peculiar kind of sexuality. But normalcy was still so essential an attribute of his ideal self that he had to presume that what he so desperately wanted was what everyone else wanted:

> Gee, I wish that I had a girl
> Like the other fellows do.

It had been Liz Reilly's fault, the last time, it must have been. She was too ugly, or too dry; unskillful; overbearing. With Beverly, or Jo, or Claudette, or Eartha Kitt, or Leslie Caron, or . . . it would be different. It would be wonderful.

And so he went on telling himself that he wanted what everyone else wanted, that he really was normal, deep down. And each morning he stiffened with joy as he slowly edged a needle-sharp shower up from body warm to hot to unbearably hot, then ever so slowly back down to cool, cold, icy cold, shivering headaching freezing cold; and then up again to hot; then stretched out to dry on the soft, carpeted bathroom floor and fingered his tingling red body all over. Normal.

What mattered to Ronald Harrington? What was, for him, important, substantial, full of meaning?

The faith that somewhere there was a world denser, handsomer, and more satisfying than the one he dwelt in now.

Bodies — his own and other people's.   Water.   Fire.

The water of a shower, of a steaming hot tub. The water of a faucet, of a fountain, of rain on the roof, on the windows; water that poured down the windshield and splashed under the tires as he steered down Eldorado Freeway through a storm. The water of creeks and ponds and rivers, back home in Indiana. Water all around him, as he swam, water bearing him up and evenly caressing every particle of his skin. Water gone mad at the ocean's edge, its primeval, barbarous, all-conquering nature rendered dazzlingly clear in the mind-fixing crest and crash and retreat, the deep breathing roar he listened to as if to his own heart, the shattered foam he watched night after night at San Francisco's western edge, parked along the Great Highway, Playland behind him, the Pacific before. Water in this, its ultimate state, mattered profoundly.

Water and fire. The fire that burned his arm and face had not been an accident. He adored fire. He had set that fire on purpose to see what it would be like to burn.

three.

Five. Out of nowhere they leap, five creatures of light, incarnated by the roar, by the cresting, bursting thirst of twenty thousand souls. Suddenly a wild, lean man in front is impaled by the spots: an apparition in black, silver, red over flesh. Now he is talking to them, some self-effacing lie about the crowd, the plane, the place, the unfortunate delay, as if they were all just friends and he a mere fellow human. His voice is a broad boyish cockney rasp, his manner one of artificial calm, of genial offhandedness belied by the red white and blue hat, the outrageous scarf, the silver belt, the twitching limbs black molded, snakelike, never still. A chord from the right rips through his pose, an exquisite plucked blinding assertion of their presence, and they are on. *Smash*, bam, rat-tat-tat, under the throbbing chord stalk cymbal and drums, relentless and unbearably right. Then a second guitar overlays piercing threads of sound, a third adds internal thumping beat, until the hall and all its heads become soundboxes pounding to the will of the five dark glowing children of light.

And He: Jagger. He is now as if plugged in himself to the wall of electronics, as if humming through every sleek fluid fiber of his limbs. The mike is shrieked to, then whipped out of its stand, its cord flicked looping out of the way like a long royal cape, out of the way of twitching, already step-kicking, soft-slippered feet. The glare from wide, unnaturally bright eyes is defiant, magnificent, the face spellbinding, theatrical, strange. The voice is yelling now, high, raw, shrill and compelling, spilling syllables at random over the happy pounding beat:

The telephone is ringin' I says Hi its me who is it there on the li-ine?
A voice says Hi-Hello-How-are-you, Well I guess I'm doin' fi-ine
He says it's three A.M. there's too much noise donchew-people-evvawanna go to be-yed?
'Cause you feelin' so groovy do you have to drive me outa my he-ad?

Hatred, confusion evaporate: knots untie, resistance goes slack, familiar griefs and tensions yield themselves to a fresh flood of passions never felt before. Ronald feels himself locked of a sudden to this freakish creature, tied by the scarlet scarf, the silver studs, hypnotized by lips, eyes, hair, arms and legs and all, seized by the wild nonhuman noises that come from its mouth.

> I said *Hey!* (Bash) *Yew!* (Ratatattat)
> Get offa Ma Clowwd!
> *Hey!* (Bash) *Yew!* (Ratatattat)
> Get offa Ma Clowwd!

and on each *Yew!* he points, with glorious menace, a long stick of a finger at some melting, guilty, giddy soul in the crowd, someone who has apparently had the hysterical effrontery to have dreamed of sharing the private Jagger cloud.

Warmed, tingling, filling with new blood, no longer discriminating, the man in P101 feels plural, undifferentiated, larger and brighter than life, as drumsticks rattle in his head, sounds vibrate through his gut, as the devil prances and points and slaps and sings.

A knee twitching, bending, poking like a knife, then sending off its energy to its brother leg, the pair dancing in place, winding with the beat, the cord flicked again and again into sine wave curves across the stage, the verses growled, shrilled, chopped, drawled out of fat drunken Michelangelo lips. Then a doubled, quadrupled rise of power from the guitars, the lead forcing him higher and higher, smashing, dashing cymbals and drumsticks defying him to meet them, the whole shrieking, crashing, driving home as the final wave of abundant noise breaks into a fine foam of compulsive applause.

A bow. A deep prancing sinuous bow from the waist, a low, rubbery, mocking bow, then a flick of the scarf, a mean sweeping wave of the Uncle Sam hat (which is now tossed offstage, having served). A word over his shoulder to the drummer, two scant prickling seconds' wait, and then *bang* into Number Two, some song everyone in the hall apparently knows by heart, for everyone seems to breathe a great happy gasp of communal recognition and delight at the third or fourth bar: one, two, one, two, a raw, rustic, wildly amplified rockabilly sound, twang-*thump*, twang-*thump*, over and over. The band seems terribly pleased with itself; the crowd is all but choking in its knowing expectation of new pleasure.

Joy: simple, infectious, gleefully happy. And when the lead singer begins striking a tambourine, and his three fellows join him in the song, swooping up a fifth for the chorus, up higher still for the next repetition, suddenly Ronald knows the song too, has known it for years; finds himself longing, like a silly kid, for the next time, and the next, feels a heart-swallowing ache each time they lift

> This could be the *last* time,
> This could be the *last* time,

then lift higher again —

> *May be the last time*, I don't know

— dropping back down on the last . . .

Why was he yielding so resistlessly? A simple A to D chord shift, in a trivial, repetitive little tune: but he *was* yielding, there was no arguing that. And, odder still, he was overwhelmingly *pleased* with himself for yielding, pleased with the whole dumb scene, the very escape it was offering him from all the things he had once thought really mattered. His heart begs for more, drinks in great draughts of the echoing air.

The song over, the star breathing hard: ". . . a little numbah we recorded a bit ago, some of you may know it. We like it, anyway."

Begins in a strange Tahitian beat, the bass guitar and drums parroting maracas, congas, finger drums, Mick twisting the long red silk wickedly about his neck and wrist, arching right and left, opening the heavy lips. The voice comes out high this time, as if sick, the words hyper-enunciated, vowels oozing over the beat.

At first, Ronald feels himself chilled by what seems to be a decipherable message, frozen in mid-flood by cerebral intervention: St. Petersburg, Blitzkrieg, kings and queens, Lucifer. Christ. Even Christ. Please, Mr. Jagger. Stop: no more of this.

I tempted Christ. I killed the Czar. I killed the Kennedys. I'm a Nazi. I'm the Devil, the Devil himself. Oh yes I am.

Please; *out* of this!

And Jagger seems to understand. Faster, campier, uglier, he abandons his posing, prancing Halloween devil role, and begins to play witchlike games with his outstretched finger bones. Ronald is teased out of thought, as Jagger flicks the scarlet scarf, twists his lips, runs a hand down his side, backsteps into the band between verses to prod his cohorts into stinging, shrieking noise. Grunting now, yelping, higher, faster, freer, wilder, the knees scissor up, the feet pounding down, up, down. Suddenly all lyrics lost in an almost hysterical scream, *Oh Yeah, aaah yeah* circling about the stage still jerking exactly to the beat, cords of the throat raw, red, knotted, neck stretched and straining, *some restraint*, body locked in a kind of choreographed spasm, *have some courtesy . . . soul to waste . . . mah name, My naaame . . . what's my name?*

> *All right! / all right! / all right!*
> *tell me baby: What's my name?*

Abandoned every shred of sense or self, Jagger pleads, shaking out of control and commanding:

WHAT'S MY NAME?

"Siddown, hey!"

forty-four

Ronald sits down. He is staring into the eyes on the giant screen, which are staring back into his.

Below, the smaller, three-dimensional human image, in garish unreal colors, is pinned to the stage and wriggling.

But it is the magnified great eyes in black and white that are looking at his, so he keeps his gaze fixed on the screen.

The singer walks off to the side, takes a big swallow from a bottle, then comes back. As he returns, a single amber spot from overstage is slowly sweeping back and forth across the front rows of the audience, following his glance as he walks up and down, scrutinizing his fans. He stops. The light stops. He points. It points, then shifts to red. He pulls off his scarf and begins sawing it lewdly across his rear, staring at one fattish little girl in the second row. Someone begins pumping a chugging rhythm out of the electric organ. One of the TV cameras onstage turns to face the girl, and there she is now on the screen: puff-faced and plain, eyes dark with makeup, strands of her hair stuck to her cheek, transfixed by the spotlight and the basilisk eye.

> (Chug-a-chug-a-chug-a-chug)-I'm-not-talkin'-
> bout the clothes she wears —
> *Lookit that stoopid girl!*

Twenty thousand docile, obedient people stare at the face on the superscreen, exactly as they are bid, and believe all the things they hear snarling over the loudspeakers about a creature no one knows.

> She purrs like a pussy cat,
> Then she turns around and hisses back . . .
> She's the sickest thing in this world
> *Well, lookit that stoopid girl!*

He has stripped her, a little nobody, up in front for all to see, and ordered them to laugh: and they do. Ronald stares at the picture of the creature Mick has elected out of their number and half wishes *he* had been the one.

The song over, Mick bends to one knee, remolding his evil

features into a mask of tenderness and concern. On the screen, the girl's giant blurred image is shaking, weeping, trying to hide in a girlfriend's shoulder. Mick pulls off the scarf he had tied about his hips, balls it up and tosses it to her with a kiss: little pig become a princess.

Song after song, then, seemed *aimed,* aimed like darts, like spurts of hot oil, at the female half of the audience. It was planned, of course, oh he realized that, planned like the spotlight on the fat girl and the tossed-away scarf; all very carefully planned. But it *seemed* like a genuine enough fit of misogynist spite.

After all, he had written these songs, hadn't he? He and that scraggly dark witch of a guitarist? Ronald imagined them vividly; a pair of sick perverts who copulate in the dark, then dream up horrible fantasies of female degradation, like Proust whipping his rats until they bled. The man *meant* every word of what he was singing, what he was so obscenely acting out.

But the girls around row P, girls above and behind, they seemed to love it. They shouted and screamed, they lapped it all up, blood and semen and venom together; they beg him for more, wet their pants with delight. Ronald turns around and stares at them, listens to their screams.

A pair of songs, now, incarnate a neurotic, high-living London bitch who had crossed the singer and is now having her whole life ripped open before this bloodthirsty mob of punks. Whoever she was, this fantasy deb, whatever she had done, she was at this minute being flayed alive in a beautiful, a near perfect act of revenge.

For it *was* beautiful. It was perfect. All through Jagger's snarling and snapping his accomplices are rolling off yards of just the right noises, cynical, threatening, even sweet. Plucked, lyrical music-box ripples, raw layers of metal sound, tinny tambourine crash; all atop the humping, raunchy beat. And the voice that rasps out the insults, the insinuations, is always under such careful *artistic* control.

But still — think: what a mad, barbaric use of art! For somewhere in those overarticulated consonants, those flamboyant vowels, in that cruel, sad voice, lives a real, blood-filled human being who means every word, every snarl, every lash of the whip!

Arching his back, now, ordering some invisible female animal onto her knees, shoving his crotch at her face. Appalled, Ronald turns into a terrified voyeur, unable to unglue his eyes from the display: groaning, writhing, whispering, *down to me!* twisting head and hips slowly from side to opposite side: to be staring at *this!* Out of breath, out of his head: *Ah, Eeeh, oh yeah! Oh* (as if in pain), *Take it-teasy babee* (whispering) . . . *Take it easy,* (lower) . . . *eee-easy.* Was he going to do something on stage? like that guy in . . . take it out and

No. No, of course not. Jagger stops, as if drained at last, and with a bounce and a bash of the tambourine reminds the house that it was all just an act, something he can turn on and turn off at will. Whatever *they* may have thought, it was all choreographed and planned to the last stinging string, the last artificial groan.

He has carried them so far now that two out-and-out sex songs that follow come not as higher and higher crests, but simply as second and third orgasms by a pair already deeply dug in, ruled by rhythms and pressures outside of their control.

> That's no / hangin' / mat-tuh . . .
> That's no / cap-pit-tal / crii-yime

The voice snarls at them all, caws loudly and lewdly of scratching and biting, of "nasty habits," of three way games with teenagers between the sheets at some musty warren full of insanity and disease.

Ronald could imagine the place: a world cruder, lower, viler (*You could bite like that*) than he had ever known, could ever know.

But, Oh pull *out* of this stew, my friend, one part of his head says to the other: there's nothing honorable or attractive about it. You'd hate it. You couldn't cope if you wanted to (*Why don't you bring her upstairs*).

But I do want to. I want to *be there* with them, to have been there (*shoots water rats*) to have known it all (*in between the*) sheets wet with vomit, racketing noise, endless crummy orgies. (*Harebrained children they are locked*) and so am I.

I could: I could, me there with them, with him, in between the, forget: forget everything else but (say it) cocks and cunts, sperm, slime. Anyone, anytime. Pull things apart, throw bottles at the wall, paint dripping down like blood: Beat Eat Meat ever, forever, lower, lower *lower* DOWN:

I can't do it. I can't.

The man shivers at his confusion, torn by the internal effort to become something he cannot be. Yet.

Although he had never seen them before, and heard them only by accident, Ronald Harrington, like a lot of other people, had come to identify the Rolling Stones with something very like the sink of vileness and vulgarity he felt soaking about his ankles even now.

Oh, he might tell himself this or that, pretend to be disgusted. But for all his flushes of repulsion, a very demanding part of his being had all along been praying that it might be dragged into precisely the agitation he was experiencing now, so devastating and so delicious.

For a long time, he had allowed himself, every so often, to get caught up in vulgar, alien escapades like this.

It had begun decently enough, six or seven years ago, with the equivocal sensuality of respectable artists: Michelangelo, Géricault. Erotic Japanese paintings followed, then pornographic eighteenth-century novels; certain French and Swedish films he could pretend he was studying seriously (and dismiss publicly as decadent trash). He watched five-dollar sex films in little dark South of Market boxes, and quit them in disgust after half an hour. New wave plays of a sort he actively hated, like *Futz* and *Oh! Calcutta!* and *Paradise Now.* Stag shows. The nude beach in San Gregorio.

Even stranger, ostensibly non-erotic things had become for him wicked and irresistible. Auctions of old junk; dog races; a destruction derby, one hot Sunday afternoon in Vacaville. Student political meetings of a certain shabby, overheated kind. Odd neighborhoods, prowled in at odd hours. Playland-at-the Beach.

For years now, Playland had been on the brink of closing down. Its rickety rides and tatty booths were two-thirds boarded up. An acrid, unidentifiable odor hovered in the air. Whatever it was, it seemed to come from the two places that still sold things to eat, electric-cooked frankfurters, instant pizza wedges that tasted of glue.

Many times Ronald had been the only patron of these rancid cafés, and he could have wept with joy and pain for the tawdriness of it all, the cold gray emptiness in the fog. Often he was the only prowler on the Midway too, but for a few sailors and drunks, the odd band of black kids looking for anything left they could still break into or steal. But he must have believed that the answer lay there, behind the boarded-up stalls. Because he kept going back to Playland every time he felt the need. And over the last two years, he had been feeling the need with greater frequency, greater urgency. He was glad the shabby old amusement park was there, glad it was just as it was. He prayed they would never renovate it, never shut or tear it down completely.

But Playland, dirty movies, dog races: all these escapades turned out in the end to be worse than useless. Each time, he was left ashamed and disgusted, full of hatred for what his own sordid compulsions were telling him about himself. And all through these adventures he lived in the stark white terror of being caught, like a boarding school freshman masturbating at night in the john.

And still he couldn't stop. For a month, two months at most, he would rivet himself to his work, to the ardent celibacy and meager socializing of the graduate student world. And then he would ache and suffer and spend sleepless nights until he had wasted time and money and self-esteem on another of his petty adventures.

Until last summer. In May he had failed — or at least not passed — his Ph.D. oral exams. A professor who believed in him, or felt sorry for him, or both, had helped him to a thousand-dollar grant from the department's travel funds, to enable him to do research on nineteenth-century vandalism in Burgundy. There he had lived two months of relatively uncomplicated contentment. He fell in love with Burgundy. He fell in love. That came to an end, in a way he did not like to remember.

He came back to Berkeley, emotionally numbed, no longer innocent, but cured, he thought, and with purer, happier memories than he had owned at any time since he left Granger, Indiana, at the age of fourteen; came back with notebooks full of many things — records copied out of French archives, speculations of his own, pencil sketches and descriptions of the ruined abbey church of Cluny, and of the lesser romanesque churches of its region: the most nearly perfect things, he believed, man had ever made. He got a job in the university library, and set to work methodically studying for his second go on the oral exams. This time he would pass. Late in the evening, he would put on a pile of records, then lie back on his bed and think about France.

And yet here he was. Mick Jagger and the Rolling Stones, beginning their 1969 American tour at the Oakland Coliseum Arena. By late October, the joy of work had begun to pale. Even the notebooks from France had lost their savor. The shell of his civilized sphere flaked and peeled over its own hollowness, the way it had so often in the past, and the old dirty urges wormed their way to the surface. He had gone back to Playland twice; got himself mugged the second time. By his sordid standards, a triumph.

But this. A live rock concert — he who hated the new music. It was a total admission of his having given in. It was his most outrageous adventure so far.

And at this point it seemed to be working. In an unspeakable, inexplicable way, this spectacle — the most sordid, most flamboyant of his escapes — seemed to be succeeding where the others had failed. It was giving him what he wanted, without remorse, what he needed, and that in spite of his repulsion.

Why, he couldn't say. Or why, perhaps, he didn't want to know. The top slice of his brain settled for the explanation that

Jagger and his friends were able to clothe vileness and cheapness and bestiality — nourishment he obviously craved — in a craftsmanship of the most exacting finesse. That way they managed to ward off the disgust that had marred all his other adventures. Disgust of a sort remained: disgust at the crowd, at Jagger's bestiality, at his crude, audience-manipulating tricks. But even the disgust was as if special, transfigured. He actually found himself enjoying it, the way children enjoy roiling in mud.

What they were doing, wherever it belonged on The Great Scale of Civilization (but then fuck the great scale of civilization), was done *so well,* damn it. So that at the same time he could pretend to reflect critically on Jagger's performance — such a safe, respectable way to deal with it — *and* engage in warm, liquid fantasies of himself and Jagger, of himself *as* Jagger, of himself as a natural part of the whole unnatural scene.

From these sleazy and satisfying reflections, Ronald was pulled back by a raw-throated yell from Mick, one that seemed almost to come as an extension of his own floating thoughts.

I'm free! is what he is yelling: *To do what I want: Any old time.*

> I'm free.
> To do what I want.
> Any old time.
> Oh yes I am.

Oh yes you are. In a burst of illumination that flowered out of envy, Ronald answers him. You probably are. Freer than I'll ever be. (Those are tears that were his eyes.)

> I'm free
> To choose who I please
> Any old time.
> And I'm free
> To please who I choose
> Any old time.

Great stinging struck strings ring out bell-like in treble sequence, loud and hypnotically simple, understruck by a buzzing bass: all exact and sure. Over them winds Mick's jagged shout, wild vines growing over taut white overhead strings. Then up, and a shift of chords, for the refrain:

> So hooold me,
> Looove me;
> Hold me,
> Love me

as Mick comes back chastened into line, joins the even, dense beat of the others for that yearning, contradictory plea. As the lead guitar spins off into solo, scribbling out whorls and spirals of electric nasal noise, Ronald tries to break his head loose and track the notion home.

Free. *Free.* Free. Yes. What else is there to call them? Not simply wild, free like wind or fire, but free *on top of,* free because of all they know and can do.

It does begin, he decided, with Mick's weird voice: an aural emission of fantastic range and quality, which seems, at least, to be an authentic sonic expression of the whole strange thing he is. It is as if an unregulated, savage way of existence, learned and led in England in the sixties, has stretched and worn and callused his throat, bloated his lips and forked his tongue, just as it has dug out hollows in the cheeks, sharpened nose and chin, hardened the large diamond-bright eyes, and fever-taught all the nerves and muscles a kind of warm, fluid, hyperresponsive motility unknown to stolid, sober, sensible mankind.

And yet surely he is as much a creature of the band's as they are creatures of his. It is they, after all, who set him up, push him, test him, who create the world of noise and beat in which he lives.

And because they can all work and play as one, at the peak of their separate skills, they *are* free. Free to create absurd fantasy songs, slivery put-ons, outrageous imitations, sex-driven thrusts, scandalous evocations of filth, violence, of the joy of rioting and brutality, of rapists, teen layers, drugs and neurosis, not as something rational or doctrinaire or journalistic, but as musical images of their own steamed-out heads, the only possible objective correlatives for the freaky, freaked-out superworld they live in. In a sense, thinks Ronald Harrington, looking at them, their bodies, faces, hair, their glory rags, then looking at the youngsters around him, shabby, phthisic, underfed copies of these supermen, the Rolling Stones are at once the symbol and the justification of everything these dumb, cultureless kids are trying to be and to do.

In a word, free.

It is, on the surface, harsh, cynical, defiant, determinedly ugly *not* simply as a statement or gesture or joke, but because that is where they come from. And how he envies them that; how he wishes that was where *he* had come from too, instead of (the cosmic absurdity of it!) Granger, Indiana. They *know*, know it all too well to fake or pretend. Know the inside of it, know where it will end and what will come next. The only thing that preserves them from suicide or explosion or total disintegration — and with this insight stabs the bitterest pang of envy — must be the incredible sureness of their craft. Either that or go to pieces. Like the rest of us cretins. The harsher, uglier, more inhuman become the worlds within and without one is trying to express, the more meticulous and exact must be the control.

> I'm free . . .
> I'm free . . . [three-four syllables all rolling into one]
> You know we're free . . .
> You know we *are* free . . .

(We?)

> You know what I'm talkin' about . . .
> You know we are free . . .
> *We* know we are free . . .

We do? Is this some kind of political . . . Or maybe he means, like, free, *existentially?*

> I want you to be free . . .
> We gotta be free . . .
> We *can* be free . . .

> If we *know* we're free . . .
> That's one thing we know, at least
> We're *aaallllll* free!

Jagger is obviously exhorting them to *feel* free, trying to arouse something from this too silent, too well behaved crowd. Long fingers pull at them to respond. Eyes and lips beg them to react.

Then someone does.

"Free Bobby!"

The cry leaps raucously out of the heights. A dozen voices take it up, on behalf of the latest imprisoned Black Hero. Shouts, cheers . . .

. . . and not for Jagger. Now they *do* feel free, the upstairs mob, free and hungry, free to enjoy the liberation of answering back, to break the circuit of seduction. Upraised fists bristle, insults explode.

A black voice from the left upstairs, loud and clear over the rest:

"Fuck you, Mick Jagger!"

Scattered cheers; a few hisses.

He has lost them, surely, Ronald thinks, turned too many against him! Divided, not united this sullen, sallow, kick-crazy crowd. But defiant, surer than sure, he shouts back:

> *I am* free
> To sing my song,
> Though it's a little bit out of tune,

and outreaches them all. Free, yes: to sing my song. Though it's a little bit out of tune. *That* kind of free.

The band builds for the last repeat. Mick stands sneering and still, asserting his political pronoun one last time.

> We are free!
> Oh yeah. Oh yeah. Oh yeah.
> Maybe we are.
> If we wanna be.

He starts to raise a clenched fist, a knot at the end of one long lean black-wrapped arm. Ronald's mind spins, grabs for an explanation: surely not a gesture of solidarity, a political . . . the upraised fist spreads, deliberately splits into two upraised fingers. He spins about before the music ends, offers an insolent backside to their hooting mix of jeers and applause.

Snap. Detached once again, Ronald is back talking to himself: Levi's, fringe, granny dresses, wads of hair, Ha! They burn down buildings too, these little punks, and don't you forget it. This is just their night off. Anyone dare step on their little revolutionary daydreams — even Mister Mick Jagger — and they'll burn him down too. "Free Bobby." Shit. As if that had anything to do with anything. Politics. Their politics, all politics. Always so stupid, so hateful.

When Ronald looks up, Mick is pulling a little bench over to middle stage. Something cozy next, no doubt, something intimate and pacifying. He's playing these people, can't you see? Playing them up and then down. They're his instrument, his orchestra. Unfazed by the whole passionate affair? — of course he is. He's staging it, for heaven's sake, writing both script and stage directions as he goes along, he and his corrupt commedia dell'arte troupe. Improvising a scenario for twenty thousand amateur extras minute by minute, and at the same time responding instantly to their reactions.

"Fuck you, Mick Jagger!" — to churn up that intensity of emotion; to lift up the bleeding activists, only to drop them on his upraised fingers, flash them his rolling ass. It was evil, it was cynical and evil, and it was brilliant.

And now watch; watch him lull these infant revolutionaries back into docility with:

"It's blues time, boys and girls. A little quiet now . . . a couple of old numbahs from befoa yoa ti-yime."

Near total silence: respect for the blues. Keith sets a simple, Hawaiian-style steel guitar pace so quiet and fine at first they all *have* to hush; then Mick pulls out his harmonica for the first time and lets loose a high, aching old-timey mountain wail that sails up into the silence and fills all the winding, empty channels of the brain.

Then for who knows how many minutes, out pours nothing

but pure moaning voice, soaring into the space over their heads in long, slow, stretched-out aching notes. Below, only the deeply satisfying strumming of a simple, slightly drunken blues beat; once a bar a soft drum tap from behind.

Nothing simpler or more formal in all music. Two short, stark lines; the same lines again; then a third. The accent pattern, even the subject and tone — the bittersweet cry of a poor man's loss — fixed for a hundred years. And yet within this cage of sound a twenty-six-year-old white British singer drives his pure, strange, whining sliding voice further than he has for the last ten songs, spreads to the uttermost his wildly mannered accents and emphases, making another nation's, another race's tradition uniquely his own, rolling free and far over the strumming, almost heartbreaking beat. And when the powerful, pure, hogcalling wail has wound and twisted its way in, too deeply in, when all is silent beyond silence, on the edge of pain, he stops, picks up his harmonica again in order to close off full circle this interlude of calm, this ice-still eye of the hurricane; and it was too much, the yearning heart's wail from a distant place, a far-off time. If one could have cried, one would have cried.

four.

In 1962, Mick Jagger was a nineteen-year-old student at the London School of Economics. That summer he and Keith Richard (who had grown up with him in South London); Brian Jones, a professional rhythm and blues guitarist of twenty, from Cheltenham; and Bill Wyman, a twenty-one-year-old draftsman (also from South London) made music together for the first time in public at the Marquee, a club on Wardour Street in Soho, standing in for the club's regular R & B group on a Thursday evening "Blues Night."

In November of that year, the four were given a booking of their own at a little club in Ealing, north of the river, managed by the same man who ran the Marquee. It was located in the back room of a pub called the Bricklayer's Arms. There they played their versions of the music of Muddy Waters, Jimmy Reed, and the other black American bluesmen they admired.

At the Bricklayer's Arms, they were heard by Charlie Watts, a twenty-one-year-old drummer from Islington in North London, who soon quit his own band to join theirs.

These five young men — Jagger, Richard, Jones, Wyman, and Watts — decided to call themselves the Rolling Stones.

At about the same time, Ronald Harrington, a third-year student at the University of California in Berkeley (who knew nothing of British blues bands) was enjoying Thanksgiving dinner with his family. One week before he had made what was in his world a major decision, a declaration of independence. He had changed his major from business administration to art history without consulting the family, and announced the fact abruptly in a somewhat arrogant letter home.

A constant drizzly wetness, more a gray damp than a proper rain, gave the streets of San Salvador a look of oily slickness. More than usually fragile, he thought, the wet white houses of Rancho del Oro. He passed unfamiliar cars lined up in front of the houses: other people's relatives gathered for the feast. He parked his own car — the green Chevy he had bought in high school — on the street, behind Hank's new red T-Bird and Uncle Fred's big black Buick Le Sabre. The driveway was taken up by his mother's and father's cars. Hers was a new yellow Mustang, his a two-year-old Lincoln Capri, two-tone lavender and gray. Ronald's was the last to arrive.

"Hello dear, Happy Thanksgiving. I'm all sticky, don't touch. Must get back to the kitchen. I've left Kate stirring." Mrs. Harrington wiped her hands on her apron and held out a cheek to be kissed. "Daddy and Hank and Uncle Fred are out in the garage playing pool, if you'd like to go on out."

"That's OK, Mom. I'll just sit in the front room."

"I think the football game's on. Oh, you missed the most marvelous parade this morning, that one in New York with all the big balloons. Dorothy Kilgallen, Steve Lawrence, everybody. Even the astronauts."

"Oh. I'd like to have seen that."

"Well, you just set down and watch the game, dear, or read a magazine or something. Would you like some root beer?"

"That'd be nice."

"I'll get it. There's some chips and dip on the table. But don't go filling yourself up now! Lots to eat!"

Ronald sank down into his father's lounge chair, brown Naugahyde, a hammock of foam, fished around with one arm in the pile of papers and magazines on the floor. He had chosen a *National Geographic* and was beginning to leaf through "Colorful Ceylon Comes of Age," when his mother came back with a blue plastic star glass full of root beer. She bent to turn on the television: large bottom, inches of slip. The game popped on, bright green with white players. She brought him over the tray of potato chips and dip. He smiled up his family smile. Hands under her apron, she stood a while looking down at him — lips pursed, head cocked to one side, brows slightly raised over sympathetic eyes. The Worried Mother Look.

It was coming. One, two three, four, five . . .

It came.

"Oh, Ronny, Ronny!"

Sad, sad, said her shaking head.

"Look, Mom —"

"All right, that's all right," she interrupted at once. "No need to talk. No point in spoiling a lovely meal, as your father says."

He looked back at his magazine. "If you want." But she didn't. Colorful Ceylon. First and ten for the Bruins. The Look of Concern still pressing down.

"Ronny, Ronny, Ronny. You're still Mommy's best baby boy, you know that, don't you?" She stopped down by the arm of his chair to rumple his hair.

"Sure, Mom." At this moment, he did feel more an infant than he liked. Helpless. At Mommy's mercy.

She gave him a wet kiss below the ear (avoiding the scar), then stood up and went back to the kitchen.

God damn it to hell!

Ronald put down the *National Geographic* and stared, unseeing, at the television screen. It flashed through a series of commercials, neon green, hot pink. The rain had begun to fall more heavily, and for a few minutes he listened with lean contentment to it rattling on the roof, imagined it soaking the roots of flowers and shrubs. Bubble up, fill the gutters; pour, run, flood us all.

He stuffed a handful of chips in his mouth, drained the root beer, and, leaving the television babbling to itself, went to his room.

A Swedish sewing machine, beige, new, sat on his desk. Cardboard boxes full of fabrics and patterns and clothes to be mended were stored in his closet and along the wall next to his bed. Since he came home only for holidays now, and the occasional weekend, his mother had turned the space into her sewing room.

But the bed, the chair, the chest were the same. His old clothes were in the closet, his old things in the drawers. Neat piles of a boy's shirts and socks and underwear, clothes he no longer wore, like the room of some famous dead person, preserved exact and intact. His ship models and fossils and high school textbooks were on the shelves, his old posters of Paris on the wall. He tipped a Book of Knowledge at random out of its case, flopped on the bed, and began to leaf through it. Then he shut the book, laid it on his stomach, and stared up at the shapes on the ceiling.

Five minutes into his fantasy, he was pulled back from Europe by the noise of the men in his family coming in from their game.

Face it, fellow.

He swung his legs over the side of the bed, roused himself to join them.

The hearty noises in the kitchen died out abruptly as Ronald joined the party. "Ah, the boy artist from Berserkeley. Come down to visit the little people, have you? Us common money grubbers?"

"Now Fred, don't start in. Remember what we said."

Ronald smiled a pale hello at his uncle and father, and perched himself on one of the breakfast counter stools. The air was heavy with the odor of unspoken opinion and roasting turkey; the pressure of falling rain seemed to close them in the more.

His mother and aunt were bustling about doing housewifely-holiday things: reaching down china and glassware from high shelves, spooning tinned shrimp and tomato sauce into sherbet glasses, washing up the already used ware.

"Whattya say, Ronny?" said his brother, who had just popped open two beers. "Have an Olie?"

"Sure. Thanks."

The smells were disorienting his stomach, on top of potato chips and root beer (and worry; gut-anticipation). But he was anxious to pacify, assert common blood. The two older men were making a big comical do of tasting gravy, stealing shrimps, joshing the women. Hank sat on the stool next to Ronald. For a little while the two brothers sipped their beers in silence.

"I don't get you sometimes," Hank finally said. Half of a blue navy tattoo showed on his forearm. "Sometimes I don't understand anything you do."

Ronald couldn't think of a useful or civil thing to say.

"I guess it's that place."

The silence dragged.

"What it's done to you."

Try.

"What do you think it's done to me, Hank?"

"Made you think you're better than the rest of us. Made you too fuckin' good for us. Give you lots of funny ideas." He looked at Ronald. "Maybe worse things."

Ronald didn't think Hank was baiting him, like Uncle Fred. At least Hank believed what he said. The word *fuck* wasn't necessarily a sign of hostility. Everything had been *fuckin'* to brother Hank, since the navy. Ronald sipped his beer and tried to find more words.

"Different, Hank. Not better. But I was different from you guys before I ever went away to Cal. I didn't care about the same things you did back in high school, even before. Back in Granger. That's why I went to college, instead of just going to work. Or joining the navy."

"Ha. I'd like to see you in the navy. They'd beat your fuckin' ass off. Fuckin' ass."

"That's just what I'm saying, I wouldn't fit in at all. Christ, Hank, you do what *you* want. So does Dad, so does Mom. Uncle Fred. Why the, why the fuck can't *I* do what I want?"

"Because nobody does things like you do. Nobody normal . . . Oh shit, *do* what you want. I don't care." Hank chugged down his beer, got off the stool, and went back to the others.

Hell's bells, Ronald glowered after his back, what am I *supposed* to do? Agree with everything they say, pretend to be something I'm not?

You are pretending. Drinking beer, saying "fuck" for Hank's sake. Just being here is pretending. You don't belong in this *house* anymore. You're going to go through a whole afternoon's act, now, watching the game, drinking more beer, laughing at Uncle Fred's jokes, playing good ol' Ronny boy over all that inedible crap.

"Out! Everybody out! Shoo! Women's work to be done in here, else nobody's gonna get anything to eat. Out, out, out. You too, Ronny. You men go watch your game, and we'll call you when it's time."

The forty-five minutes till dinner passed tranquilly enough, thanks primarily to the box. Everyone attended to it with an exaggerated interest, grateful for the opportunity it provided to avoid the shadow Ronald's "case" had cast over their holiday. His uncle either looked at the set, or argued with his brother-in-law. Henry Harrington looked anywhere but at Ronald. Henry Junior, on the contrary, kept glancing at his younger brother with uncomfortable attention.

But all four pretended to care about nothing so much as UCLA's beating Washington, and after that, half a Bob Hope Thanksgiving Day Special. During the commercials they talked about the game (or the special). During the programs they discussed the things advertised on the commercials. With the last crumbled bits of potato chip, Ronald scraped up the last smear of sour cream mixed with packaged onion soup, and heard oblique references to himself in everything anyone said. The halftime display of new 1963 Pontiacs (in living color) made him wince for what he had written in his letter about cars. Anacin presented a family at dinner, dropping dishes, saying the wrong things, getting on each other's nerves (Happy Thanksgiving), then dissolving into fizzy concord, thanks to Anacin, made like a doctor's prescription. The Harringtons at home.

Worst of all, for some reason, was a string of predictable, not very funny jokes Bob Hope rattled off about the Kennedys at the start of his show. The three others laughed, and he didn't. And the three others watched him not laughing.

Oh, perhaps he was taking it all too personally. Perhaps they meant nothing at all.

They had done a lot to the living room in the last five years.

Mom had a Barcalounger now just like Dad's, except that hers was ivory colored, his a dark chocolate brown. They had put up a bar/room-divider near the opening to the dining room (where the women were now setting out glasses and plates), with two actual bar stools and a screen made of colored glass bricks. The new three-piece sofa Ronald and his brother were sitting on, upholstered in a tropical leaf print, curved around one corner of the room. Over their heads was a giant original oil painting on velvet of The Golden Gate Bridge by Night. The walls had been repainted in burnt orange, and new tropical print drapes had been hung on the window to match the upholstery.

In front of the sofa stood a large mosaic-top table, where the chips and dip had been. Underneath it was a fluffy white rug, laid on top of the original green carpet. Dozens of ceramic birds, which his mother had been collecting since before he was born, stood on the mantelpiece, between his Americanism contest trophy and his father's Salesman of the Year cup from Ford; they also spilled over onto knickknack shelves in the corners of the room. The birds and the gold trophies, as well as The Golden Gate Bridge by Night, were reflected in an antiqued gold-framed mirror over the mantel.

A family-size electric organ stood under the front window, between the fireplace and the new TV. The original set had been traded in two years ago on a 25-inch color TV-stereo combination in a French provincial cabinet, which stood in the opposite corner of the room from where Ronald was sitting. On top of the set were bud vases, statuettes, souvenirs, ashtrays, birds, family photos in hinged silver frames, and a large monkeypod wood planter lamp Hank had brought back from Honolulu, carved in the shape of a tiki god, which spilled philodendron leaves down alongside the knobs.

By the time Mom called them in to dinner, nothing had been mentioned about his letter or his plans. The agreed-upon Order of the Day was being maintained. They moved into the dining room with relative ease and good grace, making the ritual remarks about the size and smell of the turkey ("I just don't trust these newfangled pop-out plugs") and the great bowlsful of food, enough for twice their number. ("Mmm, sweet potatoes!" "Oh, great — cranberry sauce!" Surprise, surprise.) And the milk. Two half-gallon Marin-Dell cartons on the table, to wash down the Foremost Farms turkey and Langendorf's dressing mix, the mashed and sweet potatoes, the canned cream corn and frozen string beans, the shrimp cocktails, the ruby-colored slices of Ocean Spray cranberry sauce on sale at 29¢, the Wonder bread and Mary Ellen's jam, muffins from frozen twist-open cardboard cylinders, cubes of Bluebonnet margarine on silver plastic trays.

Dad said grace, and proceeded to carve the big bird at a folding card table set alongside his place, while they all complimented him on his work. Then forty minutes were spent asking and passing and scooping out and tasting, washing it all down with more and more milk, saying over and over how *good* everything was. Then seconds, then thirds, *more* meat, more sauce, more creamed corn, more potatoes, the napkin-covered baskets of muffins and bread going round and around, the margarine and gravy, the salt and pepper trying to keep up. Another half gallon of milk was brought in. The gravy boat was refilled. Spots here and there on the cloth. A sticky wishbone got pulled. Fred won. The first protests were finally heard.

"Oh, Grace, I just can't. I really can't."

"Come on, Fred. Someone's got to finish it up. It won't be near as good tomorrow."

"Well, just a drop. Hey, a *drop*, I said!"

"Now you, Ronny. What'll it be, white or dark?"

"Don't be silly. Here, pass him this. And hand the dressing on, Hank. Come on, you're ready for more. Let's have your plate."

"More milk?"

Burp.

"Yes, please."

"Pass the butter." (Seventeen years of using margarine, and they all still called it butter.)

"Here 'tis."

And so on, stuffing, feeding, chewing, swallowing, until the better part of twenty-eight dollars' worth of groceries was packed down inside half a dozen drum-tight bellies. Another Thanksgiving Dinner was moving to its close.

"Well," said his mother, two hours after they had started. "If no one's going to have any more, we might as well get up and let that good food settle a bit. We can set in the front room a spell, and have our pie and ice cream and coffee later on. I hope you all saved room!"

"Oh, Grace!" groaned fat Uncle Fred, theatrically. "Why didn't somebody remind me?"

"We give thee thanks, O Almighty God, for all thy benefits, which we have received this day from the bounty of Christ our Redeemer and Savior." His father paused, looked up, a bit fishy-eyed. Their glances met, parted; Ronald looked down, the mess on his plate. It was customary for the host to add something original on family feasts.

"On this day of thanks, we . . . ah . . . give thee thanks for . . . this great country of ours . . . of course . . . protect her from all her enemies, foreign and domestic . . . we thank thee for this lovely house and for all this wonderful food . . . for bringing us all together again, mother, father, sons, brothers and sisters. Help us to stay together, pray together, all do well and be happy and . . . not . . . um . . . do anything to hurt each other. Now and forever amen."

"Amen."

"Amen. Very nice, Henry."

"Amen."

" 'men."

They hauled themselves up, with much Falstaffian groaning and belching and patting of tummies, and dragged their extra fat into the living room, where they collapsed on the several couches and chairs. For a while, no one said much of anything but variations on how full they were and how good it all had been. Finally, after a heavy, overlong silence — a sort of intermission — Uncle Fred brought the meeting to order.

"Well, Ronny boy. What do you have to say for yourself?"

Ronald looked over at his father, who understood his plea — Don't let him run this.

"Yes, Ronny," said his father. "Now that we're through we probably ought to talk about your plans. I didn't want to spoil that lovely meal with serious talk, after your mother and Kate worked so hard."

Ronald felt so stuffed he could hardly think, let alone explain anything intelligently. What he really wanted to do was to go off somewhere and sleep, then wake up with all that awful food digested into soft, easy shit. But the rain kept on. No escape.

His mother had turned on several lamps. She and her sister sat on the two petit-point chairs Kate had done that stood alongside the television. It poured and poured. There was nowhere he could go.

"When we agreed to let you go to the university we thought it was understood that something worthwhile was to come of it. We didn't insist on business. That was your idea. Engineering would have been fine with us. Or law, or medicine, or something like that. But college is damned expensive, Ronny, and there's no point in staying in school for four extra years unless it's going to pay off. Do you follow me?"

"Yes sir. I mean no. What do you mean, 'pay off'?"

"I mean earn you more money than you could have made if you hadn't gone, plus the cost of going and four years' lost wages. On those terms, it seems to all of us that this 'art' business just doesn't make sense."

"Earning more money: Dad, I don't *care* about earning more money. The last thing in the world I want is to be another money grubbing . . . I mean, I don't want to waste my life just making money. That doesn't get you anywhere."

"Don't you *like* this house, Ronny?" his mother joins in. "This dinner? The new organ, the pool table? The new stereo and TV? Your own car? Are these all just 'useless things'? That's what you called them, you know. In that letter."

"Well, I." Oh hell. "Maybe I didn't mean that. Of course I like them. I want them as much as anybody." Except that I don't.

"Let me read you some lines from your own immortal prose." Fred Lee, Realtor, unfolded Ronald's letter out of his wallet. (What was he doing with it?) From across the room he could see red underlines. They had obviously read and reread it many times. Ronald suddenly felt that he was playing a role in some new absurd play where all the actors had memorized their parts, except him.

" 'I don't have much respect for business, either in the class-room or as a way of life. I never have. In fact I hated it.' What is *that* supposed to mean, young man? Young punk?"

Ronald fought against doing it, but it was no use; down went his head. He stared at the two pink, hairless hands that lay in his lap, so as not to have to meet his uncle's piggish glare. Once he had bent down — and he *knew* it would happen — he began to feel as guilty as he looked.

"And this: and this too. 'Is it really any better selling cars for Mr. Bigger, however much money you make? You just work and work to keep up and make more, to buy more useless things, to get ahead of other people.'

"Is that what you think of us? Is that what you think we're doing, your father and me?"

What could he say? "I don't know. I . . . I was just trying to explain why I wanted to study art. Maybe I said some things I shouldn't have."

"Damned right you did. Your father and I didn't go to any expensive commie college, neither one of us. Nobody paid us to sit on our asses for four years and bite the hand that feeds us. Foul our own nests. Whatever it is. We worked! We worked for every penny. And we're not ashamed of it either. Didn't we work, Henry? Why, do you know how much money your dad is worth today? Do you have any idea how much real ready nineteen sixty-two cash dollars your father and I are worth today?"

"No." And I don't *give* a shit, can't you understand that? Oh, this is idiocy!

"I don't *care*, Uncle Fred. It doesn't *mean* anything to me. Like I wrote in the letter, I knew you wouldn't approve, any of you. But I told you, I can pay my own way from now on. So it seems to me I ought to be able to make some of my own choices. Is that so unfair?" He looked over at his father. "This art thing is what *I* want to do, Dad. You can see for yourself how well I'm doing."

"Yes, Ronny, that's very nice. But you're not a high school kid anymore. Good grades don't buy groceries." He liked the phrase, fresh invented, tried its ring again: " 'Good Grades Don't Buy Groceries.' What can you *make* out of all this?"

"Dad, that isn't the point. Oh, I can probably teach, or get a job in a museum or something. But it's more a matter of learning all I can about something I like, working at it because I believe in it. Like the kids joining the Peace Corps. Most of the people I know at Berkeley feel this way, that just making it isn't enough."

"You know some pretty funny people." Hank.

"I've heard the Peace Corps is just a front for the U.N.," nibbled Kate from her corner.

"Oh, I don't think so," her sister whispered.

His forces were ebbing. He hated the heat of open hostility — and he was the one who was causing it. On Thanksgiving Day. *Please* let them understand.

"I appreciate everything you've done. Really. And I appreciate how hard it's been. I went to college because my teachers in high school thought I ought to go. I went because I had the grades and could make it. You all agreed it was the right thing to do. To go as far as you can, no matter how hard it is, no matter where it takes you. I know I talked about it in terms of a job like yours, Dad, but that was because none of us knew about anything else. If I agreed to study business, it was because I didn't know anything better.

"But now I *do* know something better. I know there are better things I can do with my life than sell cars or real estate, or work for Wells Fargo Bank, better things than make money and then make more money, just save and save and buy and buy forever. To me, that's a lot of crap."

"Now just a minute here. What do you think's been paying for you to go to school for the last two years — for the last eight, twelve, *fourteen* years? Your father's hard-earned money, that's what, that and the taxes people like us have paid. Money he earned selling cars, working damned hard. It don't seem to me you're anyone to go knocking the business world. You've been living off it long enough."

How about letting Dad talk for himself, you fat ass?

"How about letting Dad talk for himself?"

"Because he's too goddam easy on you, that's why! And

don't you sass me, boy. For Christ's sake, Henry, are you just gonna sit there and take this crap? 'Money grubbers,' 'profiteers.' Listen to what he's been calling us! 'Capitalists.' What's your son turning into, some kinda communist?"

"No, Fred. I'm sure he's not doing that. Are you, Ronny?"

"Dad, I swear. There's nothing political in any of this. I don't give a damn about politics."

"That's almost as bad. What a hell of a thing to admit."

"Oh, come on, Uncle Fred! You blame me for being political, now you blame me when I say I'm not."

"It's an American citizen's duty to care about politics. That's what Democracy's all about. You're supposed to be the big expert on citizenship, I thought."

"Oh shit. You know damn well politics is just a lot of lies and bribes, and tax breaks for big property owners."

"Now you listen here!"

"I'm sure he didn't mean . . ."

"We're all getting a bit het up . . ."

"He doesn't know *what* he means!"

True. It was true. Tax breaks, property owners. What did *that* mean? Somehow the play had gotten away from him again. He was saying things that weren't in the script. If only that asshole weren't here. He was sure he could make his father understand.

"Now Ronny," his mother tried. She was dismayed by his language, as much as anything. First Hank, now Ronny. "Why don't you start again. Explain to us exactly what it is you want."

OK. He pressed two fingers against his eyelids. As the room disappeared, he saw nothing but strangely glowing darkness, felt nothing but the touch of two fingers. Maybe when I open my eyes they'll be gone.

Nope. All still there.

Tell you what it is I want? He stared at a reflection of The Golden Gate Bridge by Night, painted on black velvet.

I want white rooms furnished with a few fine things made of wood and gold and thin glass. I want to be lean and smooth, covered with sweat and dark hairs. I want to be strong and warm and hard, I want the sea cresting and crashing inside me, forever, I want to be able to do anything, be anyone, go anywhere, to run and jump, to swim, to melt, to fly. I want to get out of here. He looked at their faces. I want to smash you all.

"Mom." "Dad." Some common language. He squeezed his hands together, tight in his lap.

"Back in Fort Wayne, we used to have something. I don't know what. Something we don't have here. In Granger, too. Maybe it was just because I was a kid, and didn't know any better. The snow. Our own apples, too many of them, every year, watching them come, waiting for them to ripen, picking them, eating them. All the things we grew, all the things Grandpa grew. Corn. Chickens. Rhubarb. The kind of clouds we had, the lightning and thunder, they don't *have* those here. All the space nobody lived in or built on, all the dirt and weeds along the creek. Millions of different kinds of trees. Even the bugs. The noisy clocks. Grandma Hemann's old quilts. That little tower room.

"I know you like California better, you and Mom, and I understand. Everything's easier, everything works better. It's so much simpler to get around. You can make so much more money." Harrington's Ford, Granger, Indiana: that must have hurt. "And I don't knock it, I mean I don't *mean* to.

"But I . . . Well." No more momentum. "Do you get what I mean about Fort Wayne?"

"Yes. I guess so, son. But you can't go back."

"But you *can*, Dad, you can! I mean *I* can. In a way. There were things I liked about the old place, the old ways we did things. Things I liked a lot. And I've come to realize, the last couple of years, that I just haven't got what it takes to make it this way. Your way. Be a success, I mean, here in California. I just can't do it. Let's say it's my fault, I'm sure it is, it's my fault! I'm no *good* at selling, pushing a product, no good at running things and getting ahead."

"You haven't even tried it. Wrapping packages at Ward's, working for that fairy bookstore. One and a half summers at Wells Fargo."

"I don't have to try it, Uncle Fred, I *know* I'm no good.

What's more, I hate it. I'm so bad at it it makes me sick even trying."

"We all have to do some things we don't like, dear. You can't stay in school forever."

"Ah but you *can*, Mom, that's what I found out this year, you can do it perfectly respectably. You can even make a living at it. Why there are two thousand grown men and women at Berkeley doing it right now!"

"But is that really all you want to do?" asked his father. "Stay in school forever?"

"He means the perfessors, dear."

"Oh. Well, that's hardly the same thing as staying in school forever. If you really want to be a teacher, why don't you come out and say so? I'm sure the professors at Cal make one hell of a lot more than high school teachers, anyway. And they've got a damned good pension plan too — which is more than we've got, Fred.

"I don't know. Maybe it's worth a few more years, if that's what you really want."

OK, Dad. Thanks. Your game.

"Right, Dad, that's true. I do want to teach. And I think I'd be good at it. You make up to twenty, twenty-five thousand, eventually. And they can't even fire you."

"You're kidding." Even Fred is interested now.

"Not after seven years. If they keep you seven years, you're in till age sixty-five. Unless you rape the chancellor's wife or something."

"Ronny!"

"Ha!"

Even Hank.

"And then you're pensioned off at eighty percent full pay. Every summer off. Every seventh year off. Six hours' teaching a week."

"Hey hold on a minute! How do I get into this racket?"

Keep it up, you phony little bastard. Sell it all out, fake it up, dirty it, warp and twist everything you care about in the world to make it fit into their narrow little minds.

"That's right, Uncle Fred. And all those sorority girls in

Bermuda shorts coming to your office in the afternoon to ask for help."

"Does that sort of thing really go on there, do you think?" asked Aunt Kate, who had just started to hand around dessert. "I mean, the things you hear about Berkeley. I always wondered how much of it was true. Pumpkin or mince?"

Easy sailing, storm center passed. Nothing had been answered, nothing said. He had consciously taken the safest, smoothest course, the direction he knew would bring him out least damaged, most in line with the rest. Nine hours a week, twenty thou and up, sorority girls in Bermuda shorts.

The lower left corner of his stomach ached with a small private pain. He had lied, it was saying to him, cruelly lied. Lied against himself. He had done it a dozen times before, but this time he had sworn to himself he would not.

But it was so nice to talk easily, rapidly, over forkfuls of pumpkin pie and ice cream melting into slush; so simple to oversimplify, to reduce it all to their kind of vision. And the horror was that they seemed to crave the oversimplifications, the caricatures and lies, seemed not even to suspect that the truth could be anything more complex or difficult to tell. Not one of them seemed able to make room in his head for the possibility that their little Ronny could, deep down, be any different from the rest of them. The more he sank into warm, easy lies, the more readily they believed. He ran glibly, excitedly on, stuttering in the cozy joy of seeing them so alert, so understanding and responsive. It wasn't that much different from high school. Sex was pretty casual (and not really rough). Most of the Ban-the-Bomb types were just in it for kicks. There were professors who kept big sailboats at the Marina, who consulted for Avco at three hundred a day. Connections were what mattered. Research grants were so much easy money.

Until in the end, in the interests of Making Them Understand, he had managed to reduce the whole academic enterprise to a whorish travesty of the truth, a corrupt, ignoble, cynical, capitalistic comedy. And they gulped it down, along with the mince and pumpkin pie à la mode and the instant coffee.

Ah, but he was with them, and they were with him, and that was good. Maybe it was just for a few minutes, but they were smiling, laughing at his tales, feeding him with questions, trading analogous ancedotes of lusts and chicanery out of auto showroom, real estate office, church group, Ladies' Aid, Kiwanis, Chamber of Commerce — between giggles and guffaws and snatches of song, more pie, more coffee, more coffee, more pie.

And damn it, that *was* a good thing. He felt slightly giddy and unstrung, he would grant you, from his role-playing, his fantasy tales. But there was an honesty in his urge to be one with them that went far beyond the mere surface dishonesty of his libels on the university world. For today — for this moment — he meant what he said. He was proving to himself that he could still be little Ronny Harrington from Fort Wayne, Indiana, his parents' son, his brother's brother.

Afterwards, conversation ran in as many directions as spilled marbles on a hardwood floor. The ladies talked lady talk, the men man talk, over whiskey and mints and sweet grape wine: all sorts of local gossip and fourteen-times-told tales Ronald was now family-high enough to find enthralling. How nice to sink back, on a curving three-piece sofa, with your stocking feet propped on a mosaic-top table, sipping a cloying glass of warm sweet wine after a giant family feast, and share their enthusiasm about Berta Lawson's husband's leg, or a fuel injection carburetor, or that property near Walnut Creek that was going for twelve hundred more an acre than it had in '59.

Darkness settled, talk thinned. The ladies got up first, insisted No, they didn't want help with the dishes. "You men just set and rest." Uncle Fred decided to take a nap in the front bedroom with belt and buttons undone, and proved his contentment to the chefs with a gargantuan burp. Mr. Harrington said he was just too comfortable to move. "I'll light us a fire later on." Hank offered to show Ron his new car; the rain seemed to have stopped.

"Love to, Hank. Let's see what you're wasting your money on these days."

Out in front, Hank pointed out a few things under the hood, split cowhide upholstery, custom dash, silver fittings, some work he had done himself to the body. Ronald responded with genuine delight, not so much at the car as at his brother's willingness to display it.

"What do you say to a ride?"

"Great. Let's see what this little mother can do."

The boys got in. Hank turned on the lights, gunned the three-hundred-sixty-horsepower engine: they roared away. Ronald felt almost drunk with his success at soldering the family bond. As they drove out Coronado onto Heggenberger Road he kept muttering highschoolish phrases about the car's performance, about cars in general, about Hank as a driver. Hank said little (but then Hank rarely said much), and stared straight ahead.

"You really love these mothers, don't you?"

"Yep."

"What kind of a car would you buy if you could afford any one in the world?"

"Lamborghini. Lamborghini twenty-six hundred. Special racing Bentley engine. It's cut down like the new XKE, only lower. Bronze with dark brown and cream striping. I saw one in Honolulu."

"How much would a thing like that cost?"

"Twenty-five, thirty thousand."

"Wow."

They were on the freeway now, heading south toward the bridge, when Hank opened it up. Traffic was thick, and the road surface still oily wet, but by cutting in and out (which he liked to do anyway), Hank managed to get it up over a hundred before they reached the Alameda off ramp.

Ron was properly impressed. Hank pulled off on the MacArthur-380 exit, but instead of turning around to go home, as Ronald had expected, he kept right on 380 heading east. Neither said a word.

Ronald looked at his brother's face. It was set in a peculiar way, as if he were thinking something he didn't want to say out loud. Ronald sat back, his head on the headrest, and tried to keep up the act of having a great old fuckin' brotherly time, going fast as hell in Hank's new red car.

Now they were onto the Warren Expressway, heading south again along a shelf out into the hills. Hank spoke.

"Did you know I'm going to get married?"

"No! When'd you decide? God, that's great, Hank. Why didn't anybody tell me? Ramona?"

"Yeah. Ramona." Eyes straight ahead, staring at the road. Going very fast.

"When'll it be?"

"Sometime after Christmas. February probably." Too fast.

"That's fantastic. Really: fantastic. Gosh, imagine getting married!"

"Ramona and me were talking about you." Ramona was one of a pair of twin sisters, lean redheads with wild reputations. Hank had been going with her officially ever since he broke up with her sister Carol in his senior year. Ronald still had trouble telling them apart.

I wonder why nobody talked about it at the house. Maybe they'll ask me to be best man. Hey, maybe I'm the first one he's told!

"Don't the folks know yet?"

"Yeah, they know." Almost clipped by a yellow truck. 90, 95. Keep talking.

"Funny nobody mentioned it."

"Well. We had to talk about your plans."

"I mean, but after. This is just as important. *More* important." The trees of Chabot (picnics) flying past, gone.

"Well they're kind of tied together. We never really did finish talking about what you're going to do. Did we? You sort of steered the conversation away. Huh? Right?"

Ronald felt as if he had been slapped.

"You got joking about chicks and payoffs and stuff like that and everybody went along with it, probably to keep Uncle Fred from belting you.

"But I didn't like that. I wanted answers."

He turned his head from the road and looked straight at Ronald, for the first time.

"I still do. So does Ramona. We had a long talk about you last night, Ramona and me."

Bang just like that, right back in the worst days of high school. Knotted up, no defenses. Nobody's brother, nobody's son. "What did you talk about?" Ronald nearly whispered.

"What you do all the time. The way you drive out to places alone. Lock yourself in your room." A sideways glance, eye met eye. "Ramona asked me if you were sick."

"What do you mean sick?" Be calm. "I just like to be alone, that's all. I like to read.

"You're not always reading. Sick in the head is what she means. She wants to know if you're sick in the head."

"What the hell business is it of hers?"

"She's thinking of being my wife, that's what the hell business it is of hers. She wants to know what kind of a fucking nut case she's getting for a fucking brother-in-law.

"Anyway, forget about her, _I_ want to know. So does Dad. And I told him if he didn't ask you I would.

"So I'm asking."

"Asking what? If I'm crazy?"

"Not exactly." They turned off the expressway onto San Salvador Boulevard. They were heading back home.

"I don't suppose you'd know if you were. I just want to know what you do all the time. Why you act the way you do. Nobody else I know acts like you. I don't like thinking maybe my own brother's a . . ."

"A what? What do you think I am? A communist? Is that what you think?"

"No, that's Uncle Fred's line. Anybody funny is a fucking communist. No, I don't think you're any of that." They both waited, as silence generated silence. "Why don't you come home anymore?"

"Because I like it better where I am. Today went off OK, I thought. Maybe I was wrong."

"Maybe. Maybe you _should_ stay away."

"So I won't embarrass Ramona?"

. . .

"You spend a lot of time alone, then?"

"I've *got* to, Hank. It takes me twenty hours a week just to keep up with the reading." Not so shrill. Keep the voice *down*.

"Don't you ever go out?"

"Oh, sure; sure. I go to movies a lot, sure, plays on campus, concerts, museums. I like to go to the city and drive around. I go out to places to eat . . ."

"Out on dates, I mean."

"Well. Yeah. Sometimes. A girl named Phyllis in my sculpture class, she and I went out a few times. She's pretty scaggy, but her folks have money. Her father . . ." He stopped. They drove into Coronado Road. Hank said nothing for three blocks.

"Ramona says she saw you in the city one night with a pretty funny looking guy. Chinese."

Tony. "So?"

"The way he was dressed, for one thing. The way the two of you were acting."

"There are a lot of fine people your precious Ramona probably thinks of as funny-looking. People don't have to comb their hair the way you do, you know. They don't have to go around spewing out all their money on dumb cars and saying 'fuck' all the time to be decent, normal, useful people."

"Yeah. Well. Maybe." They were parked in front of the house. "But apparently she learned something about this guy Tony. And about your friend Koerner. And your big buddy Zack at San Salvador."

"Zack was no big buddy of mine. Ask your friend Jacobson. *He* was his big buddy."

"Watch who you're accusing."

"Accusing of what?"

Hank looked him straight on, for the second time, and asked it.

"Are you a queer?"

"Oh, for Christ's sake, is that what you assholes think?"

Ronald bolted out of the car, bursting with frustration.

"Well, fuck you all." He slammed the door hard, but it caught on a seat belt buckle and fell open.

"Tell them . . . Tell them . . . Tell them . . ." He was trying to keep his voice low. "Tell them I had a fucking *date!*" he yelled from his own car, as he climbed in and turned the key. *Start, damn you!*

"Who with? Your roommate?" Hank shouted back.

Ronald flipped his brother the finger, peeled rubber off his tires backing out of the driveway, squealed off into the night.

Happy fucking Thanksgiving.

five.

Awake. He lifted his wrist till it fell within the single bar of
light. Minutes to four.

The Dead of Night.

On his other arm lay her head. Its weight had stopped the
flow of blood. From the elbow down his arm felt dead. One
white hand curved upon his chest, soft fingers against his skin.

Trapped. My arm is dead.

No. Not trapped. That was foolish. Some tag end of a dream.
But could I (how could I) get away?

Pale bars of white light reached from cracks in the shutter
down across the floor, then crawled aslant the bed up to the
black mirror of the wardrobe. A dark room, barred with pale
light. At just before four in the morning.

He stared toward the empty place where the mirror was.
Ting-Bang, Gong. Bong. Notre Dame. A minute; then four
more. Saint Marcel. Always, for that minute, no time. Ting-
Bang, Gong, Bong, gonging in his head.

He was trapped with a girl in a dark room barred with light
in the middle of France, and the dark room smelled of thousands of couples who had lain in these very same sheets, and in
that smell was everything that was wrong. It lay heavy against
the pores of his skin, heavy against his soul. The sheets were

seventy-nine

rough, yellowed and patched; they had been used and resewn many times. He and she had rolled the fat bolster onto the floor, and it lay there now laddered with light, in a quiet heap with their clothes. It had been warm, even hot when they went to bed, so they had pulled off the quilt as well, leaving only a single sheet. Now a small chill eddied in with the moonlight. Awake, Ronald could scarcely bear its touch, cold air prickling still-damp skin. It tormented his shoulder, his free arm, his throbbing temples.

Get out, the voice said, now, while she's asleep. Creep up, clothes, slip out, downstairs, away.

He looked at her, tried to make out her difference, her sleeping form.

Jill's face lay out of reach of the bars of moon. Strands of hair fell across her features, puffed, a bit babyish in sleep. The curves of her body looked timeless and nonhuman: sand dunes; undulations.

Ronald sank back under the rough cloth, shifted one leg over her bent knee, closed eyes and mind tight against the moon. She moved up against him, still asleep, and he began once more, biting hard against the flesh of the inside of his mouth. Moon bars lay across his back, unmoving as he moved.

Escape cold, heat, light, dark. Escape the smell of this room, the black of mirror, the rasp of the sheet, the dark pile on the floor. Notre Dame and Saint Marcel still ringing inside his skull over and over, Ting-Bang, Bong, Gong. Escape them, this room, this place, France, her, him, all.

They pulled together now, talking in breaths rather than words, fearful of breaking into thought. She was still only half awake, thinking nothing, only shapes. The dark became darker, the warmth warmer, the place more tangible, more real until there was nothing else and no one else in it but the two, the very nearly one of them swimming frantically towards a haven through wet, wrinkled sheets.

Ronald grew anxious, tried too hard, came too quickly; he always did. She pulled and whispered, *more*, teased, fingered him, kissed him. "Please, Ronald." But he moved away, curled up hard on his other side, sullen and discontent. He bit down on the inside of his mouth and thrust his hand between his legs. Keep away, his body said. But she fitted herself to the back of him, and for a few moments tried with her body to ease his fret, soften his selfishness, encourage him back into her arms. But he would not be encouraged.

So she pulled the sheet tight around her shoulders and rolled back away. She must, again, sort out her private nightfeelings as best she could, seek for sleep on her own in a bed made for two.

Bitter; he felt very bitter. It's no good. There *is* no escape.

No, that's not true. In his selfishness he had to admit it, in his anger. Sometimes there is. Just not this time.

He held tight to what was left of his manhood and stared up toward the one bar of light that had reached the black mirror. Then a rush of affection for Jill poured over him. It flooded his heart, then the rest of him. He rolled over onto his back, and touched her hair gently.

"Sorry," he whispered, near to her ear.

She turned back too, smiling and cuddly, and curled up once again next to his side, her head on his arm, her hand curved against his chest.

The light from the shutters had moved, and he could no longer make out the hands on his watch.

The next day they had decided to bicycle into the country-side. Early in the morning they bought what they needed for a picnic lunch, and headed south along the main road toward Mâcon.

Jill!

Silence, silence after the blues. Hold on to her, Ronald! (but she is dead), resist (but she is dead).

> When
> I lost my baby
> I al
> most
> lost
> my
> mind

The man is charging back and forth across the stage, whirling around at the turns; slowly, sinuously moving across the lip of the stage.

> When
> I lost my

Lyrics melt like Francis Bacon faces, into something neurotic and awful, into the chattering and grunting of the mentally deranged.

Don't listen to what he's saying, don't. Try to remember *Et ton doux corps*, that song *Auprès du mien*, how did it go? Cluny.

Shaking hysterically, turning faster and faster, kickstepping as if in pain, Jagger grimaces, jabs his thin, sharp knees and elbows up, back, up, back, twitching and kicking; a nonhuman thing, a dead black reptile galvanized into life. Into the noise streak ghastly wired screams.

The hysteria spreads, irresistibly, into the crowd. People are standing now in the near-dark, sweating, twitching too, making their own awful noises, washed with a sweep of bloodred light from behind the stage, where Jagger sags wasted, his hair a wet tangle, his black-sheathed silver-spangled body limp, drained, used. He holds onto the microphone stand with both hands, stares into the bloodwashed crowd with huge hollow animal eyes. Behind, a low growl, a gentle tap, a single squeal; all that remains of the epileptic racket of seconds ago. Quiet. Very quiet.

> Don' do that.
> Noooooo, don' do that,

he whispers, looks down at the floor. *Don' do that*. Weaker. Less noise. Silence.

He drops his hands, turns around. Ronald's head is once again a cave full of this, a bloody cave full of this, and nothing else. Five men look at each other in chill, nerveless space. Not breathing: waiting; regaining strength. A drum is tapped; again. One chord is blown into the thin reed of a harmonica.

Poking, fingering, noodling around. Then a plucked, whining note on the guitar. Another. Louder.

Jagger pulls away, and before Ronald realizes the shape his own vision is taking, the star of it has unbuckled his heavy silver-studded belt and dropped to his knees, facing sideways, head bowed, drenched in a single red spotlight in the now total dark. The growl rises, low and erotic, gradually shaping into words, until now he is shouting, loud and clear and full of force.

> WEEEELLLLL:
> Ya heard about da Bos-ton

CRASH! He flings the glittering belt over his shoulder and brings it smashing to the floor in front of him. *Jumps,* Ronald jumps in the darkness, as if lashed across the back.

> Honey, he's not one a'
> *those!*

Crash! and with each smashing arc of the belt, each jarring jolt forward of the kneeling body, the band squeezes out one fat jangling bundle of noise, dissonant and abrupt.

> *JAMAIS, A DIT JOHNNY.*
> *SHEILA EST DESOLÉE*
> *BRIAN JONES S'EST SUICIDÉ.*

(Hey   fat   boy   watcha lookin at
me   nothing
c'mere
huh
i said c'mere
come over heah
what do you want
well   what do you want
hey
wassamatta fats
hey you guys
        you nevah seen befoah!

hey quit it   leave me alone
hit back fatboy   wassamatta you chicken
cluckcluckcluck
just leave me alone
where's yo mama
none of your business
where's yo mama fatboy
quit that   just keep your hands off me
you want your mama   huh
no   just leave me alone   goddamn it
hey you made him cry charlie
awwww
wanna cry some more   fat baby
babybabybaby
les make him beg
i know how to make him beg
just let me go   please let me go
hey   he beggin already pete
beg some more
we let you go fats   after you do one thing
yeah   jus one thing
right)

> *walkin like a proud black pantha*
> *knife sharp / bedroom doah*
> *a hit and run raper in angah*

No, doctor, I don't know what it means. You do but you're just
not telling me, Ronald. No, sir. That's not true. I really don't.
But it seems obvious. Obvious. Doesn't it seem obvious to
you?

> *gonna smash down all your plate glass windows*
> *put a fist through your steel front door*

No, sir. But surely you can see the connection? the connection?
the connection?

Smash down all the plate glass windows. Put a fist through the
steel front door. The sheet unwound, the body rolled down the
sand then into the water, but the eyes were open all the time.

eighty-four

Dad, I'm sorry. Break every pane of every window, pour gasoline over the furniture, watch it burn. I could do that, Mick. I could do that if you wanted me to.

Where ya headin, fellow?
Bancroft and Telegraph. But anywhere near the university will be fine.
Hop in.
Say, you look sick.
My car was just smashed up. It's at that garage, the one on the corner there. I just had it towed.
No shit. Totaled?
Yeah.
You sure you're OK?
Sure. Sure I'm sure. *My father's*
I. *I don't want to* I don't want to talk about it *you dirty freaks*
Did you
You heard him, Bobby. He don't want to talk about it.
Hey, could you let me out at that light instead? I just remembered, I just remembered *my God they're* I've gotta go back and *we almost hit that* Could you please let me off? *Dad I*

It would really be better for you to keep coming, Ronald. Things like this take a long time to work out. I know that, dcotor. But I think I'd rather try to do it myself. I think if I keep talking about it I'll just end up more screwed up. But talking about it may well be the only way to resolve it. To get free of it. I know that, doctor. But I've got to stop thinking about it for a while. I can't convince you, then? No, sir. I'm sorry. I'm just not getting anything out of this. But don't worry. I'm OK now. I can cope.   Cope.   Dope.   Hope.

Please could you just stop. I've gotta
Oh for Chrissake, Harvey. Let's let him out. You can have the next one.
A gun.   Oh my god a gun.
Take off your clothes, fella.

Harvey!
Dad I'm sorry.
Your clothes. Take them off! *I*
All of them! *The car swerved maniacally, gun barrel touched him, cold steel against his.* I will. Sure I will. All.
Hey fella, what do you think we should do with you? *laughing!*

Freaks, crazy queer freaks, laughing skidding all those people outside all those cars crazy hippie freaks with a gun, it can't, oh god please please god, please be a dream
Click.
No! Don't! *It's so stupid but it's* Don't shoot me, please! *they won't stop laughing*
Dad I'm sorry. Dad I'm sorry. Oh my God I am heartily
Get out.
Get
Out. *Leaned back over, opened the door and pushed him out, shivering.* Here, asshole! *The clothes. Then drove away laughing.*
"Over here! Over here, Helen!"
"Must be some college stunt."
"Have you ever seen . . ."
"Look at the poor bastard."
"At least they gave him his . . ."

Cymbals crash, up rises the whimpering, then whining, shouting, threatening noise, drowning out Jagger's mutters, crawling its way back up to the heavy humping heat, back on his knees, unintelligible, one white starlight emblazons him at the last (Alistair!), lurched forward doglike at the edge of the stage, snarling, ready to snap:

Gonna stick my knife right down your throat!

"I wish I could *see* all you people.
"We'd like to see how you loooook. You can see us, and we're *beau-ti-ful*, but we can't see *you!*
"Chip, let's have some *light* on these people."
Instantly the arena is bright as noonday. People stare at their hands, their clothes, at one another, as if emerging from

years spent in dark underground prisons. They turn about and look at the crowd, turn up and stare into the great circle of light.

Then they run.

Once, as a small boy in Indiana, Ronald had found himself enclosed by a mob of taller people at a circus, all running faster than he could move. It was a nightmare of the very worst kind come to life. Panicky, unable to see, he had run too fast, tripped, and fallen down in the mud. He could not even scream out, so white and absolute was his terror of being crushed to death under big people's feet. He was trod on once or twice, but the crowd was not so thick or unruly that he went unnoticed for long. A big boy in overalls picked him up, held him in his arms, and yelled at the folks around to make room. Then the boy carried him off to the side and set him down on one of the hay bales, where he was surrounded by consoling strangers. He said nothing, just sat there crying until his big brother Hank came and took him home.

Ever since, he had had the liveliest fear of being surrounded by people in such a way as to leave him no clear and easy means of escape. And that was precisely where he was now. There were no doors out and no ways to them; there was no space between the rows of chairs; there were no aisles. There were only bodies, a great crush of maniac young bodies shoving and pushing forward, trying to get to Mick. The air was filled with one gigantic six million cubic foot wad of noise.

I can't GET no

so he could have screamed out his lungs for space and gone utterly unregarded,

I can't GET no

if he fell, if he tripped, if his chair was pushed over he would simply be suffocated, covered with dust, crushed underfoot,

No no no

people were climbing on their chairs, climbing on one another's shoulders, waving their arms in the air, trying to see, trying to fly, trying to be there with Mick, who was shouting, shaking, dancing along with them in his ecstasy of

> I can't GET no
> I can't GET no
> I can't GET no

frustration.

Ronald gripped the edge of his steel chair, pulled his feet tight back on the rung. He bent his head down toward his lap to close out of consciousness the stinking crush of other people's feet and legs and thighs and buttocks, other people's clothes, other people. Curled up into a warm ball of fear, gut knotted with nervous pain, he felt dehumanized, stripped of himself, a tiny sentient ball caught up in some roiling furry thing. He closed in on the one lighted spot of awareness in his skull, and let himself be pounded and stung by the electric noise, as if in abandoning himself to what he could make out of the music he might be able to forget the other nightmare, the hot bodies squeezed in tightly all around him.

> Well I tried
> And I tried
> Yes I tried

At first, only the lowest bass noise rackets around in his skull, a great rasping sawing bee-buzz, tuba deep and snarling. He tried to yield up all his head space to this demanding, commanding buzz-rasp, low and electric, totally compelling, sawing over and over: soon he feels himself beating inside to the throb of the music. The mob is raising so much din of its own, right in his face, that he cups his hands over his ears and lets only the lowest vibrations of the music work through his skull cage, send their resonances into his connected bones, then deep into the gut, the groin, the arms and legs. Suddenly they cannot stay still, but must shiver and shake with the beat. The pit of his stomach becomes a resonant drum, his head the inside of a struck iron bell. He feels an electric current from the stage running through his whole skeleton, over all his flesh. The music is taking him over.

Halfway down the stairs, Jill had frozen. She could not see or imagine either end, nothing but steep stone steps that curved and plunged out of sight. She imagined them infinitely extending, and panic seized her limbs. In her mind's eye, then her body's eye, the steps thinned out to a single column, then sloped away altogether, until she was in a deep stone well, falling, falling down, and yet her legs paralyzed with fear, unable to move. She clutched the outer wall in desperation, tried to dig fingernails into the old stone, when a large black bug ran across her hand; she hit at it and exploded into tears. Near to her squashed bug, someone had scraped words on a stone: NAZIS BATARDS. She screamed one word, that word his name, "Ronald!"

A dissonant tremor, an intimation of something wrong, something up by the stage. Faces frown in the midst of their shouting, as the shadow moves back, row by row. A thread made up half of silence, half of angry, abrupt shouts begins to sew itself into the thick web of noise. Ronald is still attached to the center of power, still tingling in nerve and bone, but he too catches the needle's chill of uncertainty passing through the crowd. He strains to see, but cannot: some sort of commotion up by the stage. Now the Jagger voice seems to be missing from the consort of noise, and a counterpoint of angry hubbub begins to break through the music.

Suddenly he seizes a flash view of the stage: a swarm of uniformed backs, arms hitting out wildly with sticks and clubs. At what? What's going on? There: a monstrous articulated caterpillar is crawling up over the edge of the stage, resolving itself as he watches into a hysterical gang of fans who have managed to work their way through the line of guards. Now the crowd walls together. The stage is gone. The song appears to be resuming its course: he hears Jagger's raggedy voice plowing defiantly through the din,

Hey! think the TIME is RIGHT for
Palace RevoLOOO-shun!

The band has pulled itself up to a peak of dazzling, jangling acid joy unlike anything before. Together, superbly one, they are pounding/ringing/rattling out a noise of hammering ecstatic madness from the stage in Ronald's head, thrusting forward layer upon drum-chopped layer of dense, metallic, beautiful noise. Twitching free in sympathetic vibration, Ronald is shaking his head from left to right, left to right, when suddenly, just to his left, he sees somebody's body being lifted out over the crowd, hand over hand. Passed out, beaten up, dead, a human body carried backwards out of the pack by a chain of spidery arms in the air. Trampled to/ Ronald shut his eyes, clapped a hand over his mouth/ I'm going to be

graduate student was bound and cruelly beaten to death yesterday in a South of Market hotel. The body of the dead man, identified as Anthony Lum, was discovered in a room at the Wieland Hotel, 410 Fourth Street, which he had rented on Tuesday afternoon in the company of an unidentified male companion described as fifty or fifty-five, about five foot six, two hundred pounds

Up on the screen, now, great livery lips are singing the song of their life:

But what can a poor boy do
'Cept to sing for a rock 'n' roll band?

But not my life: No. I mustn't let him

Cause in sleepy London town there's just
No place for

I'm giving in much too easily, just because I . . . because I . . .

Street fightin' man!

If this is right, then everything else is wrong.
He stared around.
Thousands, packed body to body and screaming. Mindless,

screaming idiot kids. Barbarians. They run in packs, take over buildings, pour bottles of blood over library cards. Wheeler Hall, the morning after: gutted, stinking of dead smoke; a stage set out of hell. Joining forces with that.

But I'm *not!* I'm not like them. I don't want to be like them. I haven't their kind of head, their kind of blood or body. They'd never let me —

Oh, Ronald, *think!*

I don't want to think.

What do you want?

This. I want *admit it* I want *say it* I want Jagger.

But how can this make sense, and everything else not? It's not even music, it's something human, nerves unstrung and electrified, blood set on fire to boil.

To be them, to be one of them. To move in their wake, their circle, uncorking bottles, hanging up clothes. To be a servant, a valet.

Oh *stop* it. You're just gutter dragging. Slumming for kicks.

Not true. Not this time.

Just like Tony.

No. This is more.

More than death?

I don't know. An answer. Let's say it's an answer. For now. (I'm free; to do what I want; any old time.)

Stop fighting. Let it be. Let *yourself* be, creature of the noise, slave to the men.

And so he does.

His feet beat on the floor as if commanded to from stage, hands drum against the chair, against his knees. He feels ordered to do more, Mario to his magician, so he clambers up onto his metal chair and begins turning to right and to left in a sort of fat man's Hare Krishna, waves his arms in whatever space he can find, ellipses and arabesques over his head, clapping up here, then down there, obeying the neural orders of his new master. He kicks out too freely, starts to fall; a girl grabs him by the waist and helps to pull him back.

The noise of the crowd is now one continuous roar. Jagger he cannot see at all, nor the band, nor even the stage. The screen has become a wild greenlit blur. So he simply closes his eyes and tries to become part of the music, part of it *all*, to shake himself free of himself in an ordeal of frenzy.

No break, no diminution. Ronald has given up his perch, and is now trying to force his way up through the mass, closer to the man on the stage. He shoves his arms between backs and shoulders, tries to claw out of his way all these jerking jammed-together too-solid bodies. Just in front of him two girls sit on boys' shoulders, swaying and shrieking: to dash them to the ground.

But he cannot move. He cannot see anything but the backs of other people's heads, hateful hairy heads jammed in around him. He hits out, bites one bare shoulder in his way. At last he clears a tiny space, a square foot perhaps. But at once the human wall closes in again.

Now a V-shaped opening splits between two ears, and through it from time to time flash now black, now silver, now flesh, now an arm, now a fist, now the free-flying hair, now a piece of the face, flash-dancing from one side of the stage to the other, a machine on a single track gone totally out of control, enraptured itself by the rapture of the crowd, trying to urge them on to a greater and greater frenzy, and at the same time to convince himself that the frenzy is spontaneous and real: theirs as well as his

Oh, and it was, damn it. It was.

> The bass player he looks nervous
> About the girls outside.
> The drummer he's so shat-tahd
> Tryin' to keep on time.
> And the git-tar players look damaged,
> They've been outcasts all their lives

straining to see, straining to hear, straining to be with him; pressed up against so many people, so many people pressed against him; all of them straining like him, their minds riveted to the stage place

> Me I'm just waitin' so patiently
> Lyin' on the floor

yet still aware of every square inch of skin's surface rubbing against textures of cotton and wool,

> I'm just tryin' to do my jig-saw puzzle
> Before it rains any mo-ah

as thrillingly aware of the skin surfaces of each girl and boy near, as if all had been naked fleshly extensions of himself.

The vibrations of the great voice kept pining, whining, curving down at each line over the roar of the crowd, running like fingers over his skin. Images flash through the V, throbbing like sudden jolts of his own blood. There he is! Again! Again! The stinging, shattering, indiscriminate roar of all the Stones together is now taking place from inside his *own* skull, no longer music but a hallucinated fantasy of music — the buzzing of giant insects, the squeal of faraway sirens, a brain fever of noise images that was transcendentally fine, that was home, that was all.

And now Mick is waving, waving high, both hands high from the very lip of the stage, his slippers inches from their grasp, blowing kisses (No) throwing rose petals out of a silver bowl *No* and they were all waving back, blowing kisses too *No Don't* snatching for the rose petals *Please!* over the heads of those in front, waving high, Thank you Mick, Thank you people *NO NO* the bowl itself flung into the crowd, Thank you, thank you, thank you; love you, love you. Love.

Don't let it end

And he was gone. The Stones were gone.

For a high white moment they stayed, not wanting to move, not wanting to know what they knew they knew: that it was over. High, high and free for an hour and forty minutes, together and one, they would very soon have to begin to atomize, to disintegrate into single little unprotected egos, to face the fact that the Stones were gone, and that all they had left was the world.

SIX.

In February 1963, Giorgio Gomelsky, a White Russian film producer who owned a jazz club at the Station Hotel in Richmond, hired the Rolling Stones for a regular every Sunday afternoon booking that was to run on for eight months, at thirty quid a go, and establish this group of nineteen- to twenty-one-year-old performers as the most popular rhythm and blues band in London. In April, a writer for *Record World* came down the river to see them, and wrote a review hailing what he called their "new jungle music."

> The Stones are destined to be the biggest group in the R and B scene — if that scene continues to flourish. Three months ago only fifty people turned up to see the group. Now promoter Gomelsky has to close the door at an early hour — with over four hundred fans crowding the hall.

His review was read by an ambitious young-man-about-London named Andrew Oldham (who had already worked for the Beatles). Oldham went down to Richmond, listened to the music, and signed on as manager of the Rolling Stones. He dressed them in suits and ties (of a style then called "Mod"), helped them to produce their first single record (of a Chuck Berry song), got them written about in the national press, and in September of 1963 booked them on their first of many tours. For two weeks they played the big ballrooms and cinemas of the Midlands and North of England, along with the Everly Brothers, Bo Diddley, Little Richard, Micky Most, and the Flintstones. They were fifth on the bill.

[FROM RONALD HARRINGTON'S JOURNAL, VOLUME SIX]

February 12, 1963

The sky was deep blue-black and boundless, covered with a film of exquisitely shaped clouds. The moon seemed to float slowly through this film, now a mere bright reflection in the dark, now round and dim and mysterious, now burning free and brilliant silver through an opening in the clouds.

I couldn't tear my eyes from it. It was perfect Beauty, Beauty itself, untainted by any lesser, baser element. I felt nothing of the vaguely sensual content that seems to mar my love for Michelangelo's slaves, for example. Each time I looked back it was just as exciting, just as stirring. I don't know that I have ever felt anything so wonderful before.

And it had nothing to do with me. Or any man. Nothing at all. It was apart from everything else, worlds apart from merely physical moon and clouds. Man has no right to call it his, to measure it, to use it — to send rockets to it, for example, or colonize it, as the President talks of doing.

No, that would be wrong.

Why was it so moving? Why isn't it always so beautiful? Why do so few people see it as I saw it, or feel it as intensely? All this beauty, I believe, is a thing quite apart from me. But even so, might the beauty have depended on my being there to see it?

I don't think I have ever felt such a "wholly other" feeling, as the Philosophy 6A instructor calls it.

But even if I have no answers for it now, I am sure that this particular experience, so keen and so extreme, will provide an excellent point of departure for any future inquiry I care to make into the Nature of Beauty or the Aesthetic Experience. The mere memory of it, like Prince Andrey's sky, may prove the solution to many problems. And there were no degrading elements whatever in the experience. That is perhaps the most noteworthy thing about it.

Dropping for a moment to sublunary matters, there is one problem that particularly wounds me at the moment: my self-directed and other-directed sensual appetites. I keep staring at others, concocting terrible fantasies, imagining myself doing (or enduring) horrible things. I had hoped to clear this up by rational self-analysis, as I have cleared up so many other problems during this past year. But I have not been able to do so. I have the best intentions, but still I succumb. All I can do on such occasions is try to force my mind elsewhere. And so far that hasn't worked very well.

What happened last night is almost too dreadful to put into words. Tony and I read each other's Matisse and Jawlensky papers, and then I told him what I had felt about the moon. Then we got to arguing about the real nature of aesthetic experience. And all the while he was talking I found myself imagining his body stretched by ropes or cables between the floor and the ceiling, whipped with fish hooks on long threads, hooks that tore out bits of his flesh. I tried to keep my mind on what he was saying, but I couldn't. Or rather, I found I could concentrate passionately on the argument, and still keep seeing these things. I went on, fantasizing worse and worse things. I imagined his skin burned with tiny fires shooting out of silver tubes, like Zippo lighters. All his hair was set on fire, first the hair on his head, then on his arms and his legs, under his arms, on his chest, everywhere, all the hairs suddenly crackling into orangey wires and then turning into a very fine ash that disappeared, leaving behind only the horrible smell of burnt hair — exactly like that time I tried to light Aunt Emera's gas heater, back in Fort Wayne, and burned the hairs on my arm. I hadn't thought about that for years, but I could actually smell that smell, that very same smell.

I have no idea how such things come over me. I like Tony, I certainly don't want to hurt him, or see anyone else hurt him. But as long as we went on talking, I couldn't get rid of the vision, his yellowish tan skin all burned and scarred and bleeding. What's worse, I didn't want to get rid of it. I think that's why I may have kept disagreeing with him about the source of true beauty, to keep that horrible picture of him in my mind's eye from disappearing.

God, it's awful. It's really awful. But what can I do to stop?

I must, first, as in all things, determine rationally what is best for me, in regard to the goals I have already set up — understanding, self-improvement, usefulness, things like that. I must examine these psychological aberrations rigorously, and try to keep all my actions, desires, and relations with other people realistic and rational. I must not let these disturbing and senseless impulses continue. It seems an almost hopeless task! There are times when I feel that my "psyche," or whatever you want to call it, is as real and powerful a part of me as my reasoning brain. But it ought not to be so. I do not wish it to be so. I shall make my reason more powerful, more real, so that it may still these inexplicable urges. For they are bad, because they cause me pain.

I think that such a simple device as more frequent use of these notes may be a great help in silencing these cravings. (Surely I'd never do any of these things. So why does my secret self keep imagining me doing them?) Whenever I write here, my reason seems to rule.

So: I shall write in here frequently, regularly if necessary — at least, say, once a week — to keep a toehold on rational activity. Then, whenever I feel a painful situation arising, I shall force myself to recall my resolutions, with a view towards *doing what is best for me, and especially towards avoiding any sort of unnecessary pain.*

Hank and Ramona got married last Saturday at the Presbyterian church. Very big deal. Peter Jacobson was his best man, as I expected all along, but he did at least ask me to be an usher. I had to rent my own suit, and got a silver cigarette lighter for my pains, like everyone else. Very useful, considering I don't smoke. Reception at her grandparents' house, half the people drunk. The happy couple are now honeymooning at the Lees' place on the River, and I trust having fun.

April 3

Nothing really momentous has occurred since I wrote last. But this week a heaviness has set in that I can't shake off. There seem to be so few moments of happiness, so many hours of objectless melancholy. My pleasures all seem to stop short of some inner shell, never manage to plunge themselves into the heart of me, let me turn into pure joy for even the shortest time. There's a perpetual weight on my stomach, a great dark cloud in my brain. And just when I was so sure I was finding all the answers.

Something is wrong, something is decidedly lacking. I'm beginning to get an August-1960ish feeling of the unreality of everything around me. Or at least the unimportance. Everything has become so damned trivial.

I even hate writing this. It just deepens the depression. And I can't camouflage it with Gothic cathedrals, or music, or philosophy, or "Time," or writing a letter, or doing the dishes. I can't go to sleep and escape it, or walk the streets and hide.

Part of the problem is my own. I am guilty of pride, flagrantly guilty of this worst of all vices: irrational, painful, uncontrollable pride. Ever since the new semester began, I have been succeeding admirably. A—'s, A's. Even A+'s! Recognition from professors, the envy of other students, brilliant success in almost every course. Now each new triumph inflates me, lifts me up; but then I think on it, and feel the utter wrongness of my swelling self-delight; and I am just miserable.

I cannot keep from telling people how great I am, and then feeling regally superior when they acknowledge it. I promise myself I won't tell Tony of my latest A — and ten minutes later I casually drop it into the conversation, or leave my bluebook where he's sure to see the grade. A is glory for me, A+ ecstasy. B is utter dejection. A four-point semester is my dream of paradise.

And this is wrong! Abase yourself, Ronald, reduce yourself, force yourself to be humble. Or at least shut up. Remember, remember, all this means next to nothing.

Humility. God, how easy it must be for the inferior to be humble. For someone like me, it will require nothing less than an interior revolution, after all the years I have spent taking such delight in my superiority.

I must force myself into self-abasement. There is no lasting pleasure in pride. It is false, unstable, a house of cards.

April 5

What a revolution these notes represent! Whatever else may have changed, one thing stood firm through my Big Decision in November 1962 — my own adamantine sense of superiority. All the deep reasonings of later days had to work themselves around this — whatever else was right or wrong, I was all that mattered.

Even now, my feelings are not undefiled. A new pride has grown up — a pride in my newborn virtue! And a tinge of shame, unreasonable as it may seem, at my embracing something so common, so unintellectual as humility and self-abasement. But this is as nothing compared to my yesterday's crimes.

I would it were so easy to resolve my way out of my sexual obsessions, my voyeurism and sadistic longings — for I must give them that name. These have become an absolute and intense fixation, before which my better self often finds itself quite helpless. And the pangs are not lessened in the slightest by any of the rationalizations I devise. I go on staring, my eyes riveted below the belt, dumb to any reason, imprisoned in this

*invincible inner pleasure that borders on sensual ecstasy —
and sometimes spills over directly into it.*

*I keep telling myself, more and more faintly, that ordinary
sexual relations would cure me. But must I endure these waking nightmares while I wait? Panicky longings for other people's flesh. Dreams of bruised skin, splintered bones.*

*It is the nearest I have ever come to a psychotic state. If I
were convinced psychiatric help would put a stop to it, I might
even try that. If I knew how to pray, I would pray. But for
now, I must simply try very hard to stop by myself. However
much my senses delight, the rest of me suffers. I tell myself it is
not really wrong, since it does no one any harm. But still it
hurts and disgusts me. Oh, I can argue that it's all a matter of
natural impulses restrained by social taboos; but that doesn't
help. Explain it any way you like. It still hurts, and it must
stop.*

May 8. Mezza notte, by the Campanile bells.

*Sometimes I think that our lives are all fixed and finished, all
decided in advance by a billion trillion accidents. That we are
what we are, determined from before birth by our brain cells,
by our parents and their brain cells, by every tiny pressure that
pushes us this way rather than that.*

*Then along comes a day like today, and smashes this whole
notion. We make ourselves — at least we can make ourselves.
We decide what we're going to be and do. We make real
decisions, decisions that matter. We can change the very
course and nature of our lives.*

*I truly believe I've done that today. The years to come may
prove me wrong, of course, but at this moment I believe that I
have taken my life into my own hands and, by a conscious
effort of will, assumed control over a part of my own destiny.*

*It began this morning, in a reasonable enough place for
mental revolutions — Professor Heron's lecture on the German
idealists. No: even before that, now that I come to think of
it.*

*I woke up very early, feeling fresh and alert; early enough,
in fact, to read the whole 160 assignment while Tony slept on.*

By the time I had finished, morning was high, and I felt that I myself had forced the sun into the sky, radiated my own exuberant heat into a lucid and benevolent sky. Lovely hot water kept pouring out of the shower — something it hasn't done for weeks. I played sides four and five of the Callas Norma while I was in the shower, and went all to pieces, as usual, at the part in "Mira O Norma" where her voice cracks so spectacularly between ranges. Not once did the needle stop on the scratches. And then the car started, all by itself. (We've been having to push-start it all this week.)

The funny thing was, I felt that I myself had willed each of these things to perform: the hot water, the phonograph needle, the car; just as I had willed the sun and blue sky.

I drove Tony to work, had a doughnut and hot chocolate, went to Heron's class all wide-eyed and open, knowing it was going to be one of his great days. And it was. He was talking about Nietsche (sp?), among other people, none of whom I'd ever heard of. (Nietsche isn't even on the syllabus.) What anybody else in the room got out of his presentation I don't know. But it shook me so much I still haven't got over it.

What exactly he said I think I have in my notes. But what's more important is that he uncovered (or implanted) in me a totally new kind of self-awareness, an awareness of — what? Will, I suppose, in Nietsche's sense. And Power. My own will, my own power. And a sense (where this came from I have no idea) of almost sublime purposefulness or mission I've never felt before.

It came to what you might call a new creed, one that runs something like this:

I am not only different from other people — more intelligent, more sensitive. I've always known that. But elect Chosen, picked out. I can do something important, something great even, by pulling all my forces together, and I shall. I was born to. My separateness is not some fortuitous, cruel joke of the gods. I am being set up to effect some decisive change for the better. But it is up to me to do and to act.

I could let it slip, do nothing. Let the chance die. Just exist. But I must not. From now on I must receive each message, each possible addition to myself with this purpose in view. I must make decisions, active willed personal decisions, in each case with the design to make myself more fit for my great task.

It all makes sense now. My apartness from the family, the alienness I feel towards classmates. My discomfort in mediocre jobs. The wrongness of my first two years here. My response to people like Nietsche and Michelangelo. Even the physical unattractiveness that sets me so obviously apart. My having been uprooted from Indiana — it's all part of the plan—and having been dropped in this Wasteland.

Except that it doesn't feel like a Wasteland any more! More a bare field cleared for action, the action of strong men. And I must be strong.

It's a terrifying conviction, you know? I look at my reflection in the men's room mirror after class: face, eyes, all of me. Not very impressive. Not the sort of person I'd pick for my Superman. But the eyes seem to have a kind of unusual light inside them, coming from inside the black holes, almost. And when I looked into them, eyes into eyes, self into other self, I felt the full force of my Nietschean conviction return. You, Ronald A. Harrington, are going to do something, one day. Something important.

I wonder what? Actually, the feeling probably counts as much as the doing; this discovery, this seizing hold of my own will. From now on, everything I do will take on a greater force and luminosity. "Animate the trivial days / And ram them with the sun" — I just read those lines this morning, studying for Schorer's midterm. See how everything converges, fits so dazzlingly well together?

I spent the whole two hours between Heron's class and Ackerman's walking around campus thinking all this out, first along Strawberry Creek up to Faculty Glade, then around behind Le Conte to Mining Circle, and down Hearst to Euclid, where I stopped and got something to eat. Then back in through North Gate and down to the Eucalyptus Grove. What a short time ago I was feeling ashamed of my superiority, stopping up my ears to the call of my own destiny! What putrid nonsense the world can trap us into thinking. The shabby remnants of Christianity infect our very souls.

At the moment, I feel above all a great hunger for knowledge. I must ingest the whole of Western culture, languages, arts, history, people, ideas. I must learn how to discriminate, how to favor the healthy and cast off the sick.

But education is only a start. Listening to Dr. Ackerman (who was truly inspiring on Palladio), I felt suddenly sick with the frustration of being here in California, looking at slides, and not there, in Italy, looking at life.

I won't wait any longer. I must begin to take possession of my cultural past, in order to fit myself to serve. I am going to get a job this summer and then keep working until I have made enough money to go abroad. (I stopped taking lecture notes, in fact, and wrote that decision down in my 122 binder. You can see the very place.)

I will stay abroad as long as I can. Then I will come back here, richer, more mature, more adequately stocked, and continue to refine my skills and increase my knowledge through more formal education.

I am shaping my own life. I am deciding for myself, directing my life where I want it to go, for my own and the world's best ends.

June 8

I have no doubts at all, not the shadow of a misgiving about my new purpose. I can scarcely even remember having done or felt anything else. I was blind, unborn before last November, unfinished before last month. My higher self has found its place.

As for what might loosely be called my sex life, all the careful analyzing I did here went for nothing. There's something next to irresistible inside me pulling me towards freakish forms of perversion, which can achieve at times a positively frightening intensity.

With women, this last semester, I found myself wanting to hurt, to cause pain. And often I succeeded. How easily I learned to twist Phyllis's own contradictions against her, found cruel, oblique ways to remind her of her ugly bones, her pocked complexion. Julie and Alzora I would simply play with, like a sadistic puppeteer. I could get them to make idiots of themselves without their even realizing it, at Circolo meetings, or over their damned Russian raspberry tea. If they couldn't take it, I kept excusing myself, they could always leave, or learn to fight back. But I knew they wouldn't.

I never felt any great desire for them physically, I must admit, though I did go through the motions a few times with Phyllis and Alzora. When I did, though, I was bothered by a suffocating sense of their bodies, their femaleness, the warm soft roundness of them. There were times when I felt it all over me, like something melting or vegetally growing, something I had to scrape off and get clear of before it smothered me. I once woke up choking on my pillow, and actually believed for a few seconds that Alzora was sitting on top of my face, stopping up my nose and my mouth with her wet female flesh. In revenge, I imagined myself — oh, there's no point in writing it down.

With men, all I felt were blunt, glowing heightenings of feeling. I can't exactly call them "desires," since I can't identify any object for the desire, any thing I want to do. That awful torture fantasy I had about Tony Lum was probably the worst.

But for some reason, my feelings towards people I know (like Tony) never approached in sheer intensity the fixations I developed for strangers. There were times when I could not force my eyes off, order them away. An arm or leg or face or head of hair, a simple bulge or curve could drive me to near distraction.

I remember an hour I spent trying to kick my way out of one of these fixations. It was over three months ago, that weekend I drove down to L.A. to stay with Alzora's folks. I found myself staring at a fellow's arm, at UCLA, staring as if I would eat it, and I couldn't force myself back to my book. At the time I wondered whether this ugly, irresistible power might not taint my whole life, destroy my vocation, grow even greater and more fearsome than it was then.

On that occasion (as on all others), once the provocation passed — once he got up and left — the feeling passed too. Powerful and painful as they are, these urges still take up a very small portion of my time; most of each day passes normally enough. I was even able to write a fairly good poem about that particular experience, a day or two later. At least I think it was good.*

Or those two fellows in my sculpture class. I went out of my way to watch their every move, but at the same time I developed a murky feeling of hatred for them, a desire to see them made fools of, bested, esteemed below me. One of them, in particular, who always wore Levi's and a T-shirt to class, continually had learned comments to make. How I hated to hear him speak out! I had to go him one better, shut him up somehow. And at the same time his hair, his eyes, his mouth, his arms, his shoulders, legs, the way he slouched down in his seat, his voice, his walk all enslaved me, left me hopeless and hollow, burnt out inside.

Never have my perverted feelings reached the peak to which he brought them! It is the memory of this, perhaps, that leads me to dread what might come later on. That, and my torture fantasies, my playing with fire, my longing to touch people's skin.

I believe that as long as these irrational, driving forces remain, my life will be fraught with anxieties, and getting through any day sanely at best some wretched compromise. It

* (FROM RONALD HARRINGTON'S *Poetry Notebook*):

Soliloquy in a Westwood Cloister

An arm, only a strong round arm,
Of course you don't care;
Warm-lit like golden sands in the sun
    He sits
Empty across a sun-carved romanesque arcade
Full of life and living and all the fine warm being
Of long Grecian statues in repose:
Such an arm.

Why do I stare?
What is a fine arm to me,
Round like orange marble columns come to life?
Worlds were given for less, I suppose.
There comes a time when hell must be, and we let it come,
Because it must.

Forget, sink and forget, I
Sink in the numbing heat of the sun
And stare at an excellent arm.

will be utterly impossible for me to do the great deed I was born to do until I have put these monsters to rest. Either I will kill them, or they will kill me.

I rest all my hopes on a single thesis — that falling in love with the right woman will put out the fires of perversion.

July 2

Minutes into hours into long, dull days. You go through the motions of living, even delude yourself into thinking you're enjoying it. But of how much value is a pleasure that burns itself out in a minute of time? Or a life which is nothing but a long series of waits for some imagined future? Whatever I do, the days of my life will add up to no more than time spent making the best of a shabby and unsatisfactory thing.

It's such a bother to be dissatisfied, to be always dissatisfied. I sometimes wonder if the only "innate idea" in the universe is not some dark, metahuman urge for nonexistence, for the sudden snuff back into Nothing. Why else would sleep, the closest we can come to Nothingness, be the state we all long for most? The more I see of life, the more I see of lives, the more senseless and bleak the prospect becomes.

I want to drown myself in something, find an escape so powerful that the Nothingness will appear to disappear. For I'm convinced it's the kind of radical fact you can never manage to think your way out of. What I need is a mental dope, an opiate. Perhaps the rest of my life will be a search for an opiate adequate to each season. Art, or study, or traveling; writing, reading, religion, depravity. Each in its turn will wear through, and, just as the abyss begins to gape through the cracking surface, I will leap onto the next, Eliza crossing the ever-melting ice.

I must dry up my questing mind, forget about my great purpose, silence all thinking by emotional storms.

Nothing matters. Nothing lasts, endures, has value. There is no solid satisfying reason for living, for anything. We are every one of us burst into life, into a span of so many years of human existence, tangent at both ends to the uncontrollable unknown.

Why? To do what? Every value that man has proclaimed is just one more wretched attempt to hide the lack of any real

one hundred and six

value in life, another drug designed to render bearable this unasked-for existence. As long as I remained unaware of this, I could accept these various values, be they Christ's or Nietzsche's, and subject myself to them as to eternal and satisfying truths. But as I mount to a position of better perspective, I realize that the whole History of Man has been nothing but an unending cycle of desperate, futile attempts to make the best of a very bad thing.

This is what makes thinking for me now so impossibly hard. I can only go on for so long before these great boulders of truth block my path, to remind me that all activity is for nothing, that all my plans and ideas are mere daydreams and chimeras.

Last weekend, in Berkeley and San Francisco, I tried to think, as I had done so often before in and between those two cities. But I can't, not anymore. The black shadow of Nothing falls over my thoughts, and very soon I find myself asking, "Why bother? What's the use?" The only meaning anything has anymore lies in its use as a drug, in the extent to which it can dull the intellect to the barren one and only truth.

I abhor this barrenness. I crave fulfillment. I search for escape. But where? Religion is hopeless, a harmless enough drug for those who can swallow it, but useless and meaningless to me. No longer can books, art, music carry me out of myself. People are out of the question, in this stupid house with its stupid orange walls. So is sex.

Long drives to romantic places remain my one dependable escape — long drives, and long naps. Of late I turn to sleep at almost every juncture.

But I am going to Europe, for better or worse, so I must keep working doggedly eight hours a day, coming back at night to this stupid house. One month has passed already. Three and a half to go. Surely we can handle that.

July 12

A graph of my present existence would be a five-day-long line at the lowest scale, barely edging up each evening, with a manic spurt to mark the free hours of each weekend.

Little trumpets sound in my heart at the coffee and lunch

breaks, because they are tangible symbols of that many hours gone by. (I dare not look at a watch. I keep mine in the drawer.) At the start, when work was slow, I hated having nothing to do. Now I have too much to do, and I hate it even more. The noise and bother, the unbearable stickiness of Vina and Newell, my own mistake a minute, the nuisance of filing and revising and rushing — what a silly, shallow world it all is, a bubble blown of dollar signs and computer printouts. That I should have to effect concern over bimonthly credit surcharges and misread automatic deductions, over what happened to DuPont's correspondence file, over the fantastic number of overdue mortgage entries! Oh, Europe: you had better be worth it.

The last pair of weekends was like coming up for air. Berkeley, San Francisco, Phyllis and the art galleries — there is, after all, an antidote to Oakland and San Salvador. Tomorrow begins another. I'll run off again, I suppose, escape to the city and try to live for a while. Telegraph Avenue and Telegraph Hill, "L'Avventura" again (for the fourth time!) Phyllis's ideas on Europe at fifty dollars a week. Saturday night dreams at Seal Rocks, Sunday with the French Impressionists.

But suddenly a thick fog of unconcern has dropped over all. I don't care. I don't care to write, to think, to read, to listen, to eat, to sleep, to be. I knew when I began to write here that I would end this way, but I had already checked off everything else and hoped that writing would be the answer.

I don't care to put down another word.

July 14

Disgusted with this house and all within it, I hurled myself across to San Francisco again last night. As an escape attempt, it was the worst of fiascos. I envisioned another poetic evening at the Cliff House, or lying under a tree in the park, or writing poetry from the Sausalito ferry. But the city was smothered with wet, dark, gloomy fog. Phyllis wasn't home. The ferry cost two dollars, and the next one wouldn't leave for an hour. From Telegraph Hill I saw only a black sea of nothing, and got cold and wet doing it. *I stopped at a bookstore in North Beach to do nothing for half an hour with a smelly crowd of freaks, then drove out dreary Geary to the ocean, where I tried to sleep off my frustrations among cars full of teenagers making out at the beach. Fat chance. I imagined myself sneaking from car to car with a knife, scaring the shit out of all of them.*

Half being, half wishing I were not, I drove back downtown, sat through forty minutes of a pornographic movie (it was too late for "L'Avventura"), and came out after midnight to find my car towed away. Eighteen dollars. I got home to bed in the foulest of moods.

July 15

Today I read every page of the Sunday papers. The level to which I've sunk.

More than three months left to go. And then, I'm sure of it, more gloom, more fog, more miserable dog-paddling in time amid lonely old cathedrals, or in cold museum galleries, where I don't speak the language, and can't eat the food. Europe is just another piece of space, fellow, not another life! Life will go on, exactly as it always has — a damn dull agonizing bore. Can I delude myself into forgetting it any better in the Bois de Boulogne than in Golden Gate Park? If I am too alone now and hating it, I shall only be more alone there.

Maybe I won't come back. May be I'll keep wandering, or bury myself somewhere there. Do something, what I don't know; die, maybe, if I'm lucky.

I've thought a lot about dying this summer. But what I really long for, I think, isn't death so much as merely not to be. Or to be in some vastly different fashion, some very simple form of life, like a rock along the ocean shore.

I started to write an epic poem on this theme last Saturday night, leaning on the parapet looking out to Seal Rocks. I'd get back and work on it now, if I could just rouse myself one fraction of a centimeter above this wretched state, this state that can find no surcease except in sleep, or something worse.

Hank and Ramona over for dinner. Something seems to be

wrong. But who knows what's going on, once people wall themselves up in a marriage? All very mysterious and unpleasant. Naturally, nobody says anything about it.

August 11

One long, involved, unhappy month later. I've got myself tied in knots, without even a glint, a glimmer of peace, release, or satisfaction.

Hank and Ramona seem to be splitting up.

If only I could know what I was, let alone why. I can't conjure up a thing called me, I can't imagine a single meaningful entity that binds together the complex of contradictory feelings I keep on experiencing.

Even now, nothing satisfies but make-believe, and that for the shortest of spans. I've had all sorts of new chances — an honest friendship with Ted Mathews at work, whom I envied, hated, loved, and longed for for so many weeks; new friends and new adventures, thanks to him. But all this has served more than anything else only to awaken a long dormant bête noire: my hateful, odious incapacity, the shrieking fact that I am not as the rest of men. In a world like mine that prizes the intellectual, I can forget this completely. In a world like Ted's, that prizes the physical, I am slapped in the face with it every word. That, and my own evil imaginings . . .

Tonight, Ted and Ellie are hiking in to Margaret Lakes, in the High Sierra. And I am sitting on a log before a soon to be dead campfire on the road out of Florence Lake.

Why did I come? So I could tag along with them a part of the way. I feel no irresistible Call of the Wild; I don't belong here. But then where do I belong? In none of the places I want to be. I'm just wrong. I should be thrown out, erased, started over.

I am an outsider in a world that couldn't care less. I loathe others who have what I have not. I loathe myself for lacking it. I despise in turn what I do have. And I loathe life for being such a hell.

I can't make do, accept my life, accept my role. I can't rebel — rebel against what? So I dream, awake and asleep, of

one hundred and ten

the world as I would have it, and turn to aching tears and a silent half-life when the dream must end.

August 19

What is the matter with me? Ellie, for one thing. Right now I get upset just looking at the phone I only this minute finished talking to her on. "You are coming tomorrow? . . . Just got through talking to Ted — he's so drunk he can't stand up . . ." Lord, why does she disturb me so? I sit here and tell myself that I'll hate myself for going to her barbecue tomorrow, I'll get high and speak freely, lie madly and tell the truth even worse, choke up at the sight of her handling Ted, or at the eternal conversation on the eternal topic. And then come home to set the bedroom stage once again: me plunging into her naked on the bed, coldly giving in to her long-frustrated demands, as poor hopeless Ted comes in to stand, lost, distressed, watching at the door. God, I'd love that. There's nothing I'd rather do than make love to a girl I hate, in order to crush a guy I like as well as anyone I've ever known. Good old normal, well-adjusted Ron.

October 20. RMS Baronia, two days out.

The engines purr deeply on and on, the walls creak quietly inside their cream fabric sheaths, the whole ship makes the subtlest gesture of a back and forth roll. Outside, a clear, dark, star spangled night, a rich yet not cold wind. White waves forever cloven and spread by this vessel. It's so huge you have no sense of its size from inside. I feel I'm on a private new world that's neither America nor Europe, and that I've left a whole self behind me on the dock. I can see him standing there still, poor lost little American bastard. I wonder what the new Me will be like.

The sound of the engines, the quiet creak of the walls, the oddly caressing, almost mothering lurch left, then lurch right of the floor catches you in the gut of the gut, till you feel like a fetus, living in the rhythm of its mother's breathing and blood. It seems to me better than living on land. This world we three thousand people are riding on (writing, sleeping, serving, steering, whatever we're doing), this world is alive. The land back there is dead. Our closed-off, forward-moving world has a beating heart, a pulse, it lives in the same vital contingency that we do, and I curl snugly into the organic correspondence of ship to me. One's own life processes seem to take on a new vitality from those of this great and purposeful ship, which knows so very well where it's going.

October 22

Middle of the journey now, middle of the night. Back, after a time of storm, to our gentle, general rumble-creak-and-lurch, just the minimum of noise and motion to let everyone sleep securely in the warm assurance that the ship is working through the night, pulling us closer and closer to . . . wherever it is we're going.

seven.

On November 1, 1963, Ronald Harrington took a 9:45 train from Paddington Station, escaping from a gloomy London drizzle. He spent a four-hour stopover walking about Oxford, then continued on by train to Stratford-upon-Avon, where he arrived about 6 P.M. and headed straight for the Allardyce Inn, at 5 Kenilworth Lane, the cheapest place listed in his *Guide to Hotels in the British Isles*. That same day, the Rolling Stones released their second record, a jangly version of the Beatles' "I Want to Be Your Man," backed by a very explicit instrumental called "Stoned."

On January 20, 1964, the day Ronald sailed home from Naples on the SS *Nero*, flagship of the Neapolitan Line, the Stones had just released their first extended play disc, which included a live concert version of "Route 66," that old roll call of U.S. place names, shouted through by Jagger over Charlie Watts's drums. One month later English pop fans could hear their version of "Not Fade Away," a Buddy Holly number that brought the Stones' throaty, hard-driving noise to the top of the charts.

To those who came later to their music — after 1965, say — "Not Fade Away" was the earliest song that actually *sounded* like the Rolling Stones. Hesitant, slashing chords: a three second pause; then in with a steady, stinging beat, a tambourine jangle at the end of the line. After each of the sung verses came a break for this same noise—a kind of metallic, raspy *thump,* with a sour blue harmonica wailing away above.

It was all very basic. Part rhythm and blues, part country and western, one hundred per cent Rolling Stones.

ChunkaChunkaChunk. Chunk Chunk.
ChunkaChunkaChunk. Chunk Chunk.

My love is *big*ger than a Cadilla-ac
I'll try to show it if you'll drive me ba-ack
Your love for *me* has gotta be re-al
For you to *know* just how I fe-eel

(words beaten out in Jagger's near-monotone whine). And then low down for the refrain, chopped and growled to the syncopated beat:

Well, love is love, and not fade away.

Between November and February, the Rolling Stones played at thirty Odeon and Gaumont cinemas, in London, Streatham, Edmonton, Southend, Guildford, Watford, Cardiff, Cheltenham, Worcester, Wolverhampton, Derby, Doncaster, Liverpool, Manchester, Glasgow, Newcastle, Bradford, Hanley, Sheffield, Nottingham, Birmingham, Taunton, Bournemouth, Salisbury, Southampton, St. Albans, Lewisham, Rochester, Ipswich, and back to London. In the same time, Ronald Harrington had traveled to London and Cambridge, Stratford and Oxford, Windsor, Warwick and Kenilworth Castles, and Tunbridge Wells; Paris, Chartres, Versailles, Mont-Saint-Michel, Rheims, and Amiens; Brussels; The Hague and Amsterdam; Vienna; Munich; Willisau, Interlaken, Grindelwald, Kleine Scheidegg, Zermatt, Chamonix, and Geneva; Nice and Monte Carlo; Milan, Venice, Florence, Rome, and Naples.

Three times their paths crossed during these twelve and a half weeks. Jagger and his friends were in London November first through November ninth, working out of a second floor Chelsea flat and the Decca recording studios in Knightsbridge. That same week, Ronald was staying about a mile away, at a quiet rooming house on the south side of Kensington Gardens. According to the popular London press, the Stones were seen at a number of clubs and musical pubs during these nine days, either individually or all together. With several lady friends, they all attended a very noisy all-night party given in Marlborough Place, St. John's Wood, on the eighth. (The police were called in on a neighbor's complaint, but no arrests were made.) Ronald, meanwhile, was going to places like Westminster Abbey, St. Paul's, the Houses of Parliament, the Tower of London, the National Gallery, the British Museum, the Tate Gallery, Covent Garden, Festival Hall, the Old Vic, Petticoat Lane, Simpson's on the Strand, Dickens's House, and the Lord Mayor's procession, which he saw by craning his neck around Englishmen and tourists crammed six deep on the sidewalk across from the law courts in the Strand.

The Rolling Stones were present — though not performing — at a concert at the Olympia Music Hall in Paris on November 18, which featured a number of American bluesmen. That very day Ronald Harrington took a late night train for Brussels from the Gare du Nord. Jagger and Richard are reported to have been in Marseilles over Christmas (doing what, no one knows exactly). Early in the morning of December 26, Ronald's overnight train from Geneva to Nice stopped in Marseilles for a quarter of an hour.

In twelve and a half weeks, Ronald managed to see more than half the museums, churches, palaces, and ruins whose names he had entered in his notebook. By Italy and January, however, he had reached a near-saturation point for famous old paintings and celebrated old churches. His Grand Design was dissolving in exhaustion and ennui. The Brera in Milan, frankly, had been a drag.

"I planned to go on until I found one really interesting painting," he wrote home to his friend Phyllis, "and spend all my time studying that. But I never did. I ran past hundreds and hundreds of insignificant Renaissance nothings, dreamy-eyed Virgins holding misproportioned rubber dolls, ecstatic saints in swirly red robes, looking theatrically up. Christ with the bulging cod. (Mantegna. Remember?) At least *fifty* pink Saint Sebastians all pincushioned up with arrows. It was just too dull for words."

He forced himself, next, through all the obligatory art student's waystops in Florence. The Pitti, the Novella, San Spirito, San Lorenzo; the Bargello, the Duomo, the Medici Chapel. The Michelangelo statues *did* get to him, still. But Florence itself, the city he had counted on to be the high point of his tour, a city he had fantasized in clear, clean sunlit lines, turned out to be muddy, exhausting, a mess.

It rained a dribbling, halfhearted rain the five days he was there, five days spent tromping along narrow brick sidewalks or damp slushy streets from one church or museum to another; then tromping *more* miles through cold galleries or dark side aisles, trying to arouse the proper inner flame for Giotto and Fra Angelico and Della Robbia and Botticelli.

But the river was an ugly Mississippi brown. The buildings looked like prisons made of mud. The sky was dark from morning to night. And his inner flame had just about gone out.

He had allotted two weeks to Rome, but by the time he got there culture fatigue had set in. A deep-seated loneliness and self-dissatisfaction were beginning to pollute all his sources of pleasure. All he could think of was Berkeley, and the boat for home. Fourteen more days.

He went to St. Peter's his first day in Rome. He stood just inside the front portals, looked up and around for half an hour, tried to let his eyes find something of value, something that might wake up his weary soul. But the huge carven spaces giving into more huge carven spaces awakened no emotions whatever; nor the gilt, the marble, all the monumental popes. His soul, his eyes, his head, his feet, all of him was tired. Tired of art, tired of architecture, tired of Europe.

So he turned around, pushed aside the leathern curtains, walked down the many steps. He didn't even turn around to look back.

On his way to Attraction Number Two on his Roman list (St. Peter's: check; Castel Sant'Angelo: check) a terrific rain started up. In two minutes he was as wet as a full sponge. So he kissed off the Castel and took a taxi back to the Via Giovanni Amendola and his dollar-a-night room. There he shed his dripping clothes, put on clean underwear, thick wool socks, and a tartan plaid robe and, wrapped in a blanket, wrote notes to himself all the afternoon.

He never went back to see the Castel Sant'Angelo properly; or the Sistine Chapel; or the Vatican Museum; or any other Roman museum, or palace, or church. What seemed to suit his mood best in Rome were the ruins.

He liked the silence of the ruins, the invisibility of man. They were a nice blend of immensity and decay, a mixture that proved to be satisfying, regenerating. After so much effort devoted to admiring all the insistent genius of Europe, he found the anonymity of the ruins to be exactly what he wanted. He could not imagine their human builders at all, so stripped were these remnants of all utility, all decoration, all individual stamp. Renaissance Italy, most of Europe in fact, pressed against one with the pullulating, crusted-over presence of all its builders and users, their names and faces, their carven chairs and canopied beds, their golden copes and suits of armor. At times Ronald had felt himself suffocating in this excess of personality, squeezed and trampled on by the weight of too many great men.

But the mark of those who had built and then dwelt in ancient Rome had long since been effaced. Sacked, attacked, abandoned, eroded, buried under centuries of silt, then gradually, gently uncovered, detached from the encrustations of later times, these silent, useless fragments had become an almost natural phenomenon, a perfect piece of earth.

Men had designed them, piled brick on brick, lived among them once. But so long had they belonged to the soil and the sky, the water and green plants, cats and rats and pigeons and insects that they seemed no longer man's work at all. And it was this ancient, organic tranquillity, this faceless and nameless nonhuman silence that attracted Ronald to them. After the twelve weeks he had spent among the teeming and too-busy past, the ruins of Rome were able to order and ease the over-taut wires of his imagination.

Great columns fell, and were left fallen, like old trees in a forest. Flights of foot-high stone steps were worn into moss-covered slopes. Every sharp angle had been softened. Walls, like wind-eroded cliffs, had broken open into a thousand little fissures and pockmarks. Few of the buildings or monuments turned out to be the pure white or cool gray he had expected. No: tones of reddish brown, or a sad old uriney yellow had been cast over almost everything that was left. And all sorts of living green plants — shrubbery, ivy, lichens, weeds — flour-ished in the cracks, grew out between the stones, tied what was left of Imperial and Republican Rome back to the earth.

When the downpour at Castel Sant'Angelo continued into its second day, Ronald decided to abandon his art history logbook and give in to an overpowering urge to see *nothing*, go no-where. Forget about works of art. For the next twelve days, he would just read and write and rest, keep as warm as he could, and go out twice a day in search of cheap Italian meals. He would explore side streets and shops, perhaps attend a few operas and concerts with the little money he had left.

The rain eased off a bit the second evening, and he went downtown to attend to a few chores — mail from home at American Express, Piazza di Spagna; the Neapolitan Line office just up the street; opera tickets at Piazza di Colonna. On his way back, he noticed a sunken park across the street, with a railing around the sides and a stairway that led down from the street. It looked like a cozy retreat from the Roman traffic, so he decided to cross over and relax in it before going in search of dinner.

It turned out to be his first, unexpected glimpse of ancient Rome: a very minor ruin, as Roman ruins go, dug up from twenty or thirty feet under the street and railed off from the white Fiats and green buses and red neon of 1964. The excava-tion was, in fact, closed to the public. The stairway he had seen was only a *sottopasseggio pedonale*, or pedestrian subway, not an access to the romantic precincts of the past. But one could lean against the railing and stare down at two small templelike buildings (one round on a high platform, one a

one hundred and eighteen

rectangle with a semicircular apse); a row of fine columns; a flight of brick steps; some bits of wall; a couple of solitary columns rising free. Ronald stared for a long time at the ruins, his first Roman ruins; after a while, all he could make out were vague outlines among shadowy pines. When at last he pulled himself away, in search of bread and spaghetti and salad and wine, he felt his insides humming with deep and novel harmonies. He had found what he needed.

The next few days he set out in earnest, rain or no rain, to discover the rest of this quieter Rome. At each spot — the Colosseum, the Pantheon, the Imperial Fora — he had to work out ways to escape hungry cats and souvenir-selling guides, all desperate for any patron they could find in midwinter.

Then the rains stopped. By Monday a bright sun shone valiantly, if none too warmly, in a light blue January sky. He decided to spend his whole last week in Europe in the Roman Forum.

In an odd way, Ronald knew the Forum already. He had spent a month in the spring of 1962 with a plan of it pinned up over his desk in Berkeley, as he struggled to write a term paper about its evolution and design. Of course, then he had been writing about the Roman Forum whole and in use. Now what he was dealing with was a romantic green park, decorated almost haphazardly with ruins. Even so, it pleased him to be able to identify the basilicas and arches and temples; to recognize at once the three perfect columns of the Temple of Castor and Pollux, posed with exaggerated picturesqueness against their reflection in the carp-filled pond of the court of the Vestal Virgins. There was something very comforting and secure in knowing one's way about a place, after so many weeks of near total displacement. On the first two or three visits, he paced off the red dirt or gravel paths of the Forum, and named over all its buildings to himself.

But this was not what pleased him most about the Roman Forum. What drew him back, day after day, was something that all his research had never led him to imagine.

The Forum of the Caesars had decayed into a beautiful park, perhaps the most beautiful park in the world. Not a great formal park, not a huge rambling country place; but an enchanted ground one could stroll about, explore, lose oneself in, read or think or dream in happily through a succession of short Italian winter days.

At one end, the great arch of Septimius Severus; at the other, the tiny arch of Titus. Alongside, on the cliff of the Palatine, the red brick ruins of the palaces of the Caesars. Wherever he stood in the Forum, Ronald could look up and see them looking down, somber shapes softened by green ivy, their arches forming black frames for a sky now and then spotted with clouds.

The floor of the Forum undulated up shrubbery-clad slopes, down little paths or steps to green meadows spotted with white and yellow daisies and wild blue iris. Trees grew, alone or in groves.

After a couple of days, Ronald began to treat the arches and temples with less respect. He stopped naming their names, and made a point of forgetting that he knew their dates and plans and functions. As he did this, they began to move silently back into the landscape. Chunks of marble became benches for him to sit on. The high row of columns from the Temple of Concord turned into nothing more than a place to rest the eyes; a way to compose an overlarge piece of sky over the brow of the Capitoline Hill.

He discovered a headless purple statue behind the Senate building, a small brick cube in the northeast corner of the Forum: a Roman senator, he decided, half hidden in his little side garden. A block of stone the height of a chair faced the headless senator, and this gravel-paved clearing tucked away from other strollers became for Ronald a place of frequent resort.

He usually arrived at the Forum in midmorning. In his book bag were a sketch pad and pencils, a book or two to read, and a lunch of salami on a hard roll and an orange, which he bought each morning from a street vendor near his hotel. As a rule, he stayed in the Forum until the gates were shut at six, when it was already beginning to grow dark. He would then follow one of two routes: either along the Via dei Fori Imperiali, by which he could prolong for a while his day in im-

one hundred and twenty

perial Rome; or else down to the river, and a tiny park with the wonderful name of "Piazza di Bocca della Verità." This tree-shaded square had two little temples of its own, as well as a fountain made out of two mermen standing back to back, with their tails intertwined. The mermen held a great bowl over their heads, from which water spilled over their faces down to the craggy rock below. There were usually a few dark-eyed urchins careering about the fountain when Ronald arrived. Across the street was a fine old brown stone church, Santa Maria in Cosmedin. When the bells in its tower rang seven, Donald left to walk along the river, under the trees, until hunger set him searching down narrow side streets for a TRATTORIA sign, its letters spelled out vertically in green neon.

When he found one he liked, he would go inside, sit alone at a table, and order a few inexpensive things — a soup or pasta of some kind, a salad, perhaps a small piece of meat, a fruit for dessert. To drink, a *mezzo di rosso*, and (to water it down) a *bicchiere dell'acqua*. He wasn't yet up to full-strength Roman red.

These modest evening meals were one of the small but certain pleasures of his trip, glowing faintly but warmly at the end of each day. The evening search for the gasthaus, the café, the trattoria, each with its warmth and light, its thick kitchen smells, waiters in slightly shabby white coats: this was good. This was sure and certain good. A bentwood chair. A patched and spotted tablecloth. A candle, perhaps. A menu written by hand. Cheap silverware. A stout glass. A carafe. And then food. Whatever he chose to order. Many things went wrong, almost every day. But this part he always loved.

After dinner, he usually tried to find a concert, an opera, a late church service to go on to. Even a lecture would do — anything to fill up the time other people were spending at home. Some nights he could hardly bear the glow of other people's windows.

There had, in the past twelve weeks, been a few sociable exceptions. In Stratford, Paris, and Alpine ski villages he could at least pretend to be one of the artificial family of his inn or pension. In Amsterdam and Willisau he stayed with girls he had met on the *Baronia*. In London he shared a room with a boy from the ship, at least for a while. In Venice, on New Year's Eve, he met a party of American music students at the opera, and spent every night for a week in their company.

But companionship was the exception; solitude was the rule. The weariness of waking up in an unfamiliar room, in an alien city, staring at his face in mirrors or shop windows, trying to fix on his consciousness that he, Ronald Harrington, was here, here in London, here in Munich, here in Rome.

The aloneness pressed more gently in the Forum by day, or at the blessed dinner hour, or in the Galleria Centrale at the Opera. After a performance, he might stop for a while and stare at the illuminated waters of the Piazza della Repubblica near his hotel. Back upstairs in his room, he would read or write, then try to get to sleep before he froze, or before sad thoughts and exhausting temptations took over his brain.

His travels had been celibate as well as solitary, for the most part. All the bright young people in Tourist Class on the *Baronia* were doing it, he was convinced, but he never found the girl, or learned the right thing to say, or discovered the secret key everyone else seemed to possess. Two girls in the group — one German-Swiss, the other Dutch — invited him to visit them in Europe, and he took advantage of their invitations. The Swiss visit was charming and proper, very much *en famille*. The girl in Amsterdam, who lived alone, asked him to spend the night, and he did. In London, the fellow he roomed with went out daily in search of women, and usually found them. But Ronald hadn't the courage or will to join him, and when Mac started bringing chattering birds in miniskirts back to their room, Ronald moved to the YMCA.

There had been an erotic fiasco with a crowd of Austrian teenagers at the Bellevue in Kleine Scheidegg. Just two days later, he met a girl from his French 3 class at Zermatt, and was able to make up for Kleine Scheidegg.

Paris had been especially hard to take. Oh, he loved the city, of course: the buildings, the paintings, the palaces, the parks. But his third-floor pension in Montparnasse reeked of cabbage and bad plumbing and unwashed sheets. The stairway was filthy and feebly lit. The wine made him sick, and the one toilet was a foul place to have to be sick in. He shared a room with an engineering student from Normandy, a handsome, well-built youth who appeared never to bathe or change his underwear.

But in some disturbing and undetectable way, the strongest odor of the place — of the whole city, in fact — seemed to have something to do with sex. The iron curves of balcony railings, soft brown hair that grew down the napes of people's necks, morning mists, Jacques Brel songs, roast chestnuts in front of Notre Dame. The leaves, the red wine, the loaves of bread, full lips shaping unpronounceable vowels. All those lean bodies in brown knit fabrics and suede, bodies of men and women who moved like cats. Never had he known a city so at ease among the mysteries of sex, or one so cruelly closed off to the nonparticipant.

Why are you here? it seemed to ask. Why did you *come* to Paris, if not for the things of the flesh? The Monets in the Jeu de Paume, the very windows of Sainte Chapelle enjoyed more sex than he did. After three weeks, it was easier to go than to stay.

The American opera lovers he joined in Venice on New Year's Eve were male homosexuals. There were five of them, American music students studying in Vienna. In Venice, they had picked up a sixteen-year-old Italian boy who seemed to be the property of a different member of the group every night. The air around their party was always thick with sexual innuendo, but Ronald pretended not to notice. They appeared willing to accept his company on his own terms, whatever terms he chose. He ate and drank with them, talked music and art, then left them each night at 1 A.M. to find his own way home, down the dark alleys of Venice, along the little canals.

Whores seemed to be everywhere in Europe. He had never seen them parading so freely before. In Rome, he never got back to his room at night without a few invitations from the ladies of the evening who lingered behind the arcaded crescent at Piazza della Repubblica. He said nothing, or said no, and went on his way, until the night before he was due to sail for home. He was sitting on a bench near the fountain. Behind him, Verdi's *Otello* and a cappuccino. A prostitute walked out from behind a parked car and sat down beside him.

"You all alone?

"Is no good to be all alone."

True.

He looked her in the face. Very dark eyes, thick black hair, thirty-five, perhaps forty. Full bosom pushed into deep cleavage over her blouse. Only a light sweater over her shoulders. How did she know I spoke English?

Somebody's aunt. Somebody's mother, even. A gold cross on a chain nestled in the crevice, where he wanted to put his hand.

She touched his arm.

"Gotta cigarette?"

"I'm afraid not."

"Want one of mine, English?"

"*Grazie. Americano.*"

She gave him a cigarette, and bade him light hers as well. As he bent over to do it, she put a hand on his thigh.

"You cold, English?"

"*Si.*"

"Got any money? I keep you warm."

She moved her hand nearer the place.

He had been terrified of whores, ever since Tijuana. But she seemed . . .

"How much?"

"How much you got?"

He took out his wallet and counted. Ten, fifteen, seventeen thousand lire. He knew it was foolish, but he told her.

"But I'll need ten thousand for my hotel tomorrow, and money for food and train to Naples." There were still two last traveler's checks back at the hotel.

"You go to Napoli! Is my home, Napoli!"

"I'm taking a boat from there tomorrow. A boat for home."

"Home is where?"

"California. San Francisco." No one had ever heard of San Salvador.

"Ah, San Francesco! *Città bella. Come Napoli.*"

"That's what people say."

"For you, English, t'ree t'ousand lire. Because you go home tomorrow. Because you go to Napoli."

eight.

The voyage home, which lasted for ten days, was not particularly pleasant. But Ronald so wanted to enjoy it, was so ready for what he imagined to be the romance and relaxation of sailing home on a great Italian liner, that memory and imagination conspired to turn the voyage into a happy one.

A white-jacketed trio from First Class had played "Arrivederci Roma" over and over, up on the aft end of the sun deck, as the ship moved away from the dock. Everyone cried, and smiled, and waved good-bye to Italy. But things began going wrong before they reached Gibraltar. Even before Cannes.

As advertised, the *Nero* was full of contemporary Italian art. The entrance foyer in Tourist Class was lined with bright tapestries of classical motifs. Yellow sunbursts were woven into the white carpeting of the grand staircase, and repeated in a hundred other places. A hammered steel bust of the Emperor Nero, double life size, stood on a marble pedestal between the dining-room doors. The lounges were furnished in tones of ivory and blue, and fitted out with colored glass and inlaid wood. There were banks of living plants in the main lounge — even a white art nouveau birdcage with live birds. A mural of some imaginary Italian village ran the full length of one smoking room wall, under perky little awnings on poles. The whole Roman Forum, put together in mosaic tiles of purple and blue, had been installed behind the long starboard bar.

Ronald's own berth was one of sixteen in a men's dormitory on E deck. His cabin mates hung lines of wet washing between the bunks, and piled cardboard boxes in the aisles. They came and went at all hours of the day and night, drunk and sober, sick and well. All of them were Italian, many of them were loud, and most of them smelled. The men's toilets and showers were half a ship away.

Up on deck, and in the public rooms, Ronald listened to the complaints of the other non-Italian passengers, who had quarters far more lavish than his. They all seemed to find their cabins too small, to dislike the exposed pipes and peeling paint. Beds were unmade. Drawers wouldn't open. Closet doors banged each time the ship rolled. Hot water didn't work. Stewards were rude, or impossible to find. The *France* had been so much nicer. (Or the *Nieuw Amsterdam*. Or the *Empress of Canada*. Or the *Bremen*.)

Two-thirds of the passengers in Tourist Class appeared to be members of lower-class Italian families who had never been to sea. Old women in black camped from early morning until late at night on the white couches and molded armchairs of the lounge. Old men spat on the decks. Vulpine Italian teenagers took possession of one's rented deck chair and refused to leave. Italian waifs raced free all over the lower reaches of the ship.

The Sicilian family to whose table Ronald had been assigned had brought along its own food, untrusting to the last. At the first evening meal, Mama rejected all but the soup course, and then doled out from a sack great hunks of her own bread and cake, and pieces of fruit. When Ronald stared in wonder, she glared angrily back. "Itsa home make!" she cried. "Itsa home make!" It was their only spoken communication of the trip.

The various Americans, Canadians, British, French, and Germans, in all about fifty, found one another by the first night out. At once, they began to form into little groups, staking out for their own use the writing room, the card room, and the starboard half of the smoking room with its bar. There, amid a corps of their own kind, they could bitch openly about these dreadful Italians, which helped make the first few days of the trip almost fun.

The Italians, meanwhile, slouched in their lounge chairs, or sat on the floor, in the main lounge and in their half of the smoking room. They observed these brightly dressed foreigners as though they were a part of a floor show or a pageant provided by the line for their amusement. The foreigners, on their part, seemed to be trying to live up to the roles the Italians had assigned them. The voyage looked to be grim enough; on that they were agreed. But since they were stuck here for a week and a half, they decided, almost all of them, to play Ocean Traveler to the teeth. They wore every stitch and snapper of their new Franco-Italian travel wardrobes, and promenaded the decks with deep breaths and great determination, proud of their sea legs on the motionless Mediterranean. They drank and played and laughed and partied as though they were traveling First Class on the *Ile de France* and it was 1929.

One group of the non-Italians played bridge and canasta. Another danced. Another set for itself the goal of making life miserable for the staff, and demanded odd foods at odd hours. There was a small athletic set, all Ping-Pong and brisk workouts and the early morning swim. Two English academic families with children merged for mutual support, and did everything they could ("Trevor! Sarah! Come away from there at once!") to keep their little ones away from the Italians'. The Germans and the over sixties kept pretty well to themselves, though one white-haired widow from Düsseldorf hopped from group to group, with rings on her fingers and bells on her toes.

The group that made Ronald most welcome were the card players, so he got in a lot of bridge and canasta his first five days at sea. He tried some Ping-Pong and deck shuffleboard, too, but *that* crowd struck him as a bit humorless and over-competitive, so he gave up active sports. He didn't dance, and he wasn't about to make a bad trip worse by leaguing with the steward baiters. He talked quite a lot at the bar with an alcoholic medievalist from Texas, and traded travel notes with a group of Junior Year Abroad girls from St. Mary's College in South Bend, Indiana, on their way home from a year in Pisa. For some reason, he chose not to tell them that he had once lived very near South Bend.

The set he most envied was made up of six young people, three British, two French, and one Italian girl, who had taken over the best row of deck chairs, aft in the sun, and the one big round table in the bar. Like all the little groups, this one had formed by spiritual affinities. Their binding ties were cleverness, a dash of politics, high spirits, high style, and a taste for champagne and mild malice. The leader of the group was a thin, brittle Englishman who always dressed in white. Toward him Ronald Harrington found himself developing one of those dreadful obsessions that had troubled him so much at school the year before.

The ship made its way effortlessly enough through the Mediterranean to the Canaries. Ronald played his hands of cards, talked Gothic cathedrals, drank bouillon and tea and Vermouth Cassis. He wrote postcards and letters to his mother and father, to Phyllis and Tony and Alzora, to Ted and Ellie, to Professor Ackerman. Out on deck, he read from a book of Scott Fitzgerald stories, and looked at the waves. But all the time, he was watching and listening to the Englishman and his friends. He wished that they would take notice of him and ask him to come over.

He did, in fact, get his wish. But it came about as the result of a pretty dire circumstance, and did not have the happiest conclusion.

Two days out from Gibraltar, the SS *Nero* steamed into the worst storm the Southern Route had seen in over two years.

The sky had been foul all that afternoon, Very few people

were braving the cold on the open deck. Perhaps ten hardy souls, mummy wrapped in their white and green blankets, reached out chilled fingers to hold a book, or accept a cup of tea.

Ronald felt a bit queasy after lunch, so he decided to stand outside and breathe the cold air. Walking the deck, he found, had become more difficult than usual. One had to tack from one side to the other, first pushing uphill, then scurrying down. Standing at the railing, he realized in horror that the two Italians alongside him were in the process of being sick, so he walked quickly back inside.

Already telltale patches were appearing here and there among the carpet sunbursts. Stewards hurried to cover them over with sawdust, which they then scraped away. Great numbers of Italians were going below, but smoking room starboard was bearing up.

"Bit of a swell out, then?"

"Yes, a bit. Nice to have a touch of weather, really."

"Oh, I agree. Livens things up."

"Mmm yes. It was getting too smooth for my taste, didn't I say so just yesterday? Coming over on the *Mary* now, we really had a blow. Why, you couldn't keep the cards on the table!"

"That's my idea of transatlantic travel."

"It doesn't seem to be that of our immigrant friends. Half of them seem to have abandoned ship."

"I met two out on deck, getting rid of lunch."

"Ha ha!"

"Oh, here's Gerta. Gerta! Over here! Shall we have a game?"

And so it went on, the sky getting darker, the sea rougher. The ship had moved into decided pitch and roll, and was beginning to make painful creaking noises. The fifty foreigners stuck earnestly to their card playing and drinking and letter writing, their bright, brave seagoing chatter. Each time one of their number got out of his chair to zigzag out to the deck, or down to his cabin, he came back with more tales of fouled carpets and sick Italians. Each began secretly to believe that it would be not only unpleasant, but distinctly degrading — letting down the side, as it were — to give in to the storm.

one hundred and twenty-nine

The rough seas continued through that day and night, and by late afternoon the following day even the Evanses agreed: the *Queen Mary* had been nothing like this. The dining room was less than half full at lunchtime. Almost no one went on deck. Windows were battered by spray, even on the promenade deck. Doors were difficult to open. Open deck spaces were dangerously awash. Ronald went out once, for just a few seconds. He held tight to the rail and marveled at how far *down* the side of the ship seemed to go each time it rocked, and how very long it took to come back. Back inside, he watched the horizon line sweep up to the top of the smoking room windows; stay there; then slide quickly and heavily down, giving place to a sky almost equally dark. Then up. The window space fills up with ocean. Pause. Down, and the sky. Pause. Up, and the ocean. Pause. Down, and the sky. He stopped watching.

At the card tables, ice cubes rattled loudly. Then glasses began sliding across the marquetry tabletops. At one creaky lurch, four separate piles of cards shot onto the floor before anyone could catch them — all four players had reached for their glasses instead. They laughed, after a breath, gathered up the cards, began to shuffle again.

Talk became louder and a bit more shrill, and it was loudest and most shrill at the table of The Six, who had ordered champagne and were composing a song of interminable French and English verses about seasick Italians. At 5:05, a steward spilled a tray of drinks over two of the girls from South Bend. At 5:15, or shortly thereafter, during one of the ship's steeper portside dips, Frau Ellendorf laughed with a trace too much abandon and tipped herself onto the floor. At 5:22, the first visible breach was made in the foreigners' ranks: Trevor Billingsley ran up crying to his mother and was sick all over her lap.

At six, the bell boy came through with his little xylophone, and the loudspeaker announced dinner.

Il pranzo / per i signori passeggieri di classa
turistica / primo torno / è servita. Il pranzo /
per i signori passeggieri di classa turistica /
primo torno / è servita

Deener / for Touris' Class passenger / firs'
seeting / ees now be serve. Deener / for Touris'
Class passenger / firs' seeting / ees now be serve.

The foreigners without children all ate second sitting, an
hour and a half away, but the little bells automatically evoked
the prospect of another thick Neapolitan Line dinner —
something most of them preferred not to fancy just yet. They
sat hard on their chairs, nibbled pretzel sticks and peanuts,
and drank on with an almost Puritan determination.

The Billingsleys had left after Trevor's mishap, and had not
come back. Their friends the McCulloughs and their children
had quit the scene too. Henry Armbruster, from Toronto, was
seen helping his wife (who looked very pale) out of the writing room in the direction of the elevator. Mlle. Tourcoing
slipped and fell in an unsawdusted puddle of sick, which made
her sick in turn. Daisy Burgess excused herself in haste from
her canasta table. Her companions exchanged sympathetic
looks. Stories came up of a very unfortunate event (involving
two of their German friends) during the afternoon movie; of
whole *rooms* awash in First Class.

Les Six went on writing their song. Then an argument arose,
and the fellow in white went below in search of some records,
pretending to dance a samba as he zigged and zagged his way
across the floor. He returned, and gave his records to the Italian hostess to play on her discotheque. Then he and his friends
got up and proceeded to bump and grind about the dance
floor, more or less in time to the music. It was a peculiar sort of
African or Indian dance they all did, in which each person
seemed to be dancing by himself and yet responding in some
way to a partner. The music was repetitive and loud, and very
heavy on the drums.

Soon the whole smoking room, Italians and non-Italians, was
watching the dancers. Shoulders, elbows, hips moved with a
quivery, semicircular shake. There was much stumbling and
bumping about as the ship rocked in counter motion to their
patterns. Their freedom and high spirits delighted the Italians,
while at the same time they antagonized many of the other
foreigners, who scarcely dared let go of the arms of their

chairs. The Italian girl, Renata, was able to balance a champagne glass on her forehead and dance their quivery, novel dance at the same time. "*Brava!*" the others cried at her feat. "*Brava*, Renata!"

By the time the second sitting xylophone came donging round at half-past seven, the number of foreigners was down to about thirty. The ship was pitching about with as much fortitude as they were devoting to staying still. This time, when a couple of the chairs toppled over, no one came to right them. A rattling crash was heard from the lounge. A bandsman's drum set and cymbals had fallen off the stage. A few magazines and ashtrays went sliding across the floor. The stewards had long since given up trying to keep up with seasick passengers. In fact there were very few stewards to be seen. One had to watch very carefully where one stepped.

The foreign contingent, what was left of it, went down to dinner in a tight little band, holding on firmly to chair backs and stair railings and each other's hands. They took their places at table at almost exactly the same time.

During dinner, the roll grew so extreme that the dining room stewards, awkward enough at the best of times, could not keep plates of food balanced on their trays. Dishes started sliding and crashing down in several corners of the room. At first it seemed a joke; then an embarrassment; in the end, a bit frightening. Tablecloths were saturated with spilled water and wine, with the *ossabucco* gravy, *pastina in brodo* and tripe stew. By eight-fifteen the place was a shambles of broken crockery and the trodden remains of food, through which stewards and departing passengers had to pick their way. Children were crying, parents yelling. Someone was throwing rolls, and wet wadded-up napkins. By eight-thirty the staff had abandoned the menu. All they were offering (to those still hungry and able to eat) were safe, dry things like cold cuts and celery and grapes.

The last holdouts included The Six (whom nothing seemed to faze), and Ronald, who sat eating grapes and drinking white wine until nine o'clock. By that time, he was alone in the room except for half a dozen shouting stewards with mops. Whether by constitution, or miracle, or sheer force of will, he had numbed his stomach lining and the nerve ends of his inner ear into ignoring the most violent assaults the south Atlantic could mount. When he finally rose from the table, he felt freakishly stable. His whole system was spinning and screaming quietly, like the still center of a whirling gyroscopic toy.

Thus poised, thus unnaturally alert, he climbed down to E deck (the elevator was out of order) to use the toilet and change his clothes. Then he climbed back, one hundred and sixteen steps, to the *ponte della passeggiata*. The ship was creaking now as if in pain, and rocking like a bathtub toy. The stairs were littered with filth, mops and dustpans, left-behind clothes. Everywhere there were lone passengers being or about to be sick. Ronald met two lost little children crying in one corner of the stairs. He tried to talk to them, but they just crouched in the corner and kept sobbing in Italian.

When he reached the level of the Tourist Class public rooms, an unusual sight met his eyes. The white spaces had been stripped. Chairs and tables were now lashed against the bulkheads by thick elastic straps, which he now realized had been there all along. In the main lounge, even the great birdcage was gone. A pianist was playing to an audience of perhaps a dozen Italians, all sunk as if dead in the long white settees along the wall. Stewards out of uniform, tripping over each other and cursing, were in the process of stringing ropes at waist level from one side of the lounge to the other, tying them to rails along the outer walls — ropes by which, Ronald presumed, one was supposed to haul oneself from starboard to port, like a mountain climber on a violently moving cliff.

His center brain felt the triumphant fixity of the nearly drunk, or the lightly stoned. He stared directly in front of him, blue-white diamonds of eyes, and walked a dead straight line through the card room and writing room to the smoking room door: straight, though varying markedly in forward speed, as the ship's hysterical plunging and leaping either impelled or retarded his course. He had by now won out over the side-to-side roll. He could walk precisely parallel to the ship's keel by a simple, involuntary adjustment of weight from right foot to left, without having to Z-bend back and forth across the deck like some ludicrous music hall drunk.

one hundred and thirty-three

Inside the smoking room (which was already stripped of its furniture, and spiderwebbed with ropes), the foreigners were reduced by now to a dozen brave souls. An old German couple sat on one of the couches fixed to the forward wall; they appeared to be praying. Ed, the medievalist from Austin, was gesticulating wildly from a bar stool with one arm; with the other he held tight to the rail. Next to him were Mr. and Mrs. McCullough, who had deposited their children below. To Ronald's surprise, his own regular bridge group was still up — Gerta Bloewenstein from Hannover, the Evanses from Bognor Regis — and Gerta waved to him from their regular place beneath the mural.

But she was not the only one waving. So, to his even greater surprise, was the lean young Englishman in white. Ronald stood by the smoking room door, fixed to the floor as straight as a mast, while the elegant lad he had been constructing private fantasies over for a week rose from his seat, waved a bottle of champagne, and bade him join the Round Table.

Ronald felt flushed and triumphant, and pretended he hadn't seen Gerta and the Evanses. Choosing his angle of approach, he walked straight as an arrow to the round corner table by the bar.

"Bravo! How on *earth* do you do it?"

"Do what?"

"Walk a straight line like that. We've been watching you all day. No one else on the ship seems to be able to do it, and we want you to teach us."

One of the girls, French to hear her talk, was gazing up at him with large moist eyes shadowed in blue. "You seem to be able to choose a target, then make straight for it as if the ship weren't moving at all. Now teach us how you do it."

She handed him a glass of champagne, filled to overflowing, and moved over to make room for him on the seat.

"I don't know. I saw some Italians getting sick out on deck right after lunch yesterday, and I decided then and there that the only thing to do was to face this thing down. Mentally, I mean. Outthink it. Beat it by . . . by . . . ."

"Willpower?"

"Something like that."

"Well, huzzah. Here's to willpower, sick Italians, and Mary Baker Eddy. Have a pretzel stick. My name's Alistair."

Ronald looked into deep eye sockets, and seized the hand warmly.

"Ronald Harrington. From San Francisco."

"Ronald Harrington from San Francisco. Right. Marie-Josée, on your right; lovely Helen; Renata; my friend Simon; and François. We are trying to survive this wretched excuse for an ocean voyage, and have asked you over to pick your brains." He sipped. "Such as they may be."

"American?" The girl who had handed him the drink.

"Yes — Yes, I'm American."

"*C'est drôle, ça.* I've never known an American."

"Don't believe her."

"She collects them."

"And then eats them."

"*Mais bien sûr.*"

"Peekled."

"Do you like being an American?"

"I . . . I've never really thought about being anything else."

"But I mean you aren't *ashamed* or anything?"

"Ashamed of what?"

"Oh you know. Peanut butter, killing Negroes, the assassination. Being so violent and uncultured. Everybody telling you to go home."

"Nobody told me to go home. No, actually. Everyone I met abroad seemed very friendly."

"Until now, you mean?"

"Oh, leave him alone."

"You shut up."

"For God's sake, Simon!"

Was something wrong?

They were far ahead of him now, of course, but if he just tried a little longer he was sure he could fit in. After all, they *had* asked him over. He drank some more champagne, and vowed to act mature.

They asked him about himself, about his travels. They

seemed genuinely fascinated by his ideas about each of their countries. Murmurs of appreciation arose each time he mentioned favorably some famous building or work of art he had seen in England or Italy or France. Alistair made him describe in great detail the Lord Mayor's procession in London, which none of them had ever witnessed. Ronald refused at first to believe that the Italian girl — who *came* from Rome — had never been to the Roman Forum. But when she swore to the Blessed Virgin and convinced him that it was indeed so, he stood up and identified for her all the monuments represented (several erroneously) in the blue and purple mosaic behind the bar. They all applauded, especially Renata, the girl with the beautiful nose and long red hair, who could balance champagne glasses on her forehead.

They sang for him their "Andrea Doria" song ("But he was sick, the little spic"), the one with all the verses they had been composing that afternoon. They tried to explain the pattern each new stanza was supposed to follow, so that he might contribute too; but he never got the hang of it, and after a few minutes they gave up.

This led to talk about the *Nero,* and Ronald gradually learned that things on board were in much worse shape than he had imagined — worst of all, apparently, in First Class.

"You've not been upstairs? Oh, you must. Alistair, he must. We must sneak him upstairs tomorrow, very first thing. Don't you have any nicer clothes? Oh no matter, you're American. You'll love it. You'll simply love it. Won't he love it?"

"I think he could pass." Alistair's friend Simon. "That air, that sophistication, that *je ne sais quoi?*"

"*Je ne sais quoi* indeed."

"Pass for what?"

"For First Class, *espèce de con!*"

"What exactly is happening in First Class?" Ronald asked, trying to ignore the asides.

"Oh my God, it's too much," said the English girl, Helen, touching his arm. "The sea. They can't take the sea. The floors are soaking wet and they're dying like flies, they're puking all over their Puccis. Some American senator's wife has apparently gone stark staring mad and broken the leg off a Giacometti."

"A *what?*"

"A leg. Off a Giacometti. It's a statue."

"I know, I know. But a real Giacometti? I mean an original?" The vision was too much. A Giacometti with a broken leg. On the high seas.

"Of course a real one, what did you think, a plastic kit? One of those tall skinny men with the long bumpy legs. She panicked when the storm came up and threw a chair or something at it and it snapped, just like that." She cracked a pretzel stick.

"Good God."

"Oh that's just the beginning of it," said Renata. "They had the captain virtually imprisoned all this afternoon."

"Imprisoned? What for?"

"To explain the mutiny, or whatever it is. The seamen's revolt. *Risorgimento marittimo.*"

"What seamen's revolt?"

"My God, Harrington," said Alistair. "Where have you been? Surely even your canasta friends know about that?"

Ronald glanced around in embarrassment. He looked back quickly, but his guilty eye was caught by Gladys Evans.

"That old whore from Düsseldorf knows. The one with all the jewels."

"That's why she's in the ship's hospital now."

"Along with the cardinal."

"Wait a minute." The chaos they were intimating seemed almost too much. "Wait a minute. Start from the beginning. What mutiny, first of all? And what cardinal? And what happened to Frau Holthauser?"

"Well, to begin with," said the English girl — they seemed to be taking him in turns — "have you noticed how many fewer stewards there are now than there were at the start?"

"Well — I suppose so." He looked around. Two. "Maybe they're sick. Like everyone else."

"Ships' crews don't get sick. Even Italian ones. One of the seamen got beaten very badly by an officer, and now the others are refusing to work. That's why everything is so hopelessly run."

"There was a great battle royal down in the kitchen," put in

François. "Knives, pans, chopping blocks, everything. The ones who want to keep working versus the ones who don't."

"And what happened to Frau Holthauser?"

"A fight with her stewardess. The stewardess said she was on strike, and refused to bring her new towels and clean up her room. Your glittery friend called her a stupid dago bitch, or something equally tactful, and so the stewardess shoved her down against the side of the toilet. She's in the ship's hospital now with a broken hip."

"And people in First Class know about all this?"

"I'll say they do. They got together a delegation to see the captain, led by some official of the Italian government . . ."

"The Minister for Culture . . ."

"The Lord Chief Justice . . ."

"Well, somebody. But then the storm broke out, and now they're convinced the ship can't be run properly without a full crew. So they kept the captain locked in the lounge all afternoon trying to force him to apologize to the crew and settle the whole affair before we get into serious trouble."

"But if they keep the captain locked up, who runs the ship?"

"Who ever runs ships?"

"Mermaids."

"Or rats."

"Only Italian ships."

"Gnomes. Little men with pointed hats. I've seen six."

"Yes, they're blue. Blue all over. They go naked."

"You should see their . . ."

"I mean seriously."

"I really don't know," said the French girl, tired of the game. "Frankly, this one doesn't seem to be running very well."

And to tell the truth, it didn't. With each deep pitch forward now, Ronald could hear a great thudding whine, which was followed by the whole vessel's shuddering in a rapid, teeth chattering vibration. The propellers must be coming up out of the water. The windows were pitch black. For a moment he imagined them all deep under water.

"And the cardinal?"

"Food poisoning."

"In *First Class?*"

"So they say."

They talked on and on, obliquely, desultorily; drank more champagne. Ronald gradually forgot his fears, both of them and of the ship. They were European, after all, fresh, original, self-assured: his very image of cosmopolitan youth — the world he had just discovered brought to a fine, keen, twentieth-century point. They laughed so musically, they gestured with such style. They seemed to know everything easily. They slipped at times into rapid French or Italian he could not follow, although he tried to look as if he did. He risked a few remarks in each language in his turn, and was decorated with praise for his efforts.

They were in fact most generous in every regard, and Ronald began to feel ashamed of his apprehensions. He excused himself around eleven o'clock, and paused on his way to the toilet to look out at the sea and sky through an open window on the sheltered promenade.

But there was no sea, no sky: they were walled in by fog. He leaned his elbows on the window ledge, and put his head out into gray damp. The *Nero* tipped steeply sideways; paused; returned. He could feel the fight it was making against a violent sea, somewhere out under the fog, a sea that coated windows and decks with its foam. But whether it was the champagne, or the company, or the fact of feeling one of a very small group that had overcome all nervousness and fear, the elemental war going on just outside his reach seemed nothing exceptional. It seemed appropriate and right.

When he rejoined Alistair and his party, they had restocked their buckets with more bottles of champagne. This time, they got him onto America, about which they were unable to learn enough. In point of fact, Ronald was amazed at their ignorance. They asked him about the most obvious things, all of which he tried to explain. Las Vegas. Lee Harvey Oswald. What Americans ate. How much they made. Why, he knew more about each of their countries than they knew about his! But then (he thought) perhaps a European would feel little compulsion to inform himself about a nation so shallow and so young.

2 A.M. His brain felt wadded in fuzz. Words were pouring fluently out of his mouth (minus the odd syllable or diphthong) without any part of his thinking mind knowing exactly which words they were. He had a dim sense of keeping a tired watch over someone like himself, through the wrong end of a drooping and out-of-focus telescope. Whoever he was, this eloquent, sober person he was observing managed to explain the federal system, American racism, and what would happen to Australia and Hawaii if the communists were allowed to win in South Vietnam, while Helen kept pushing his right hand away from her bottom.

"Ish all very simple."

"To the simple mind. Oh Alistair, do send him away."

"No no *no*. I find him enchanting!" Ronald gazed back with glassy satisfaction. "Don't we, Renata?"

"*Non è più comico.*"

"Oh, nothing is funny to you," said the French girl.

"You shut up."

"Listen. Take him to bed if you want, play your silly game, all five of you. But let's stop this nonsense."

"Wha nonsense?" Ronald heard himself asking, over and over: Nonsense nonsense nonsensh. The Italian girl and the French girl were into a nasty exchange of insults in their respective languages. Just as Ronald was beginning to explain to Helen what was wrong with American women, while rubbing his hand up and down her back, one of the two girls slapped the other an evil-sounding crack.

"Stop it!" he shouted, and tried to stand up. "Jus shtop it!" He fell across the table, then propped himself up on his hands. "I donno who you people are doing but just stoppit." He slumped back into his chair, falling heavily. Their faces were staring at him, weirdly lighted around the edges like mechanical monsters that suddenly pop up before you in the old Tunnel of Horrors at Playland. They looked like masks, all of them, the eyes little electric lights sunk in papier-mâché holes, the faces painted cartoons, the bodies mere stuffed plaster puppets

one hundred and forty

that would fall back on their hinges at the push of a hand. He wanted to throw softballs at them, knock them all down and win the prize.

"You're sposed to be so European and . . . and European, and you just go around hitting people and making fun of everybody else. England, Italy, Fransh, England. Big fucking deal. You don even pay attention. I tell you, you let the communists in the consitution. You gotta consititution? No. Well, we do. So *c'est la guerre* and fuck off."

"Bravo! And hip hip, hooray. Well said, Ronald." Alistair poured him some more champagne. "Couldn't agree with you more."

"Oh don't, Alistair! Can't you see he's had enough?"

"No one ever has enough. Why, just listen to that noise. I'll be surprised if this idiot ship makes it through the night."

Drunk as he was, Ronald received the notion with a very real, wet chill. He saw his bare body waving like seaweed, somewhere under water. He sat up, looked around as far as he could see. No one else in the smoking room; no one else in sight at all. They were alone. An eggshell of drunken people talking through the storm, lost in the middle of fog and black sea.

"Oh nonsense. That proves you've had enough, in any case. Ships don't sink any more."

" 'But he was sick, the little spic . . .' "

"Don't be morbid."

"Who's morbid? The Italians don't know how to build or sail ships, and that's a simple fact. The wop crew all piled into the lifeboats of the *Andrea Doria* and left the passengers to drown. And they'll do it again. Before morning."

"That's simply not true."

"Oh don't go getting all Italian of a sudden, Renata. It's true enough."

"Well, we're not going to sink."

"Then what's that noise? And where is everyone else?"

"The noise is simply the normal sound of stressed metal. And everyone else is in bed, where we ought to be."

Ronald was so far drowned in champagne he could scarcely put two ideas together, but one thing he knew. He did *not* want to have to go back to a dormitory full of groaning, puking Italians, seven decks below. He couldn't make it to the door, let alone down one hundred and sixteen stairs. He didn't want the others to go away and leave him, either, alone in his empty eggshell in the middle of the sea, in the middle of the night. With the flashlight bulb of lucidity he had left in his head, he began to work out a marvelous scheme of salvation.

"Well. Burp. Who gets to sleep with me? Here on the couch?"

"Listen to that." "That Great American Lover."

"Renata?" Lovely nose. "Whaddya say? Do we do the dirty deed?"

"I doubt he knows how it's done."

Why don't they answer me.

"*Regardez-donc notre petit Casanova.*"

"Marie-Josée, then?" The breasts. The blue circles.

"What do you have to offer?"

He started to unzip and show her, but François poured a glass of champagne in his lap. He stared open-mouthed at the puddle, and became very cross.

"Why you do that? Huh? Huh, Frenchie? The lady asht me a question."

They laughed mirthlessly, smiled out of boredom. It was very late, and very rough, and only Ronald was drunk enough.

"Oh François. To cool all that ardor."

"*Ah, c'est assez gros déjà. Comme ils sont des cochons, vos américains!*"

"All v'you then. Boys and girls together!" He tried to focus on Alistair: grinning teeth, sharp bones, dark eyes in deep sockets.

"Would you really like that, Ronald?" White suit, white shirt, white tie. White all over. "Would you?"

"*Vive l'Amérique!*"

"Sure I would. Vive Lamreek."

"Up the flag."

"Up the flag!"

"Oh, for the love of God, mate, don't you know when you're being insulted?" Helen was exasperated at his denseness; tired of the game; tired period. "I really think you'd better go."

He stared at her blankly. "I don think I can."

"My Lord, he's stinko. Oh, Alistair, you are such a *fool*." She turned and shouted hoarsely toward the empty lounge.

"Steward! Steward!"

By the following afternoon, they had steamed clear of rough seas, and the ship and its passengers began to pull themselves together. Ronald returned, after a day's rest, to his bridge mates, cured of his infatuation for the boy in white and his sophisticated friends.

interlude:
8½

She might as well be dead.
Are you dead?   Then open your eyes
And tell me not to stare.
No eyes. Two bumps instead of eyes.
A fine pink foreskin
Stitched tight by long thin eyelash hooks
Over two dead bumps of eyes.
I wonder where she is,
Stretched under somebody's sleeping skin.

The mountain blanket moves
And someone in me screams

one hundred and forty-four

To peel it down
And drag her back to morning.
(FROM THE *Poetry Notebook*, 1964)

In the months that followed the assassination of John Kennedy, the tangible quality of life in many parts of America began to change. In the short time that Ronald Harrington had spent in Europe, the temper and style of his country had already shifted considerably. The result was something he found strange and uncomfortable. He was frequently to feel, in the next few years, that he did not possess the resources required to accommodate himself to the change.

In the early months of 1964, the city of Berkeley began to shelter a new breed of citizen — thin, sickly young people whose like he had never seen before, dressed in work clothes or farm clothes, clothes from army surplus stores or St. Vincent de Paul.

The place was full of them. The papers were full of them. One's own head was full to aching with them.

And they terrified Ronald. Their very bone structures, their complexions were foreign. They bared scrawny, fleshless frames under the California sun, and seemed incomprehensibly ugly and out of place.

Ronald tried to stare through these skinny barbarians, tried not to see them at all; to keep, at all costs, from taking them seriously. Surely what *mattered* would maintain, beyond their waves of spittle and noise. They were still kids, after all, soft, untested kids without roots or creeds. Surely thumping shouts and blaring noises were not things to analyze and worry about. Surely a seventeen-year-old kid with long hair was still only . . . a seventeen-year-old kid. With long hair.

But then why was he worried?

Something was shaking very hard at his whole sense, so painstakingly assembled, of what mattered. Whatever it was in fact, the visible proof of it lay in these could-care-less students, with their scorn for nuance, complexity, civilization, tradition, their peculiar private lives, their freedom, their slogans, their grunts and loud music. This music, the surface noise of the new barbarism — the same shapeless din Ronald had heard

for the first time on the *Nero*, on the English boy's records —
now came blaring at him from public loudspeakers, translated
into the ubiquitous buzz-blatt of a million Jap transistors.

He had come back from the sure center of civilization onto a
hostile new planet full of dread.

"L.B.J.! L.B.J.!
"How many kids did you kill today?"

In the world of popular music, most of the press and public
at this time was still fixated on the Beatles, a group of four
musicians that had exploded out of the English underground
in 1963. For a long time both the Beatles and the Rolling
Stones (then the Number Two group) were regarded by most
of their friends — and their enemies — as shaggy-haired kids
who made noise. Many things came later to complicate that
image: drugs, groupies, tens of millions of dollars, visionary
films, otherworldly electronics, pronouncements of radical re-
jection; wives and lady friends, the Maharishi and Yoko Ono,
Lennon Remembers, Mick's arrests, Brian dead in his pool. But
to most who had heard of them in 1963, even in 1964, Mick,
Keith, Brian, Charlie, and Bill (like John, Paul, George, and
Ringo) were just Pop Stars, the mod style gone musical, this
season's *monstres sacrés;* lads who sang and posed and played
guitars or drums, and were blown up all out of human propor-
tion by managers and publicists and the sensation-seeking
popular press: a kind of cellular multiplication of earlier, no
more reasonable Hit Parade phenomena like Dion, or Fabian,
or even Johnny Ray.

By 1965, though, and especially by 1966, many people
thought they saw a difference. For one thing, the craze had not
passed. It had taken root, in fact, grown tall and firm, put out
branches that bore fruit. A semidocumentary film on the
Beatles was written about as a work of genius. A stomping,
arrogant, near inarticulate shout released by the Rolling Stones
in the summer of '65 became (in the minds of certain cultural
pundits, at least) the rallying cry and creed of a whole genera-
tion, a profound revelation of Western malaise. Fans in Paris
(and Oslo and Munich and Manchester and Chicago and

Sydney and Tokyo) tore up seats and ripped up clothes, tried to storm the stage just to touch the performers.

By 1966, one could find professional critics who professed to see these wild children *not* just as Mickey Mouse Clubbers ever so slightly grown up, but as portents and omens, as the incarnation of deep new human needs.

But if Ronald Harrington heard about the Beatles, or the Rolling Stones (or Chubby Checker or the Byrds or the Beach Boys or whoever), it was for the same reason that most people did during these years. He couldn't avoid them. Whatever paper he read, there they were. Searching for music on his car radio, it was *their* music that kept coming out in between. It came out, interminably, from other people's nasty little portable sets. It came out of the television, out of loudspeakers in front of record shops and supermarkets, as background to noon rallies in Sproul Plaza. By mid-1966, a person who lived in or read regularly of any part of the active Western world could not *not* have known of them. And if he had ears to hear, he had probably heard their music as well.

Why did people stand in line all night to see the Rolling Stones? Why did eighty million people buy Hula Hoops, or watch Jack Paar every night? Why do dogs run after sticks? Why do babies like balloons?

Mr. Jagger was charged with being in possession of four tablets containing amphetamine sulphate and methyl amphetamine hydrochloride; these tablets had been bought perfectly legally in Italy, and brought back to this country. They are not a highly dangerous drug, or in proper dosage a dangerous drug at all. . . .

We have therefore, a conviction against Mr. Jagger purely on the grounds that he possessed four Italian pep pills, quite legally bought, but not legally imported without a prescription. Four is not a large number. This is not the quantity which a pusher of drugs would have on him, nor even the quantity one would expect of an addict. In any case Mr. Jagger's career is obviously one that does involve great personal strain and exhaustion; his doctor says that he approved the occasional use of these drugs, and it seems likely that similar drugs would have been prescribed if there was a need for them. . . . It is surprising therefore that Judge Block

one hundred and forty-seven

should have decided to sentence Mr. Jagger to imprisonment. . . .

There are many people who take a primitive view of the matter, what one might call a pre-legal view of the matter. They consider that Mr. Jagger has "got what was coming to him." They resent the anarchic quality of the Rolling Stones performances, dislike their songs, dislike their influence on teenagers and broadly suspect them of decadence — a word used by Miss Monica Furlong of the *Daily Mail*.

As a sociological concern, this may be reasonable enough, and at an emotional level, it is very understandable, but it has nothing at all to do with the case. One has to ask a different question: has Mr. Jagger received the same treatment as he would have received if he had not been a famous figure, with all the criticism his celebrity has aroused?

— from *The Times*, July 1, 1967

nine.

Henry Harrington, Senior, lay in a hospital bed, propped up on two large pillows. Midday sun filled his ward with light. A nurse moved silently into the room, and whispered in his ear. "It's your son." Sun? "He's come to see you."

Moon face, ears sticking out like jug handles. Old scar. New moustache. Ronald peeking around the corner.

"Hi, Ronny. C'mon in."

He held out a hand. Ronald took it.

"What you been up to?"

"Not much."

He pulled a chair up alongside the bed.

"Studying for the exams mostly. How are you, then? You're looking good."

"No I'm not." He pulled on the skin of his neck, under his chin, lifted the chin to show sagging wattles. "Did you ever think your old man would end up like this? Huh? Did you? Look at that." He pinched the loose flesh, pulled it back and forth violently, proudly. "Just look at it."

Ronald struggled for appropriate words, but none came. He was sure his father said things like this on purpose, just to make people uncomfortable.

"I got a postcard from Hank." He took a folded card out of his jacket pocket and handed it to his father. "Yesterday."

The postcard dropped from his father's hand onto the sheet, picture side up. Some motel it was, with a giant pink statue of a dinosaur in front.

"Where's that supposed to be?"

"Vernal, Utah. It's near the Dinosaur National Monument."

"Vernal Utah? Is that where he is?"

"That's where it's postmarked from. Aren't you going to read it?"

"Course I am. Give me a second." He managed to stop his hand shaking and turn the card over. Vernal Utah. What the hell's he doing there?

Henry focused his eyes to make out the words, a diagonal scrawl across the left half of the card. Wrote like a little kid.

Billie Jean and I are staying with this guy whose got a place in the desert. Our engine block cracked coming up out of Salt Lake so we junked the car and hitched, which is how we met this guy. Tell the folks I'm broke but OK. Blew all our money in Reno. I'll write more when we're settled. Hank.

Red ballpoint, a red blur, a smear of blood. He let his eyes drift back out of focus.

He picked up the card, bent it backwards in two, folded it back and forth.

"Why did he write to you, do you think?"

The sordid banality of the message had left him disoriented and peevish. "I'm the one who ought to know."

Well now you do.

"I expect he was too ashamed to write you, Dad. Embarrassed or something." Christ, don't ask *me* why he doesn't write to you. "He wanted to let you know he was OK, but what with the car business and the money he must have felt he

one hundred and fifty

didn't have any good news." Shit. "If he wrote you a letter he'd have to explain things."

"He doesn't have to explain anything to me. I just want to hear from him, that's all. Just one word. Christ, my own son." He glowered at the window.

"Do you think he knows how sick I am?" God, listen to him: self-pity, that's all it is.

"He couldn't, Dad, else he'd be here quicker'n anybody. You know that." Pathetic. "You seemed pretty good the time he left, remember. Getting stronger, eating more. Nobody thought you'd be back here so soon."

"*I* knew how sick I was. Even if nobody else did. Half a stomach left, puking up everything I ate. How he could just up and leave at a time like that I don't know. *I* couldn't have, if it was my old man. Christ Jesus's sake: his own father. His own father's going to die and he won't even be here for the funeral. Out in the desert somewhere with some . . . whatever she is. Some goddam hippie whore. Is that right? I ask you, Ronny: is that *right*?"

Ronald could think of no answer to that one either ("Yes"? "No"?), so he sat and waited, his eyes fixed in the region of his father's stomach.

"Do you think they got married?"

"They went through Reno."

"Yeah, well. No proof they got married. Lotta kids go off these days without getting married." He stared out the window for a moment, then decided to ask.

"You ever meet this Billie Jean?"

"Once. At a bar. Hank asked me to come and meet her."

Hank had never allowed his parents to meet her, and neither of them had ever mentioned her to Ronald before. He felt peculiar talking about her now.

"At a bar, eh? What's she like then, another whore like Ramona?"

"No. Not like Ramona."

He remembered the meeting. "She was wearing jeans and a man's work shirt. Long hair, no makeup. More a pizza and beer place, actually, not a bar. Hobie's, down by San Pablo. She's from Oklahoma."

"Yeah, so I heard. An Okie hippie. Just what the family needs. What's she really after, do you think?" It was himself he was asking, really. "What does she *want?*"

"Just Hank, far as I could see." Her hand, rubbing the inside of his brother's leg under the table; he flushed at the recollection. She had played whiney old Hank Snow records on the juke box, one after another, the whole time they were there. "She really seemed to like him."

"Like him, eh? Well, God knows why." His father turned back and frowned at the sky. Fair, unfair. God knows what's right.

"Oh, he's a good boy, I suppose. You can't blame him for falling for an old pro like Ramona."

"I think you'd like Billie Jean better than Ramona."

Hank Snow songs and beer mugs and knotty pine walls around a booth. He could feel her presence, all but touch her long hair. "She'd been all sorts of places. Mexico, Central America, all over the states. She left home at fifteen because of her stepfather, she said. She's been hitchhiking and working around ever since. Plays the guitar, gives lessons sometimes, works with kids. Cooks in restaurants. She's only nineteen, but she can take care of herself." Better than Hank can.

"I don't like it. Hitchhiking, wearing jeans, going to bars. A girl like that. What'd she do with my fifteen hundred dollars? That's what I'd like to know."

"I thought it was Hank's."

"Well, his *and* mine, don't sass me. What happened to it, then?"

"Maybe he's the one that lost it. Look what he's done with money before. Look how many jobs he's had and quit."

It's not fair, goddammit. Stands up for Hank no matter what.

"I thought he was gonna stick it with that electrical supply job, didn't you?" He was going over it all again, trying to make it make sense. So many times. "Then there was that car wash thing with Peter. He talked a lot about that. I'd a helped him out there, if he wanted me to."

Ah, but then Ramona ran off. With a black man.

"At first I blamed the navy, all that drinking and dirty talk, 'fuckin' this and 'fuckin' that. Drove your mother bats. Join the Navy and Learn a Trade. Learn to waste your life, that's what. Learn about drinking and whores and dirty talk. Learn about bumming around.

"Then I blamed that gang of his, his old high school friends used to hang around at Ernie's. Bunch of good-for-nothings they all seemed, nothing but cars and cars and cars and those Mexican girls down at the bowling alley.

"But now I don't know. A lot of them have straightened out. Pete's got four car washes now, his dad tells me. A rich man at twenty-eight, married, settled down, three nice kids. Jimmy Savo. Number two man in the shop. Married Pete's sister Julie.

"*She* was hot for Hank once, remember? You went on your first date with them, ha! With Julie and Hank and her little sister, what was her name? To a drive-in movie. Boy, did we get a laugh out of that! You in your purple shirt.

"Why couldn't Julie have married Hank? He's a whole lot better looking than Jimmy Savo. I could have got *him* a job in the shop. He knows cars as well as Jimmy does.

"But no, he just wants to ass around, marry some redheaded twin from San Diego who can't keep her hands off other men." Other men's cocks. Specially black ones. "I hear tell she's working at one of those topless joints in the city now. Ramona Sainsbury. Christ. Who would of thought?"

I would have thought. Ronald was bitter, selfish and bitter; I knew it all along. The rest of you people were just too dumb to see her for what she was. Oh, not Ramona. Not our precious Ramona.

"Almost thirty years old, and he's hitchhiking around the desert with a hippie bitch from Tulsa Oklahoma I've never even met without a dime in his pocket. Sweet Jesus God. His mother would die."

Die, his mother would die, his father would die. Henry rolled his head back from the window to look at his other son, who was still staring down at the sheet, in the region of his stomach. Must be needling him, all this talk about Hank. He shoved the postcard under his pillow, tried to concentrate on Ronny.

Always be fat, I suppose. Not wiry like Hank. He held out a shaky hand for Ronald to clasp.

"And what about you, son? You gonna run off with some floozie too, and miss the old man's funeral?"

"Oh Dad, come on. Don't talk about that."

"Why not? Somebody's got to talk about it. Somebody's got to think about dying and funerals. And it sure isn't going to be your mother!" Or Hank either. "Look at me! Look at that skin. Tubes in my arm, tubes in my you-know-what. Plastic gut. I can't eat, I can't go the toilet. They wash me like a baby. When they remember to do it. Why, I'm two-thirds dead now. A worn out old skeleton they're keeping alive by tricks.

"But they've just about run out of tricks, Ronny. Look at the way they treat me!" He waved one skinny arm, one stick poking out of the oversized sleeve of a hospital gown. "Look who they put me with. Look at old Popeye over there!" A hairless old man in the bed across was staring at them with great egglike eyes.

"All of them!" He waved the stick/arm again, then let it drop. "Wheezing old geezers twice my age making messes in their sheets. Old geezers nobody comes to see because nobody wants to look at them. Nobody wants to know they're still alive. And this is where they put me."

He dug fingernails into the palm of Ronald's hand, dug hard till it hurt. "You know what they call us? 'Terminal cases.' End of the line, that means. Terminal cases. The only way we're supposed to go out of here is in a box. And the sooner the better. Clear out the bed, roll in the next one.

"Remember that fat guy across there, Harvey, the one that kept falling out of bed? Same bed Popeye's in now? Dead. Genesco, the old Dago crook owned the supermarket? Died last week, rattling away. Sounded like two dried peas rattling around in a can. And Sal, the guy from Indianapolis, always going on about My Son the General, and My Son the Professor, dead as a doornail."

His father's voice had started out low and confidential, but now he was shouting. The man in the bed behind Ronald grunted and turned over on the other side, rolling a pillow up over his head.

one hundred and fifty-four

"Dad."

"Oh, I know."

He released his fingers from Ronald's hand, dropped his own hands on the sheet, flopped his head around on the other pillow. "You're not supposed to talk about these things.

"But do you know *why* you're not supposed to?" He turned back, made a weak fist. "So's you won't upset the healthy people. They're the ones who can't bear to think about it. Makes them uncomfortable. Makes them a little queasy, maybe, thinking about people like me turning into pulp in a box under the ground. Makes them a little sick to their stomach. Sick to their stomach. I'll tell them about sick to their stomach! Be goddam glad you *got* a stomach to be sick to, not some rotting mess of puke and pus and plastic."

He placed a flat palm on his own abdomen, swollen beneath the covers, looked down at his white-draped shape. Then he lay back, wretchedly depressed. I'm going to die.

"Your mother's the worst." His voice was low again now. "She won't hear about it. She won't even let the doctor tell her what's going on. She won't listen. She just keeps telling him about how well I look, and how we just gotta have faith in the Lord. It near to drives me crackers.

"You know what she did last week? Your dear mother? I shouldn't tell you this. Last Sunday it was, same day you came. She was coming in as you were going out, with that big yellow shopping bag and her hat on. All dressed up for church.

"And you know what she did? She runs out in the hall and tells the nurse to give me some pill to shut me up. Tells her to put me to sleep. Said I was raving, didn't know what I was saying. Then runs off to her church meeting.

"And you know why she did that? Because I told her the truth for once, that's what I told her. I was just fed up to *here* with her babbling on like some hysterical female, about how much better I looked and how she was gonna make all my favorite foods when I got home and we could have barbecues in the patio with the Kennedys and the Lawsons and maybe I'd want to get at the garden again, the roses really needed it, and when should we plan on going to the River this year, and I just couldn't take it any more.

one hundred and fifty-five

"So I grabbed her hand tight, see, and shoved my fingernails into it like *this*, see, till she finally shut up, and I said, 'Go home? Go home? I'm going home in a *box!*' That's what I said. 'In a box! A wooden box! Can't you get that into your thick head, Grace? A wooden box.'

"I kept saying it, over and over, and you know what she did? She started praying. I swear. Right then and there she drops on her fat knees, right where you're sitting, and starts in on her Dear Sweet God and Holy Baby Jesus, with her hands together and her head leaning against the side of the bed, and I'm banging on her with my fist and telling her the truth, about the box I mean, and she up and runs out in the hall and tells the nurse I'm crazy.

"The only one around here who tells the truth, and I'm supposed to be crazy."

He was looking straight before him, complaining to the world. But the world didn't care.

"Then she waltzes off to her church meeting and comes back in next day all sweetness and light. Starts right in again about the aphids on the rosebushes and going to the River in August and who-all shall we have over to dinner.

"I give up, Ronny. I tell you I just give up." He closed his eyes, shutting out a whole world of disagreeable things. Just the way Grace did.

Ronald felt stifled, as he almost always did in the presence of a will much stronger than his own. Even as it died, his father's will was eating up his air, encroaching on his being space.

He got up and walked over to the window and stood there looking out. In the street, seven stories below, kids were just coming out of school, and he followed their paths with the fascination, mute and untimebound, of a born ant watcher. Each single person's steps and gestures seemed to be random and personal, but the overall pattern, the changing tributaries of movement, were exact and predetermined, predictable as the silver trickling of a broken ball of mercury along the worn grooves of a wooden desk. Three-fifteen, the bell after home room, walking down the old path along the creek. Nobody else there.

They don't use wood for coffins anymore, I don't think. My father dead. He tried to face the notion properly, feel something filial and profound, but nothing happened. He felt guilty, then annoyed.

What pisses him is that it's only me that's here, and not Hank, that's what he's really upset about. That Hank's off in the desert with his new woman, not back in San Salvador making his Daddy proud. Running car washes, some big deal like that.

Doesn't really matter what Hank does though; *he* doesn't care. Fucking Prodigal Son. He likes to think about him screwing. I'm sure he does. Ramona. Helen's sister Julie. Dozens of them, maybe hundreds. Now Billie Jean from Tulsa.

> I don't hurt anymore,
> All my teardrops are dried;
> No more walkin' the floor
> With that burnin' inside.

Probably dreams about it. Diddles his own old thing and pretends that it's Hank's. (*Stop.*) Reliving his youth. "Living vicariously." Doesn't want to live *my* life vicariously, ha! He'd rather be dead.

Well let him die. Come to see him ten days before my M.A. orals, and all he wants to talk about is Hank.

"Ronny."

What.

"Come here." He had been looking at the boy's back and thinking.

"You know what ole brother Hank used to think about you?"

"Yeah, I know. He told me once. One Thanksgiving."

"Well I want you to know that I never believed that. Not for a minute." He reached out for one of Ronald's hands, but the boy held them stiff in his pockets.

"Not for a minute. Neither does Hank, anymore, I bet. Else he wouldn't have sent you that postcard from Utah, now would he? But I never believed it. I told him he was fulla bull. I just wanted you to know that."

Ronald felt stung, felt his face redden. What's that supposed to be, some big fatherly pat on the head? Welcome home, boy, I don't think you're a faggot. Well, fuck you.

Ronald stared at his father, trying to give voice to some nasty remark, revenge for the old man's tactlessness, something that would deflate and upset *him* for once, wipe off that self-satisfied grin.

"Thanks, Dad," slightly strangled.

"I . . . I appreciate that."

"I mean." Don't say any more. "I mean I knew you . . ." Don't.

"I won't let you down."

Oh my God what a thing to say. What a stupid thing to say.

"That's my boy," said his father. In a wan show of heartiness, he reached up one arm to give his boy a slap on the side, but the fingers contracted into a claw as he lifted them and all the hand could do was scratch feebly across the boy's hip and fall again on top of the sheets. Ronald felt a flush of pity, and closed his fingers around the fallen hand.

"I better be going now. Exams."

"Oh, sure. Sure. You run along. Good of you to come, son. And thanks for the card. Hey when's the exam again? I keep forgetting."

Sure you do.

"A week from Thursday. So I may not make it next week, Dad. I mean maybe not till after the exams."

"That's all right, don't you worry about me. You got enough on your mind without that. You just dig into those books, hear? And knock 'em dead. Champ." He squeezed back on Ronald's hand.

"Right. Well. I'll see you then." Ronald let go his fingers, and started backing towards the door.

"And I meant what I said, Ronny. About knowing you were OK. Straight. I mean, any son of mine!"

"Yeah. I . . . ah. Yeah."

Thanks a lot.

"So long, Dad."

"Bye, Ronny."

Ronald felt rotten all the way down the elevator, all the way across the bridge. Bitter about Hank, depressed by the sight of his father so little alive, so nearly dead. Partly guilty, partly angry, partly embarrassed, partly confused. Mostly just rotten.

Back in his room in Berkeley he went straight down into his notes on neoclassical theory. Before he went to bed at midnight he had them pretty well under control. But still he felt rotten.

In the middle of the night he got up and was sick to his stomach, and vomited his dinner in the toilet. It always took him a day or two to recover from a visit to his father in the hospital.

Ten days later, Ronald passed his exams. It was his second try, and final chance. The vote had not been unanimous. He drove over to the hospital in the late afternoon.

A large-bosomed black nurse warned him to keep it short. He watched her as she continued down the hall. Then he peeked through the door of his father's ward, but his view was blocked by a giant bowlful of orange gladiola alongside his father's bed. He had telephoned his news first, so the old man was expecting him. He smiled a tired smile through the wall of orange and green.

"C'mon in," he whispered hoarsely. "Congratulations, Master. Howja like the flowers? They're from Fred and Kate. First I've heard from them in over three weeks. Read the card."

Ronald picked up a card that lay on the table, next to the big vase. A pinkish rectangle from the florist's, decorated with a little poodle, who was saying in a cartoonist's balloon, "Get well soon. Fred and Kate." The joke was that most of the rest of Henry's stomach had been taken out just two days before, and everyone who cared knew he was only just holding on.

"Pretty clever, no?"

Ronald nodded, put down the card.

"How are you really, Dad?" he asked.

"Not good."

"No."

"I look awful, don't I? I look like I'm dying."

"Yes." Ronald forced himself not to turn away, and gently picked up a light hand from where it lay like cardboard on the top of the sheet.

"I look dead." The older man had set up a round shaving mirror on the table next to his pillow, alongside the green and orange, so that he could always look over and see his own face. Sewn loosely over the angles of his skull, the skin of his face had taken on a mottled, bottle-green cast, almost like mildew, which looked all the more lifeless for the flaming young flowers. Around the chin, a bristle of whiskers had needled through flesh that looked much too dangerously thin to shave. The undertaker would do it for him, thought Ronald.

"I tried your mother's trick on Tuesday, before the operation. I prayed. Prayed I would die, under the anesthetic." He closed his eyes, after a few seconds opened them again.

"Those *Reader's Digest* people don't know what they're talking about." (Mrs. Harrington had been sold on the Power of Prayer by an article she once read in the *Reader's Digest.*) Ronald couldn't take his eyes off the whiskers that prickled about his father's chin line and jowls. He imagined a tall young Irishman in his shirt-sleeves with a long rubber apron on, lathering the whiskers, then pinching the dead skin to pull it taut, scraping off the whiskers with a straight razor, as his father's body lay on a mortuary slab, half covered by a sheet. He washed off the dirty lather and whiskers into a bowl of hot water at his side, a thin-walled hemisphere of silver, and then went back to his work. Ronald shook his mind, tried to stop thinking of his father as dead.

Henry seemed to doze off for a moment and Ronald wondered if maybe he should leave. But when he tried to unfasten their hands, his father only clutched the more tightly. He opened his eyes a slit.

"Don't go." Henry tried to rouse his mind from its swamp, think of words to say to keep his son. Son. "The nurse'll tell you when you have to go. She won't let anyone stay more than ten minutes." Only son left. Talk about . . . talk about exam.

"How'd the exam go?" he whispered.

"Not too good. They asked all the wrong questions. I was sure I failed again. But I didn't."

"Good boy." God, even his successes were so pathetic. If only he had a little more . . . balls. "What comes next, then?"

"The Ph.D., I guess. They gave me 'Permission to Proceed,' which means I can sign up now to take the Ph.D. exams any time. But I'll have to study for a year or two first. Then the dissertation."

"That's it, then?"

"Right. That's it."

"Quite a ways to go yet."

"Yes."

He opened his eyes wider, in order to focus his mind more intently. "You still happy about it? All these years in school?"

"It's what I want, Dad." Damn near dead and he still wants me to Get married, son, run Harrington's Ford of Granger, Indiana. Have two big strapping sons to carry on the name.

Dad smiled as best he could, tightened his weak grasp. "I'm sure it is." Then he closed his eyes again.

Ronald stared at the orange stalks to keep away the man with the razor. With his free hand he turned his father's mirror around a tiny bit, till it reflected an enlarged image of the center of his own face. Blond moustache, upturned nose, blue eyes sunk just a bit deeper with the strain of all his twenty-five years. He pulled back his lips and looked at the yellow teeth, watched the nostrils that moved each time he breathed. The dots about the jaw where he had shaved just that morning. The scar. Being alive.

He picked up the mirror delicately, and looked closely at its reflection of his eyes. Convex white jellies, slightly reddened, over which lay watery membranes. Light blue rings rayed with slivery streaks. Black holes in the middle. That's where it is, whatever it is: inside those two black holes.

"You hear any more from Hank?"

Ronald put down the mirror without a sound, turned it back to where it was. "No. Not a word." Until the second he heard his answer, he hadn't known whether he was going to tell or not. He didn't know why he lied, even now. He watched himself and waited, to see and hear what he would do next.

"You heard anything, Dad?"

"Me? No. He never writes to me."

Silently, as if casually, Ronald reached into the pocket, fingered the wadded-up letter; her hand touching his flank. He tried to evoke an image of big brother Hank out there in the desert, doing whatever it was he was doing. A picture of Hank's dry bones kept changing into one of his father's.

Blooms, soft bosoms. A black nurse had crept up beside him. Time to go.

Henry Harrington's eyes looked as if they were crying when he turned them up at his son, but that may just have been part of the way he was: streaming out his life from every hole. Well. The letter Ronald was touching in his pants pocket wouldn't make him feel any happier.

"So long, Dad." Ronald forced out some last words. "You do what they tell you. I'll be seeing you in a day or two."

"So long, son. Congratulations. Say, you wouldn't like these damn flowers, would you? To celebrate?"

"No thanks. Give 'em to the nurse."

"Good idea. I will."

"And sleep well."

Once Ronald had left, Henry did sleep, as clear liquids dripped into him through amber tubes. The high bed supported his slight frame exactly, as the sky supports a cloud, the sea a resting gull. He felt one more layer of linen himself, white, stiff, antiseptically clean. A white thing, in a white envelope. Unfeeling, flat, folded, and still.

He began his going-to-sleep exercise, a methodical abandoning of all awareness of his physical self. He tried to concentrate, ever so gently, on nonconcentration; on dropping off all knowledge of his toes, one by one, his cold feet, his lower legs, his knees, his thighs. Each in turn disappeared; unfelt, unthought about, no longer there. Then fingers; hands; forearms; upper arms. Groin. Stomach. Chest. Neck. Mouth, nose, face, eyes, till all that remained was the dark chamber of consciousness itself, round black walls glowing dimly with flashes and spots of an almost metaphysical red, wherever light ran together with blood. Gently, very gently, he tried to remove any wisps of thought his mind was still wearing, set aside the small images, tissue-thin rags of emotion, quietly as any wandering ghost. Consciously, unconsciously, not distinguishing which, he walked the thin tightrope between, anxious not to tear the gossamer web, make any noise of will or gesture of cerebration too loud or too sharp, all the while dimly troubled lest this very anxiety might impinge too heavily on the still, gradually thickening fog. Drifting, easing, holding his intellectual breath, till all was reduced to one spot, one pin point of light in the dark curving wall of his inner skull. Focus on that. The white light. There is nothing but that. Now there is nothing.

After a blessed space of pure nonexistence, the inside walls of Henry Harrington's head became aware of a confused dream that involved a number of girls he had known 'way before Grace. A waitress. Girls from the schoolyard, down below. Old friends.

On a stone terrace overlooking the Pacific, in Mexico or somewhere like that, the girls were all wearing skimpy bathing suits, even Grace, except that Grace was fat and old and covered with a red spotty rash. The young girls crowded around him, with their smooth, tight skin, pleaded with him to take off his hospital gown and dive off the balcony ledge for them into the ocean hundreds of feet below, a great roaring sea full of rocks, and he did, and as he dived he heard Grace explaining to them how her husband was fifty-two years old and dying of cancer of the stomach and bowel, how he had to be fed through intravenous tubes and drained with enemas every day.

And then it was Hank who was diving and not he, Hank about sixteen, handsome and tanned. Henry was back on the terrace in his bathrobe, sitting next to his wife, surrounded by tall green bamboo stalks hung with orange paper lanterns. They each had a bowl of chicken noodle soup before them, but it had turned cold, and little globules of yellow fat were collecting at the top.

Number Two Son, meanwhile, had pulled his car over to a curb alongside the Golden Gate Park panhandle. He stopped the engine and put on the brake. He had meant to wait until he got home to reread his letter from Utah. But it weighed in his pocket like a piece of dead meat, like a cut off hand. So he stopped the car before the freeway approach, and took out the letter. It was written on cheap binder paper, which had already begun to go crumby and soft, come apart at the folds. Some of the writing was smeared.

Dear Ronny,
     Your brother is sort of out of it right now, strung out on

some stuff he took trying to get into a trance. But he gave me your address and asked me to write: We fetched up at a kind of ranch in the hills here, where this fellow Hunter runs a kind of religious center for people he likes. There's about 12 or 15 people here, mostly kids but a few older ones, all freaks. The scene is part Mexican Indian part Hindu I guess describes it, but Hank is digging it and wants to stay.

It's a big place, pretty run down now. I think it belongs to someone else, but Hunter gets money from somewhere and there are rooms full of Indian jewelry and pots and old silver stuff, robes and masks and all sorts of drugs for the sessions.

He expects everyone who stays to contribute, and that's the problem. Hank and I are both broke, after what happened in Reno (he said he told you about that). We're supposed to put in at least a hundred each a month, and he wonders if you could ask your Dad for 600 for another three months. He thinks he still has it coming from an insurance policy.

He should mail it to us c/o Hunter Johnson, P.O. Box 8, Vernal, Utah 87112. A money order would be best, since Hunter doesn't believe in checks. And soon, or else we'll have to leave before the end of the month.

Love to you all,
Billie Jean Dougherty

P.S. It was nice to have met you. I wouldn't have thought Hank could have such a sweet brother. I really mean that.

Play a record for me sometime at Hobie's.

A gang of youngsters had begun to lean against Ronald's Pontiac while he was reading, kids with long hair and pale, pockmarked faces. Ronald looked up through his windshield with a start; he hadn't seen them come. They were laughing quietly among themselves, handing back and forth a wet-looking homemade cigarette. A girl with violet-lensed glasses was standing at his side window. She caught his eye when he looked up, then made as if to offer him the group's cigarette, waving it pinched between two fingers. Ronald shook his head, shoved the letter back in his pocket. He rolled up the window, and turned on the ignition. Languid, unhurried, they detached themselves from his car, like suction creatures in a slow motion undersea film; laughing still, waving their weeds, blowing their smoke. All of them waved at him, long beads dangling, tiny bells ringing, waved smilingly into his rear view mirror as Ronald drove with a jerk into the street and downhill toward the freeway approach. He tried to imagine they had never been.

> I've got a broken heart,

went the Hank Snow song;

> I've got a tangled mind.

ten.

Henry Harrington, Senior, had been right about one thing. Young Hank didn't show up for his funeral. But then nobody had written to tell him the old man had died.

So Ronald sat all alone with his mother in the front pew of the right-hand bank, one of those decorated with a great black ribbon rosette. The pews of his parents' church were arranged in three angled banks, down gently sloping, rose-carpeted aisles. Ronald already knew who was sitting directly behind them; Kate and Fred Lee (Fred had lately gone into politics), the others who had flown out from Indianapolis the day before. They had all come up to him and his mother as they arrived, to shake hands and kiss and say a few words. Henry's big brave gesture ten years before, when he had signed away his share of the family estate, had proved to be a prudent gamble after all.

A set of theatrical spotlights in the chancel ceiling focused thin tunnels of amber and rose down onto the casket, which intersected precisely where the upper half of the casket had been left open, like a Dutch door, to reveal the upper half of the corpse. Around the casket, covering the carpeted sanctuary, was a sea of white gardenias, yellow chrysanthemums, pink roses, their stems stuck into metal screens or stapled onto backboards in the shapes of books or hearts or giant life preservers, propped up on easels and then swagged over with purple or black ribbons, "Sympathy," or "Requiescat" machine-printed on each ribbon in gold gothic letters. The one just behind the coffin, wheels within wheels of fragrant, pastel wheels, was from the Lees. It said so in large letters on the ribbon itself. The next biggest, an open-Bible shape of white and pink carnations under the pulpit, was from Val Bigger Ford. Not Val Bigger: Val Bigger Ford.

Behind the whole scene, the summer sun had been broken into geometrical spots colored sea-green and copper and magenta by two stained-glass windows at the acute angle of the church. The fan-shaped arrangement of the pews allowed Ronald to watch the mourners taking their places, as an electric organ moaned from above.

Val Bigger and his wife had the first pew of the center section all to themselves; he in pin-striped dark gray, white tie atop white shirt; she in sable, black fur for black occasions.

Spencer, the Jasons, the O'Neills. The other salesmen from Bigger's. Crofoot. Grigg. (Who was minding the store?) Ron O'Neill caught him staring, and winked. Orange and purple paisley tie, great fat knot, striped purple shirt, orange and purple handkerchief spilling carefully out of the pocket of a blazer with the Val Bigger crest.

Caroline from the office. Willie Whatsisname. Mr. Cecchetti. Some people he didn't know.

Local merchants in the next pew, Elks, a few neighbors from Rancho del Oro — the Kennedys, the Lawsons. The Noriegas. The backyard barbecue set. The shrubbery was taller now, in

Rancho del Oro. The better-off had repainted their houses in darker colors, added rooms on for Grandma over the garage, grapestake arbors out of *Sunset* — even swimming pools. The Kennedys had one of those big plastic jobs you just fit into a hole in the ground, and then spray with something to keep the water from leaking out.

Tom and Angie. Angel Flores from the liquor store. Doctor Heenan. A black woman in a green satin dress, tight around the swelling bust. Green feather hat with a veil. McCabe from the TV repair store was staring sideways at the bust: white flowers, black skin, one smell drowns out the other.

A young clergyman with long sideburns and large eyelids was extemporizing now from the steel pulpit, composing a fictional biography of Henry Harrington. A son of the soil. Lover of flowers and his garden. Married in God's house to his childhood sweetheart, union blessed with two fine sons, his own and Christ's, both men themselves now, soldiers in Jesus's army.

Rotting flowers, rotting flesh, rotting lies. Two old people at the other side, bent over, wearing black. Not many people wearing black. Even Uncle Fred, Assemblyman Lee he was now, was wearing brown, a rich brown with tiny red flecks, under a coat with a fur collar. Mr. Heany from the drugstore. His wife had died of cancer, too, eight years before. She was the first person Ronald had ever watched die.

Church people. Creditors. Ernie from the bar. Funerals and weddings; sex and death. All that churches were used for anymore. Old Mrs. Sorenson, nosey old witch. People who came only to see who else came.

Go away, he wanted to cry, all of you. Jimmy Savo and his wife Julie. Her sister Helen, with some man. His own rotten past, grown older and more rotten. He felt like that guy in the last book of Proust.

Peter Jacobson, King of the Car Washes, forced to wear a suit and tie for once in his life. A pew full of his kids. Three little Peter Jacobsons. Jesus Christ, Beverly *Polestri*, with some tall guy in glasses. Bev Polestri. Liz. And Jack Brady, I'm sure it is, Jack Brady, and *Ted*, and Jerry, and . . . and Walt Dubois, there with that . . . Oriental girl. Walt Dubois, with a leather coat and a moustache, Walt who had held the wet rabbit in Tijuana.

The whole of Trinity Methodist was filled with characters from his own life, but all of them horribly changed, adult upstanding citizens with houses and children who had come to his dead father's funeral.

WHY HAD THEY COME? What was his dead father to them?

His father was gone. But they were still here.

Trapped in a pale pew with a black ribbon rosette. Trapped between a weeping mole of a mother and his dead father's corpse. Between his uncle and his uncle's flowers. Between globous holy eyelids and all of San Salvador High.

If he looked forward, it was to a gunmetal box with a half-open door, awash in a sickly sea of bloom, a sliced fraction of dead profile resting on white satin.

If to the right, to a curled up sowbug covered in black, his mother sobbing softly into a wadded-up hanky embroidered with poppies.

If to the left, to the rear . . . No. He couldn't look back. He couldn't bear the thought of their looking at him. It was as if *he* were the one lying in the coffin, all rouged and eviscerated, waiting to be gawked at, to be fingered by them all . . . How he *hated* all these people, the sure and satisfied ones, the blond and blue-eyed ones, the hard simple fools who had run San Salvador High, and now ran the world: there, now, staring holes in his neck.

His uncle rapped him on the shoulder.

"Get up," hissed in his ear. "You're supposed to go first. And help your mother."

Ronald turned around to see what he was talking about. Wet red balloon in a fur-collared coat.

"The service is over. You're supposed to view the body before they close the coffin."

"I can't."

"Don't be silly. Everybody does. We're all waiting for you." His right arm was clutched softly.

"Ronny?" his mother was whispering, so quietly he felt rather than heard her say it. "Ronny."

He couldn't see her eyes through the veil. "Do you really want to, Mom?"

"Of course, dear. We have to view. Your father would want it."

What a stupid thing to say.

"We'll be right behind you." Aunt Kate, exuding Miss Dior.

They stepped out of their pew, Grace half leaning on his arm, half pushing him along. They were staring at him, all of them, the way they always did, waiting for him to do something wrong: shout, trip, play the fool, expose himself.

Stop. Right now. Shove off her arm, turn around, tell them all: Go home.

Get out. All of you! GO HOME!

Liquid smirk leaked from under eyelids bulbous, holy, red, loose, round like chicken eggs. You too, pious asshole: *out.*

Slam shut the steel door, kick down all the flowers, stand guard at the step so no one could come near him, none of these people.

GET OUT.

You Mrs. Sorenson. Glare back until she looks away. You, Mrs. Bigger, Mr. Bigger, you most of all. You and your purple tie, O'Neill. You, you rats at the back. Helen. Beverly. Walt. Ted. Melt, pulverize, LEAVE: ALL OF YOU!

Ramona, her arm clutching the arm of a tall Negro in green. smiling at him, she was, the filthy ghoul. *Waving* at him. He felt sick.

"Will you get along!" snarled his uncle, shoving him unpleasantly from behind. "We haven't got all day. And try to stop staring."

Ronald swallowed a wave of nausea and hate back down his throat. If he had a long-handled hatchet in his hand, he would hurl it at Fred Lee's forehead, at the flowers, into the rose-carpeted floor. Send its blade stabbing sharp and tight, split it apart with its steely still-quivering heft. He could feel his arm doing it: lifting, hurling, shaking with the force, the impact, the *crack* he had made.

But in fact he was walking up rose-carpeted steps, between

one hundred and seventy

white banks of offending bloom. At his side, his mother was holding onto him so tight he couldn't escape. Priest and priestess, Punch and Judy, bride and bridegroom; two victims of some sacrifice yet to come. The crowd at his back would start throwing any minute, warbling loud cries and throwing hard, pointed things. He could feel them in his neck, in the tender vale of his spine, in the calves of his legs.

His mother detached her claw and went to kneel down at a small prie-dieu alongside the half-open door of the coffin. It was placed so that one's own face peered directly into the dead person's from a distance of just a few inches.

After a few moments' prayer, she pulled up her veil, leaned over the top of the kneeler, and tried to kiss her dead husband. But she couldn't quite reach Henry's face with her mouth. So instead, as everyone watched, she pulled off one glove, reached one bare finger, and ran it slowly and deliberately in a line down the forehead, over one eyebrow, both closed eyelids, the bone of the nose; now the sunken cheek. He had been shaved closely, then colored red, and powdered white. The lips, now, first the upper lip, then the lower. Ronald watched aghast, reached next to him for support to a tall wooden stand. It wobbled, tipped, a topheavy bowl of white gladiola began to slide off the top. Fred Lee shoved past him to try to catch it, but it crashed to the floor, splashing water over the arm of Fred's coat, and over Ronald's trousers and shoes. Murmurs filled the churchly air; waves of disapproving noise. Uncle Fred said nothing, went back to his place radiating chagrin.

Ronald felt the dampness of his pants leg like a hot discharge, like a great running sore. To be swallowed up, not to be here. Now his mother was at his side again; "Ronald." She whispered his name, touched his arm with that same bare finger. He shuddered at the feel of dead flesh. "Your father." And she nodded a tiny nod towards the open door. The boy felt rooted like a figure in a dream. He longed to tear out a scream, *wake up* out of all this; but instead he went, knelt down on the prie-dieu, and laid his face on his folded arms.

Dad I'm sorry. Dad I'm sorry. He kept saying it, Dad I'm sorry, not really sure what he meant. The repeated words were enough to make him cry. Dad, I'm sorry. He looked up at his father's face through stinging wet eyes, and tried to think of something to think of.

The eyelids, the lips he saw; then a clear vivid line where his mother's finger had run. She must have cut it, he thought, cut it with a fingernail sharp as a razor. Scratched cold flesh clings to dead bone, amid the cloying jungly gas of the gardenias.

Inside that envelope of dead skin there he was, had been, once, thinking live thoughts inside a dead head. "I'm me," he could have thought, if he wanted to, a week ago, there inside that head. This body, these eyes, these organs, this hair, the itch on the sole of this foot: all me. *Lift, arm,* the brain could have whispered, in the wordless way of brains, and the left arm would have lifted.

No motion has he now, no force. Ronald pinched the flesh of one of his own hands with two tight fingers of the other. Flesh of my flesh. Not to be able to move, not to be able to feel, not to be able to think, not to be able to pee, or to itch even, or to breathe up and down. Not to be able. Not to be. Not. Just a corpse that somebody else had to shave and wash and dress, a store window dummy with stiff limbs and soft skin. Undo the tie, unbutton the shirt, reach inside and he's still there, see? Even if the heart *doesn't* beat the way it used to. White hairs on the chest, dried up little nipples, sharp, hard bones of ribs. Veins along the arms, fallen, drained, filled with formaldehyde instead of blood. Open up that other half door. Unbuckle your father's belt, undo his trousers, pull down the undershorts. Touch *that,* if you dare, O Mother of Mine! Run your cursed red finger-line down to there why don't you, down to where he might still feel it? Nothing more dead. Ronald shuddered at the thought. Soft flopped flesh, cold dead stump never rise again; decay it will into soil-like brown bits, flake off and crumble away. His: mine.

Still connected, still whole, nestled under soft layers of cloth, locked up in the lower half of a pearly gray box. Useless, icy cold. But *still there.* Reach inside and feel them, rub *life* back into them; my life, my own pulsing blood, my warm fingers; the life of *this room,* of these flowers, of this alien crowd. Rouse it up, hold, force it to throb and spill out again. The night I began, his son. *Dad I'm sorry.*

one hundred and seventy-two

A shiver from hell's wide-open window: Surely there could be nothing on earth more horrible. Dead man my own father, flesh become mine. The boy had to fight with himself, to keep hand from trying to reach in and feel soft dead sliding male skin, from opening up all those discreet protective coverings and laying it bare. My father dead.

Gardenias, spilled gladiola, damp spot on his leg. He felt ill. Thin red razor line scratched on his father's face: disappeared. He thought of the young Irish undertaker in his rubber apron, scraping off the dirty whiskers and cream. Wanted to prize open the box, rip off the wax museum clothes, wrap the body in sheets, nothing else, one huge sheet, around and around. Then he could carry it himself, out the door, away from all this. This place, ha! this place would fill with dirty brown water up to the ceiling, like an aquarium, drown all the people and the flowers inside. They would float around like turds in a stopped-up toilet. But his dead father's body would be saved.

He would put the body in the back of his car. Right. Then he would drive to the ocean, take it out and carry it down to the sand. There he would wash it gently with cupped handfuls of soft sea water, roll it over and wash the back, wash the hair, the ears, the fingers, gently wash the private parts. Kiss his father's face. Wrap it all back up in the sheet, wait for the evening tide to carry it away.

Oh, they would come after him, in their black limousines, of course they would do that. Try to take the body away and bury it first. Hank might get there before him, Hank and Billie Jean, and Helen, and Ramona, and the Negro man in green. Hank would be there at the beach, waiting. That was why he wasn't here. On the sand, he could see him, Hank in his red swimming trunks, standing behind a black rock, watching all his careful attentions to their father's body.

And when he had done with his washing and his wrapping, Hank would come out and stand over their father's body in his red trunks, feet planted wide apart. He would reach down and pull roughly at the sheet, unwind the white winding wrapper, and roll their dead father's body back down toward the sea's edge. When it was rolling free of the sheet, he would kick it and kick it and kick it again, down the slope of sand, laughing, faster and faster towards the lapping surf, the slow reach of white ocean's fingers, till at last, naked and white, eyes open but unseeing, their dead father's body would roll cold and shriveled back into the cold sea.

Let them have the body, he thought. I don't care. He looked up from the coffin, back to the church, stood up and returned to his pew.

"No. No, I'm not going," he told them after, in front of the church. The sunshine was blinding. "But you'll be the only one not there." "I'm sorry. I'm not feeling very well."

Driving home from the church, he suffered — according to subsequent medical reports — the equivalent of a mild nervous seizure, just where cars coming off the Bay Bridge merge into northbound traffic on the freeway up from Oakland. He told Dr. Ford later on that he saw a giant sheet of flame rising off the roadway, just at the junction. He swerved to avoid it, and drove broadside into two lanes of oncoming cars off the bridge. His own car was hit twice and spun around. It rolled off upright onto the shoulder, and crashed against the steel upright of a billboard, dimming the giant overhead lights on their curving steel necks. On the billboard a huge picture of a boy with tangled locks: "Beautify America," it said; "Get a Haircut."

His four-year-old Pontiac Catalina was transformed in two seconds into thirty-five dollars' worth of scrap. Ronald himself was very badly shaken, and bruised about the left shoulder, side, and arm, but otherwise visibly unhurt. After sitting very still for a minute, he climbed over the back of the seat and got out by the one undamaged rear door.

By the time he was out the door and on his feet, two Highway Patrol cars had arrived, an ambulance was on its way, six lanes of northbound traffic had slowed down to stare. But the great sheet of flame was gone.

eleven.

"Come in, Harrington. We're all here. Or almost. You know Professor Thorneson, I'm sure. Professor Hardy. Mr. Schultz has agreed to be your Neoclassical man, since John Wilderman is ill. You knew about the substitution?"

"No, sir," shaking hands, one by one, around the table. Wilderman is ill.

"Well, no matter. And of course you know Professor Ackerman. At the moment we're lacking only your outside man, outside *woman* I should say, yes, Madame, ah, Duplessis, from French. Do you know her?"

"No I don't."

"Nor do I. No matter. Well, sit down, sit down. Harrington. Anywhere you like." Out of two empty chairs. "Smoke if you wish. We've just been going over your dossier."

In fact, Eugen Schultz, whom Ronald did not know, of whom Ronald had heard horrible things, who looked awful, a death's head, had not yet looked up at him or accepted his hand; he was still leafing through a pile of varicolored papers clipped into a brown manila folder. Grade transcripts, carbon copies of letters of recommendation he had had to ask for over the years, reports scribbled or typed on pink or green forms of his performance in seminars and tutorials, his work as a teaching assistant. Things he had written himself: his statement of purpose of five years ago, applications for grants, loans, part-time jobs, the fat bluebooks of his preliminary exams, an abandoned dissertation prospectus. There was a three-page report on his dismal show at the first M.A. orals in '66, and one almost as long on his second, barely successful try shortly before his father's death. The second one had been typed, in fact, by the same man who faced him as chairman now: Professor Shoemaker, author of four separate monographs on the Pergamon Altar, who was pretending to remember him as little as he decently could. On that second occasion he had held out for forty minutes against a Pass, and finally yielded only to save himself the annoyance of having to draw up and justify a minority report, and to shut up Thorneson's intolerable yapping. Professor Shoemaker had written the transparently hostile "Bare Pass" report Schultz was now perusing, which expressed more than anything else Shoemaker's own impatience with the obstinate folly of inexperienced and permissive young colleagues.

"Ah, Madame Duplessis." Scraping of chairs, turning of heads, raising of bottoms off seats. Ronald rose. In the doorway stood a squat, fish-faced creature, twisted forward over a pair of aluminum crutches. She was hunchbacked, fat, and short. She wore a gray suit, generously cut and drooping. One thick leg was bent at an ugly angle, and it dragged behind as she pushed herself into the room on futuristic metal props. Huge watery white eyeballs bulged under an unbroken ridge of bristly brow, eyeballs that stared out of a sagging face of

one hundred and seventy-six

uncertain age, stained here and there with liver spots. Wisps of rusty-white hair had been combed over a freckled scalp. She was very nearly bald.

"And zees must be ze young man!" she turned herself abruptly around to Ronald, thrust out a hand, and stared up at him with her great poppy eyes. "Ow-do-you-do?" His hand was damp and boneless; hers was a clamp. When she spoke wet lips curled open and shut over inward-bent teeth, making her look all the more like one of those ugly Mediterranean fish whose heads you find in authentic bouillabaisse. Her voice was shrill to the edge of screaming, a rusted machine full of sand. The French accent was thick, at times near to impenetrable. Her academic specialty was, in fact, French pronunciation. In speaking the English language, she made few concessions to its crude and un-French ways of dealing with important consonants and vowels.

Her appearance before a new assembly could not help but be melodramatic, disorienting. Quasimodo walks into the Senior Common Room. They were all, all but Ronald (and Professor Shoemaker), stumbling to help her to her seat; of course she needed and wanted no help at all. She shoved herself sideways off her crutches, letting her squat bulk down into the remaining armchair at Ronald's right. Out of a huge brown purse she pulled a notebook, a few books and papers, pencils and pens, and a distinctly ticking pocket watch on its own tiny easel, all of which she set up neatly before her. That done, she glared a smile of sorts at Ronald, then swung around and nodded at Professor Shoemaker, giving him permission to commence.

He commenced.

"You've all had a chance, I hope, to look at Mr. Harrington's writtens, which Mr. Ackerman, Mr. Wilderman, and myself judged, ah, 'acceptable' last month. Do feel free to raise any questions you might have regarding his answers on those.

"This will be one of the old-style exams insofar as Mr. Harrington applied for Permission to Proceed before the fall of sixty-seven. This means that each examiner in a general period is given a maximum of thirty minutes for his questions, while the examiner in the field of concentration (Walter Ackerman, for Medieval) may take up to an hour. The outside member is invited to interject questions at any time, to go over any material from any period at the end of the examination, and to make his, ah, her own judgment of the candidate's performance all along the line.

"It is our custom to take a short break halfway through the exam — which should be about four o'clock — at which time Mrs. Haberreiter will bring in coffee and cookies. Do you have any preference, Harrington, as to the order of the exam?"

"I beg your pardon?"

"Would you prefer to proceed chronologically, taking your major period in order? Or would you rather do the general periods first, and save the Medieval for last?"

"Oh. Ah. Chronological, I suppose."

"Very well. I shall go first, then, with the Classical, followed by Mr. Ackerman. Then our break, after which Mr. Hardy will do the Renaissance, Mr. Schultz the Neoclassical, and Mr. Thorneson, finally, ah, the Fine Arts of Yesterday and Today. Are we all ready, then?"

Shifting of chairs, recrossing of legs, puffing on pipes. Madame Duplessis seemed to belch, or grunt, and scribbled a violent note on her pad.

"Very well, then. Two thirty-three." Professor Shoemaker set his wrist watch down before him, tapped out his pipe, and looked straight out his office window. The exam had begun.

"You know, of course, Gisela M. A. Richter on *kouroi.*"

?

"Richter: Gisela, M., A., Richter; on *kouroi.*"

Jazella May. Mind, get in gear. Oh, her: Gisela. "Yes." On *kouroi.* "Yes of course." He should know. They had read it just last quarter in Shoemaker's class. Good first question.

"My intention *was* to start gently. Tell us something about her categories, then, her means of dating, general lines of development. That sort of thing."

Six groups. Sournian, Melos, Ptoon. Oh, start. They'll come to you.

"Um. She starts with pre, ah, well, whatever you call the period before Archaic, examples, out of Crete and places. Then she divides the rest into six groups, each one named after the, the *provenance* of the best surviving examples. Sournion is the earliest. The key statue there is in New York. Then Voluman-dra."

"No."

"Melos?"

"No."

"Then I don't know." Strike one.

"Orchomenos-Thera."

"Oh. *Then* Volumandra?"

"Yes. Tenea-Volumandra."

"Then Melos." Four. "Then Anavysos-Ptoon twelve" (five), "then Ptoon twenty" (six). "These last two are named after particular finds from the Ptoan Sanctuary in Boeotia during the eighteen eighty-five dig."

"Eighteen eighty-five and after. Very good. I don't suppose you could date these six periods?"

"Each one ran about twenty years, as I recall, between about six hundred and five hundred B.C."

"Close enough. Now tell us something of their development. Or at least" (a tap of the pipe) "Miss Richter's theory of it." *Aha:* he doesn't agree with her.

"She *likes* the early ones well enough, sir, finds them very . . . monumental. Kind of Egyptian. What they are still, is they're four-sided blocks of marble, obviously, carved into formalized frontal *versions* of human beings. But they're all wrong. I mean anatomically. Like the ears."

"What about the ears?"

"Well, they don't look like ears. More like scrolls, or volutes, not the least bit like our ears. Or the hair. It's weirdly stylized, cut into lumpy braids, perfectly symmetrical. The heads and the eyes are too big. The shoulders are too broad. They leave out all kinds of muscles. It's almost as if they hadn't reached the stage of caring about physical realism."

"I see."

"But as they went on they seemed to start caring more and more about getting things right, you see. The statues start looking more and more like real men, even though they held the same pose for a whole century. According to Miss Richter, none of the Greeks did actual dissections till the time of, ah, till much later, so they must have started *looking* more and more closely at naked athletes in the gymnasiums. Because by the fifth century they had hit on even the most obscure muscles, veins, tiny anatomical details we don't even usually think about."

"Such as?"

"Well, I don't know the scientific names. But the muscles in the neck, like the one here." He felt for it. "And here."

"Sterno-mastoid and trapezium. All right. So the trapezium was commonly indicated, then?"

"No, sir. But by the end they at least knew it was there. And also these funny little flaps in your ear." He wiggled his.

"Tragus. Antitragus."

"Right. She makes a big deal out of those. It took sculptors a *long* time to spot them. Then, let's see. Well, apparently the inside and outside of your knee and ankle aren't really symmetrical." He touched his knee. "And there's this little tear thing in the inside corner of your eye" (he fingered it). "They had even caught *that* by the final stage. And, ah, mmm: this bump down here just below the middle of the chest. Some bone you never see, even. And your second toe being longer than your big toe, I mean, not yours, some people's aren't, sir, ha, but, well, yes. They started doing that too. Making the second toe larger. Mine isn't." He was feeling himself all over for their benefit. A living, breathing, twentieth-century *kouros*. Overage, asymmetrical, unathletic. Distinctly unideal. Sitting down. Dressed. "The way your collarbone curves backwards. The sort of hollow we all have on the side of the um, hip. Here." He touched the place where his hollow would have been, were it bare and not buried in flesh. Me, the Greek athlete, born 2500 years too late.

"The great trochanter."

"Yeah."

Shoemaker spun his swivel armchair round from the window — he had not *looked* at Ronald all through this recital — and waggled a pipestem.

"I see. And what does your Miss Richter identify as the most significant change of all: when does she have it taking place? Can you tell me that?"

Think. "The end of frontal symmetry, I suppose. Somebody

realized one day, in Anavysos-Ptoon twelve, I think, that when the left leg is extended forward, as it always was in *kouroi*, the hips and torso are shifted slightly, one up, the other down." (*Stop* feeling yourself. The French lady is staring at you.) "The buttocks too." (So is Schultz.) "The line down your middle, here, through your navel, sir, here." (*Please* stop!)

"That was, ah, second to last period, so about five forty B.C. Once they hit on that idea, Miss Richter says, we come to the end of a thousand-year-old tradition." Silence. "It was probably very satisfying."

"Indeed."

Shoemaker turned his profile against the window again and methodically relit his pipe. The glass space was now full of blue, a fierce blue Ronald imagined as Aegean.

A golden-tan beach of almost powder-fine sand, molded by wind and water into undulating dunes, baked into dust by much too much sun. A sea laps its edge; a sea of slow, constant, bone foamy crests. Behind, a cliff. Behind that, another world. The swollen curve of a calf between his hand. Fingers trailing through a fur of golden hair.

". . . listening, Harrington?"

"I." No.

"*Do* you, I repeat, on the whole accept Miss Richter's scheme?"

Accept it? "Well, I, ah, really hadn't gone into the subject deeply enough, I'm afraid, to be able, uh, to evaluate . . . I mean she *is* the authority."

"Indeed: is she? Very touching, your faith. Still one should at least inquire whether or not one's authorities merit such blind devotion. For what contributions to classical archaeology of the later period — 'my' period, if I may so term it — are we indebted to Miss Richter?"

God, he must hate her.

"Well, nothing terribly important. Most of her conclusions struck me as being rather second-hand."

"Do you recall any of her remarks on later statues in the Roman collections?"

"Well, I don't know if this is what you're getting at, but she got very upset somewhere at the Renaissance popes for . . . for desecrating Greek and Roman statues."

"Desecrating?"

"They thought them indecent."

"And . . . ?"

"And had the genitals hammered off. Or covered up. The Barberini Faun."

"Ah, yes. The Barberini Faun. And how highly does Miss Richter rate the Hellenistic sculptors?"

That's his game, is it.

"Not nearly high enough, in my opinion. She adopts the usual art-historical fallacy of a kind of biological or botanical sequence, archaic to proto to early to high, you know, each one better than the last, each all unconsciously aspiring to the condition of high, from the *kouroi,* to the ah, Charioteer, to the Discobolus to the Parthenon: Polyclitus to Phidias to Praxiteles. Then downhill by stages into decadence, you know, according to this fallacy, purity and vitality giving way to mere showiness and mannerism. That's where she'd put the Hellenistic. All very faithless and gutless and cynical. Same thing most nineteenth-century and early twentieth-century critics did with the Middle Ages and the Renaissance, romanesque aspiring to be Gothic, you know, Gothic collapsing into flamboyant; Simone Martini and Botticelli, all naïve and innocent, struggling to be Raphaels and Michelangelos, you know, and then *their* energy and faith sort of trickling down into facile showmen like Parmigianino and the Venetians. You know."

"And you don't accept that idea?" Hardy; green eyes peering over horn rimmed glasses.

Christ, he probably does. Shoemaker or Hardy? Shoemaker.

"No sir, I don't. Not that simply. I really don't see much point in moralizing about the rise and fall of art in such a pat, schematic way. People only began to see the Sienese painters properly, or the romanesque church builders, or . . . or Corot, to understand what they were trying to do and appreciate what they had accomplished when they *stopped* thinking of them as only incomplete and inadequate stages on the way to Michelangelo or Chartres or Cézanne. And the same thing holds for so-called decadent periods. There's a fantastic kind of realism, almost surrealism, in Hellenistic sculpture; a . . . a very moving psychological expressionism, if I may call it that, a sense of physical and mental suffering the Golden Age Pericleans simply couldn't touch. If you get yourself stuck in a sort of Kenneth Clarky late-Victorian box about the great inspiring tranquil masterpieces being the be-all and end-all of art, then you won't be able to see the equally valid claims of things like the Laocöon or . . or . . or the Pergamon Altar." Damn! He could have bit his tongue off. The Pergamon Altar! He had scoured his brain for another example, but couldn't come up with one in time to end the sentence. And had been going so well! Now they would all see through his answer as sucking up to the chairman. Oh, fuck him and his Pergamon Altar.

But Shoemaker, at least, was smiling — out the window, of course — and relighting his pipe. (Why did people smoke pipes if they never stayed lit?) He spun back and gave a tiny *moue* of victory to the heretic Hardy.

"All right, good, let's move on. Could you read this over, Harrington, and tell us who wrote it?" He handed Ronald three typed paragraphs on a white sheet of paper, then passed a sheaf of carbon copies to the other examiners round the table. "Take your time. And think carefully."

Oh fuck. German.

Diese Aufmerksamkeit greichischer Künstler . . . Greek artists. *Aufmerksamkeit?* Attendance, attention, *auf die Wahe der schönsten Teile*, beautifullest parts, OK, Greek artists paid attention to beautiful parts, *unzählig schöne Menschen*, of innumerable beautiful persons. Oh the *bastard. bleib nicht auf die männliche und weibliche Jugend allein*, got it, *eingeschränket sondern ihre Betrachtung war auch gerichtet auf das Gemächs der . . . Verschnittenen. Der* what? What's a *Verschnittenen? Versch*, divided, lost, deteriorated *Verschmelzen, Verschlossen.* Shit. Was not limited to male and female youths alone, but their observation was directed also to the conformation of *Verschnittenens, zu welchen man wohlgebildete Knaben wählete*, for whom well-built boys were selected. What the hell?

"Having difficulties, Hannington?"

"Um yes sir. I'm not quite sure what a *Verschnitten* is."

"A eunuch. Gelding. Castrato? You *do* know what that means?"

"Oh, yes, of course. Yes. Thank you very much."

Christ. The conformation of eunuchs. Fuck, I don't know German. But all art historians. *Verschnittenen*. Those *zweideutigen* beauties, in which the *Männlichkeit*, manliness, through the behavior of the *Samengefasse*, the who? Where's the verb, find the verb . . . *sichderweichlichkeitdesweiblichengeschlechtsinzärtlichenglichernundineinemfleischigernundrunclicherngewächsenähertewurdenzuerstunterdenasiatischenvölkern* hervorgebracht. That's it: *hervorgebracht*. Produced. Those *zweideutigern* beauties were produced among the Asiatic people first, I'll bet they were, filthy Chinese, *fleischigern und rundlichern Gewächse*, fleshy and roundish growth, God this is sick. I wonder what *Samengefasse* are? Seed vessels, Oh I get it. Spermatic ducts like.

But what has this to do with classical art?

Shoemaker was fingering his watch. Madam D's ticked away like crazy.

"How are we coming?"

"Oh, coming. It's about the Greek artists' use of the, um bisexual object."

"Are you ready to attribute and discuss it, then?"

"Ah: not quite."

"Do get on."

Panicsville. Where was I? To the rapid race of fleeting youth as Petronius says *einzuhalten*. Greeks of Little Asia, Asia Minor, boys and youths of this sort were to Cybele and Diana of Ephesus *gewidmet* yes manly youths . . . under the Romans stop the *Bekleidung* of Manhood with the juice of Hyacinth *Wurzeln* cooked in sweet wine their chin and other parts. Christ this is insane. Boiling boys' private parts in sweet wine and hyacinth berries.

Skim the rest. Quickly. Maybe something will make sense. They're all looking

Die Kunst ging noch weiter, art went still further

"That's four minutes we've waited, Harrington."

"Yes. Yes." Yes. SHUT UP THAT CLOCK, LADY!

Jointed the beauties and *Eigenschaften* of both *Geschlechter*, races, sexes, in the figures of *Hermaphroditen*, aha, that's the game. Just hit the nouns now. Hermaphrodites in size, position, artists, mixed nature, image, beauty, *hoher Schönheit*, a higher beauty, *und dieses Bild war idealisch*, right: I get it. *Geschöpfe*, creatures, hermaphrodites, the philosopher Favorinus of Arles in France, according to Philostratus, oh my God *hurry*, a parenthesis, skip it, *nich ein jeder Künstler Gelegenheit haben*, ah, verb, *zusehen*, not every artist can have the occasion to see a so rare *Abweichung der Natur*, and Hermaphrodites like those art etcetera, are probably never begotten. Christ I hope not. Quick, Quick. *Alle Figuren* of this kind have a girlish bust, yeah, *nebst den Zeugungsgliedern*, what the shit, forget it, on

"Please, Mr. Harrington! We have so many more things to cover."

"Yes yes. One minute. No more." Oh fuck if they find out I don't TICKTICKTICK

Bacchus as a *verschnitten*, what was it, what what, with fine round limbs and with the full dissolute, no exuded, something, heft, *hips* of the FEMALE SEX, what in heaven's name, the forms of his limbs as soft and flowing as though with a gentle breath informed, inflated, this is repulsive

"Time: please."

"Of course of course." *In der schönsten Natur eines Knabens und in Verschnittenen*, then again. This whole thing is They're all staring.

"Well?"

"Well, ah, he says that this type of Bacchus is a beautiful boy, who is the, ah, spring of life and the youth touching the limits in whom the, ah, impulse of, oh, lust, like spitz of a plant . . is, I, um, between sleeping and waking . . . in a dream!"

"What on earth are you talking about?"

"Excuse me, sir. I was trying . . ."

"You *do* know German?"

"Yes. Yes, I. I mean, well. It's about the . . ."

"Who: who wrote it, first, when, in what text. That is your first question. And do get on. We have *centuries* to cover."

one hundred and eighty-five

Not contemporary, Lord, hundreds of Germans could have said something like that: the sexual ambiguity of classical ideals. Leap:

"Goethe?"

"Goethe?" Eugen Schultz whipped his head around, a mask of cynical disbelief. "*Goethe?*" the umlauted vowel swooped and sneered all by itself. "'Do you know anything of Goethe's style? Or for that matter of his opinions on classical art? The *Propylean,* the Art and Altars of the Rhine, Eckermann . . . ?"

Not Goethe. Think. Eighteenth century probably. Art-historical, myths, Asia Minor. Forms. Bisexual forms. Types of Bacchus. Stackelby. Moritz. No. Lessing.

"Winckelmann?"

"Of course Winckelmann," said the chairman. "Now would you care to venture a guess *where* in Winckelmann, and approximately when?"

"Early. Seventeen seventy. Seventy-five.

"He died in seventeen sixty-eight."

"Oh. Earlier then. From the, ah, *Geschichte.*" The only title of Winckelmann's he could remember.

"Correct. Congratulations. Seventeen sixty-three, although often dated seventeen sixty-four, but in either case hardly 'early.' Though of course he'd been working on it since fifty-six. Now would you be so good as to comment on the quotation before you."

Eunuchs. Hermaphrodites. *Fleischigern und rundlichern. Jungfräuliche Brust.* Full and extended hips. He caught the Frenchwoman's fishy glance again, this time recognized it for what it was — a lecherous invitation. Imagine her hips, her bones, the texture of her dugs, press the cheek against her still virgin parts . . .

"I . . . It's related to [*stabbed to death by one of his lovers, by an Italian thief, or was that somebody else*] It's related to Winckelmann's [*depravity, sickness, lust, that's what it's related to*] theory of the ideal. [*German Greek-lover turned priest, covering up, trying to hide.*] Like the painter Zeuphis —"

"— the painter Zeuxis."

one hundred and eighty-six

"— the painter Zeuxis who was, ah, supposed to have put together an ideal image of Venus —"

"— an image of Helen."

"— of Helen by combining the best parts of several different women —"

"— And Winckelmann's theory?"

"— was that the idealized human image was *better* than anything in nature. The artist, Zeuxis, say, or Polyclitus, had an idea in his head, some concept of man or woman so sublime that no living model could live up to it. And that was what he tried to paint."

"Or sculpt. And what, pray tell us, has that to do with the text on the table before you?"

Oh that. "Um. Well, I suppose if you pushed it far enough, you could say that the ideal *human* image might combine the best parts of men *and* women, just as the ideal female image, say, would combine the best parts of several women." The Frenchwoman's private parts kept moving around in his head. Anus, nipples, vulva, pubic hairs.

"Is that what Winckelmann is saying here?"

The words. He looked down, they blurred into a bristly clot of German. Christ, I don't know. He tried to separate them, remember what he had read.

"Yes, I think so. He says here that eunuchs, for example, the . . ." He searched. *There:* "that these, um, amphibious, two-faced beauties, *in* them, the masculinity, manhood, they, um, approximated the softness of the female sex, in the superior delicacy of the, ah, parts, and in a greater fleshiness and roundness generally."

"Mmm. Which isn't precisely the same thing. Does Winckelmann approve of these 'equivocal beauties'?

"He says the Greeks did. Or the Greek artists. Some of them."

"Does he indeed? As I read it, he writes that they *observed* them merely, paid attention to them."

"Well, he seems pretty fascinated himself."

"Oh?"

"The language, I mean, sir. That passage about Bacchus." Where where where. Bacchus. "Here." He pointed it out, reversing his page and shoving it to the center of the table. "This part here. It strikes me as pretty, ah, poetic. I mean, like love poetry, almost." (Murdered by his) "Like he was fascinated. Smitten." Smitten with *verschnitten.*

. . . mit feinen und rundlichen Gliedern und mit völligen und musschweifenden Huften der weiblichen Geschlichts. . . . Die Formen seiner Glieder sind sauft und flussig . . .

"Mmm. It does rather, doesn't it? 'The type of Bacchus is a lovely boy who is treading the boundaries of the springtime of life and adolescence, in whom emotions of voluptuousness, like the tender shoots of a plant, are budding, and who, as if caught between sleeping and waking, half-rapt in a dream of exquisite delight, is beginning to collect and verify the pictures of his fancy.'" Shoemaker cleared his throat, preened slightly, a sleepy Siamese cat, at the suavity of his translation and reading, and posed once more in profile against the blue rectangle of light.

"What do you make of Winckelmann's 'poetic outburst' there, then?"

I don't know. Hell. A sick frustrated sexless little Germanic scholar like the lot of *you* who fell in love with a bunch of old statues. The curve of a rounded belly, cold beneath his sweating hand. A line in Yeats.

"Well?"

"I.

"It's sort of like Yeats, I mean Keats, the idea of stopping nature in its tracks, like Grecian urns, like, freezing it right *there* at some ideal point, a moment of perfect round ripeness. That's always fascinated artists. Some of them claim it's what art's all about. I think that's what turns Winckelmann on."

"Does what?"

"Turns him . . ." Ronald waved his hand about, reaching for an acceptable verb that might just be floating through the air. "Agitates him. Excites him. Pleases him. Makes him write like that. The idea of youth just on the brink of manhood: all the softness and freshness of a boy, still, almost of a girl, even, but a boy, like he says, 'as if unconsciously dreaming of,' um, maturity, half knowing what's in store, what's coming next, the soft child's flesh all readiness for . . ."

"For?"

"For . . . adulthood. Manhood." He shifted uneasily in his seat. The Ephebe of Kritios, alone in the desert without hands or feet: fringe of curls, baby-fat face cocked slightly to one side, the hollow eyes, the full pouting lips; swelling chest, round curve of the stomach . . .

"Do you know of any works of classical art that measure up to Winckelmann's rapturous description?"

Yes.

"No. No, not exactly. The rapture does seem to be in his perception, which is really more eighteenth-century romantic than classical Greek."

"But the classical Greek artists shared this fascination for 'fleeting youth,' as you say?"

"Well, yes, some of them." Buttocks rounded, even fattish, seductively shifted. "But only as part of a much larger world view, spiritual as well as physical. A Bacchus, an Apollo meant so much more to them than, ah, what was it," he looked, ran his fingers down — *Schöner Knabe* — "a 'beautiful boy treading the boundaries between the springtime of life and adolescence.' Athletes at the games earned their statues by their victories, their achievements. They weren't just beauty contest prizes."

Oh get off this. He'll be asking me about the fucking hermaphrodites next.

"Well, I was going to ask you something about the hermaphrodite theme in paragraph two, but since you took so long on the translation . . . Let me see:" He looked at a small list of topics he had tucked beneath an ashtray. "Egypt."

Oh no. Please no. Please God no.

At that moment, Madame's little easel clock dinged a tiny ding. Directly after, the bells in the Campanile rang three.

"Oh, goodness, how we've lingered. Three already. Well, Harrington, you've been spared Egypt."

Thank you, God. He tried to formulate a tiny prayer of thanksgiving.

"One small set of questions, then, and I'll have done. As we've altogether neglected Persia, Assyria, Egypt, all the Western civilizations outside of Greece and Rome, this little sliver will have to serve. Give me the approximate date of each of the following: The Hanging Gardens of Babylon."

"Twelve hundred B.C.?"

"More likely sixth century. The Step Pyramid of Gizeh?"

"Two thousand?"

"Much earlier. The Sarcophagus of King Ahiram of Byblos?"

"I . . . I never heard of it."

"Abu Simbel."

"About thirteen hundred B.C.?"

"Correct. One for four. The Winged Bulls of Khorsabad?"

"Ah . . . uh. Late . . . no. Nine hundred B.C."

"Late eighth century. Stonehenge."

"Neolithic."

"Of course. More specifically."

"Twenty-five hundred?"

"Or four thousand. My heavens, Harrington, try to guess closer. This is all undergraduate stuff. The Temple of Edfu?"

"I don't know."

"Solomon's Temple?"

"Tenth century B.C."

"Correct. Two for eight. The Palace at Knossos?"

"Twenty-two hundred."

"The Archers of Susa?"

"The who?"

"The Archers of Susa."

"I don't know."

"Three for ten. Not very impressive, Hannington." A frown of annoyance. He put his papers back in their folder. "Well, that's all for me. Exactly" (he consulted his watch) "two minutes past three. All yours, Walter." And he set about busily emptying and refilling his pipe, for the third time in less than an hour.

"Are you in there, Ronald?"

"Yes. Be right out."

"We're about ready to start."

"Right."

Nerves. That's all it is, nerves.

No. No, it can't be just nerves. I was even doing well that last part, wasn't I, pretty well, anyway? With Ackerman?

one hundred and ninety

Everybody must feel sick at a time like this.
No.
Not sick like this.
Petty minds, idiotic questions.
Don't go back.

See it through. Just see it through.

"A more 'creative' question, then, since you seem to be balking at serious scholarship. You've been asked to conduct a seminar on, let's say, Eastern European iconography of this period. Monasteries, manuscripts, the lot . . .

"*Berenson's* attributions, oh come now, that's very Princeton . . .

"But surely you've read Neugebauer's *reply* to Van den Haag? . . ."

"Now I'd like to know what refinements on Butt subsequent scholarship was made. How can we distinguish, for example, a Mantegna manuscript engraving from a mere *School* of Mantegna, confining the discussion . . . ?

"But obviously, if all you can cite are Wittkower and Wölfflin . . .

"If you don't mind, Professor Hardy . . .

"Just the *basic* critical works, Mr. Harrington, I don't think I'm asking for anything very esoteric. Do you think that's unreasonable, Eugen? No, I don't either. This *is* supposed to be a Ph.D. . . .

"Please, Thorneson, *please:* may we leave politics out . . .?

"We're not really interested in your judgments of Renoir, Harrington, one way or another. Stick to the critical history. You had got as far as nineteen thirty-nine."

"And do speak up."

"Are you all right, Harrington?"

"Ronald? Ronald."

"Would you like a few moments to . . ."

The air.

"I can't. I can't."

He was crying. He was sick. He couldn't breathe out.

"I'm sorry." He pushed back his chair, it fell, he rose, ran, stumbled out of the room.

Late that night, Ronald Harrington awoke from a dream, uncomfortably like those of the lost last year. He opened a can of chicken noodle soup, cooked it on his hotplate, spooned it up steaming from the pan. Opened a bag of chips. Something: something. He unlocked the closet door, dug out the phone from where he had buried it under pillows, turned it back on. No ring now, nothing; no one. Smothered to death. He reached along the closet shelf until his hand came to an expensive scholarly volume on erotic Japanese art.

He sunk back into his chair, his feet on the unmade bed, and stuffed clumsy handfuls of salt chips into his mouth as he stared at the pictures. Delicately drawn concubines split open their vaginas, to receive the oversized red penises of their fat, smiling lords. The phone started ringing again, but he kept turning the pages of his book, staring deep at all the monstrous, alive-looking phalluses and cunts on tipped-in colored plates of the most elegant color, the most exquisite finesse.

The ringing stopped, and then started again. He counted, wondering how long whoever it was would keep trying. Twenty-two rings. It stopped, and started again: thirty. He wondered if they were counting too. Then it stopped, and did not start again.

He finished looking at the book, then took off his shoes, lay back on the sheets, and began to seek his own warmth. He fixed his eyes on the eyes of his favorite-ever painting: a neurotically intense dandy sprawled on his chair in a twisted, mock-casual, artist-in-a-garret pose; alongside him a skull and a foot and a severed head. Soft vulpine face, sharp boned and thin skinned, nervous as a horse in heat. Ronald kept his hand moving, felt the dagger of a nose, bright knuckles and high cheekbones, the pouting unnatural upper lip. Into bored, seductive, dark-shadowed eyes he stared: the dead Frenchman stared back: pupil, assistant, model, the beautiful boy who had lived with the artist through that whole awful year, when Géricault had nearly driven himself mad, closed up in his studio surrounded by decomposing cadavers, trying to finish his great work. The boy was in that painting too, lying naked and dead, the beautiful head bent backwards over the edge of the raft over the ocean, the bones and veins of the neck stretched and protruding beyond the point of pain, begging to be broken or cut.

He came, rested, cleaned himself off, clicked off the lamp, and then lay there in his room, dark but for a streetlight's glow through the window, the tiny orange glow of an incense burner under the picture.

When the phone rang again half an hour later, it woke him out of a second dream as evil as the first. He answered it first ring.

"Hello."

"Oh, Ronald. I'm so glad I got you. This is Walter Ackerman."

"Oh. Hello."

"Are you all right, Ronald? People have been trying to reach you ever since you left, since six o'clock. I was about to call . . ."

"Yes. Yes, I'm all right"

"You're sure? I was — I mean, we were — quite worried."

"No, no. Something just. I'm sorry I . . . for the way I."

"No matter, no matter at all, as long as you're all right. I explained to the others that it may have been some sort of slight recurrence of . . . your nervous complaint. I hope you don't mind."

"No. Thanks."

"Do you think that's what it was?"

"I don't know."

"Ronald, do you think you could come to see me, as soon as possible? Tomorrow, even? I've got a plan, a way to pull something out of all this. Could you come?"

"I don't know. I'll try."

"I've been talking to the others, and it seems we might be able to cancel the whole business today. Treat it as if it never took place. Would that be all right with you?"

As if it never took place. "Sure."

"And then get you some time off, maybe even a travel and research grant before the next go. I really think it would be the best thing, don't you? I have a particular piece of research in mind, in fact, a few weeks' work in France. It might just appeal to you."

"Uh-huh."

"You will come by tomorrow?"

"If I can."

"Ronald? I'm awfully sorry about this afternoon."

twelve.

The town of Cluny lies off the main road from Paris to the South. Not far off, mind — just a little loop to the west, between Chalon and Mâcon. A thousand-plus years before Ronald Harrington arrived there, it seemed to some people the perfect place to build an abbey: a cupped palm of land half-encircled by a river, high green hills to the east, low green hills to the west. The abbey grew, and prospered mightily, and a little town grew up to serve it, a row of tile-roofed stone houses that wound its way along the abbey walls, westward from the river to the hills. But the abbey died, finally, and then the town had reason to lament its tranquil situation, which was all very well for the works of God, perhaps, for praying and chanting and suchlike, but not very useful for works of men.

Up and down bigger rivers, boats carried fat cargoes, towns grew into cities and joined the brave new nineteenth century. But Cluny's little river, the Grosne, was shallow and slow. Old men fished in it, boys threw stones at frogs, pale cows stood knee deep in it, cooling their feet. After the last monk had packed his things and gone away, the town slept in its handful of land, between its green hills, its occupation gone. A useless, out-of-the-way village huddled around a gigantic hulk of a church, around the walls of a six-hundred-acre abbey where nobody lived anymore, where nobody worked, where nobody did anything.

So they tore it down, most of it, sold the pieces for whatever they could get, and let the government have the rest to fill up with things like stallions and engineering students and tourists, which at least helped a bit.

It wasn't like the old days, granted, when emperors and popes had come clopping into the abbey forecourt with trains of attendants, to be entertained in and impressed by this great thing Hugh of Semur had built out in the backlands of Burgundy. But it was better than nothing. Better than just sitting there and running to seed.

Now there were big brown and silver buses in the town square, buses full of German tourists here to do the Abbey Remnants in thirty-five minutes, between the wine country and lunch. Tourists and students. Three hundred fifty engineering students full of sap, from the suburbs of Lyon, who got frustrated at the village torpor. the one movie house and eight cafés. So they got drunk in the cafés, and went roaring up the narrow *grand-rue* on their motorbikes and *deux chevaux*, whizzed about the parking lot where the abbey forecourt used to be, between the so-called Stables of St. Hugh and the so-called Façade of Pope Gelasius. Every year, at least one student was killed in a smashup.

In the summer of 1969, Cluny was still being treated as a backwater. It did have a train station, on the wrong side of the river, over by the furniture factory. But passengers could no longer use it. They had to take a train to either Chalon-sur-Saône or Mâcon, and then a bus from there to Cluny. There seemed to be no end to the city fathers' chagrins.

By the time Ronald boarded it in Paris, the 14:32 to Chalon was already packed with French passengers and their suitcases, their valises and children, dogs, newspapers, magazines, string bags and paper bags full of food and wine and bottled water.

In the corridors, students and soldiers leaned out of the windows, smoking, drinking beer, staring at the fields and factories as they passed by. Ronald found an unoccupied open window, leaned his elbows over the edge, and put his head out to look for something French.

Highways ran parallel to the tracks. Along them cars raced with the train, and always lost. New apartment blocks had sprouted between the fields. Clean new factories, blue or yellow sheds, bland modern villas "French" only in their closed shutters and tile roofs and grillwork. The iron paraphernalia of a railroad. *Bornes-kilométriques* (whatever they were), old ladies in black, beer ads on café awnings, the odd steeple: things French.

Sens. Migennes. A long stop at Dijon. Half of the train was painstakingly uncoupled to be shuttled on east to Belfort. Ronald's half continued south toward Lyon.

A Frenchwoman in his compartment offered him some of the paper-wrapped sweets she had been feeding her little boy, then opened a bag of sandwiches and a bottle of wine and shared them as well. In return, Ronald jumped out at Beaune to buy them oranges and chocolate.

Chagny — the woman's stop — came very soon after Beaune, and Chalon very soon after that. The bus was waiting at the station when the train arrived.

After half-filling with a mixture of very local looking folk, the bus began to grind its way out of town and into the country, along that little loop westward between Chalon and Mâcon. N 481: *Route Touristique*. It climbed and turned with what sounded like great effort, stopping at each village or crossroads. Two chattering crones got off at a country cemetery near Buxy. The road then closed in between high hedges, they crawled through tunnels of leaves. After a few more kilometers, the view opened into a valley between fresh vine-covered slopes.

Ronald kept his face close to the bumping glass, trying to drink it all in. Grizzled fat-bellied farmers out of Cartier-Bresson photographs sat at wayside café tables, wearing bright blue overalls and berets. Muckledung-plastered houses, their doorways hung with bright-colored plastic strips. Aperitif signs fading on walls. Shirtless farm boys playing basketball, tots in blue smocks, loaves of bread on the back of bikes. *Cave Coopérative.* Chickens. Cows. Tractors. Farms like old monasteries, iron entry portals guarding ivy-covered stone walls. Among the sunbaked tones, red geraniums here and there in pots.

Bissy. St. Gengoux. Malay. Cormatin.

After Cormatin, the landscape spread out into a silvery spaciousness, like a composition out of Claude or Poussin. Each distance was delineated by lines and clumps of green, punctuated by tall poplars, black cypresses bent by the wind. In the last distance, soft hills rose to meet darkening skies.

At Taizé, a group of young pilgrims got out. It was here that Ronald looked around and discovered that there were only four others left in the bus.

Across the aisle, a few rows ahead, a young couple was kissing. After each long kiss, they would separate their lips and look into each other's eyes, run fingers over cheekbones and ears and stray curls of hair.

Behind them, a girl about sixteen lay back almost asleep. Short hair, dark eyes, swelling breast under half-unbuttoned sweater.

In the very back of the bus (he twisted around to stare) slept a boy about her age, wearing nothing but black jeans. His legs and bare feet were stretched out in the aisle.

The bus pulled down the side lanes of a lost village, and came to rest in front of a big old house, eighteenth century maybe, shuttered up, overgrown with weeds, hidden away in a

one hundred and ninety-eight

little glade the sun could not penetrate. The driver opened the bus door, got out, urinated against its wall. The two lovers got out. The man peed against the wall too. He took a key out of his pocket and opened the front door of the building. The two went inside.

The bus backed out of the glade, made its way up the road. A wooded hill rose on the left. On its crest stood an old red brick château: fat round towers at the corners, window slits, crenellations. A dirt road lined with trees ran all the way up from the highway to the château. The driver stopped the bus. *"Eh, Jean-Luc! Ici!"* he cried. The boy in back woke up, leaped down the aisle, jumped out of the bus. He crossed the road, waved to the driver, then ran on up the path. Ronald followed his form up the dirt road till he could see him no longer.

At the next stop there was nothing but an *"Arrêt Autobus"* sign. Not a building, not a crossroad. The driver stopped. The girl got out. Ronald's glance followed her too, her shoulders, the sway of her hips.

They rounded a bend, and there it was: a big tower and a little tower, the abbey church of Cluny (all that was left of it), rising over the rooftops of a town. But then the bus turned another corner, and both towers disappeared.

A bus stop alongside a narrow river. Ronald pulled down his suitcase, gave the man his ticket, and stepped down, alone, into a faint rain.

The first time you take an unknown road, it can seem endless in the taking. You have no notion, at each turn, how much farther there is to go. The whole experience can seem quite out of time. A glimpse inside a wine dealer's storehouse takes on the enchantment of an otherworldly dream: dark, reeking of wine dregs, damp with wine-soaked straw. A man in the shadows hauls barrels onto a wagon. Behind him, dim shapes of tuns.

A young girl walks very slowly into an alley not more than six feet from wall to wall, an alley that curves off to the left. She looks at you over her shoulder. Now she is gone.

Cafés, antique shops, bookstores, banks, boutiques, past them all you make your way, pressing slightly uphill, still in the dream. The drizzle grows more dense. You stand for shelter under an arcade before a pastry shop window. Gift jars of plums in Armagnac. The abbey towers on a candy box lid. Next door a dried up public fountain. A very old looking building, bits of timbering and columns stuck into plaster and stone. Posters for a circus that had come and gone; for a students' Quatorze–Juillet ball; a yellow *France-Dimanche* poster on a newsagent's wall:

> *JAMAIS, A DIT JOHNNY*
> *SHEILA EST DESOLÉE*
> *BRIAN JONES S'EST SUICIDÉ.*

The sky clears, you go on.

The parish church. Martyrs of the Resistance. Panorama de la Ville, Tour de Fromages, Visite 1F. "À l'Abbaye."

Around the corner, a sham Gothic façade: ÉCOLE NATIONALE SUPÉRIEURE D'ARTS ET MÉTIERS. Over an insignificant doorway to the left, *"Entrée à l'Abbaye."*

And that was it. From the parking lot–plaza, you couldn't even see the towers.

That first evening, Ronald risked no more than dinner and a bath at his hotel, hanging up clothes, sorting out notes.

It rained through the night, but the sky was clear blue when he opened his shutters to the seven o'clock bells. As soon as he left the hotel in the morning, he discovered that he *could* see the abbey towers from the square. In fact, he could see them perfectly well from the hotel steps. He could see them from almost everywhere in town, looming up, gray and outsized, circled by crows. The big tower, Eau Bénite, he came to imagine alive, with a heart like some great-grandfather elephant's, a gigantic wrinkled lump deep inside that throbbed perhaps once every twenty seconds, and vibrated through the ruin.

For some reason he didn't yet feel up to going inside the abbey, presenting his letters of introduction and getting to work. Instead, for three days he explored the streets of the little town, surveying the towers from every possible angle.

After dinner, in the evening, he went upstairs to his room

and tried to sort out what he had seen. He drew maps, using different colored inks for the different centuries. By the morning of the fourth day he had a pretty good idea of what used to be where.

"*Ah, Monsieur Arring-Tone! C'est déjà trois jours que nous vous attendons. Nous avons su que vous étiez descendu à l'hôtel, c'est Monsieur Gosse qui nous l'a signalé.*" The concierge at the École handed back his letters unread as soon as he saw the name on the envelope, shushed his stuttering excuses.

Would he be so good as to come upstairs? M. l'Intendant very much desired to make his acquaintance.

Doors were opened. Hands were shook. One bowed. One was enchanted to meet him. He was to regard himself as the guest of the École Nationale Supérieure d'Arts at Métiers, to come and go as he pleased. His work was, *naturellement, très intéressant, très important,* and if he, M. l'Intendant, could assist him in any way . . .

At the Musée Ochier, at the Hôtel de Ville, exactly the same reception. Ackerman's letters opened doors. He was given his own key to the museum library. He was to spend all the time he wished in the city's archives, which were filed on the shelves of a small tower room in the Hôtel de Ville.

Within a week, Ronald had devised a satisfying routine. The twin bells of the town churches awakened him at seven. (One always rang slightly after the other.) He bathed and shaved, then wrote at his worktable till eight, when the maid knocked and brought in breakfast. As he ate his croissants and drank his coffee, he watched the morning activity in the innyard below, smelled the morning smells. Then he dressed and went downstairs, greeting whatever members of the proprietor's family were about. He admired the abbey towers for a ritual minute, then walked up the hill to start his work — by nine, if he could make it, arriving along with the earliest comers of the mayor's staff.

At the twenty-four noon bells, he closed up whatever volumes he was copying from, and walked back down to the square. There he would drink a vermouth cassis at the café, outdoors if it was fine, and watch the passersby till he felt hungry enough for lunch. At first he took lunch at his hotel each day, and spent the afternoon exploring the south transept and the rest of the abbey buildings. By the end of the second week, he started venturing farther afield, either taking his lunch along or buying it wherever he happened to find himself when he felt hungry.

Many days he went no farther than the town itself. He would begin by looking in at Notre Dame, the parish church; buy bread and cheese and wine and fruit from a grocer nearby; then climb uphill to the cemetery, past the stone cutters' yards, the old city gates, the cattle market green. From the green, a tree-shaded promenade ran off along the town's southwestern rim, overlooking the rooftops and towers and the soft hills around, distant villas and farms, cattle and horses and sheep. The road ended at a leaf-tented belvedere, where Ronald might lie down for a few minutes on the grass, to look up at the blue through the green, and listen to the birds. Then he walked back downhill, through narrow lanes of old houses, to moldy St. Marcel, and from there up the *grand-rue* into town — the same road he had taken from the bus stop his first day, denuded now of its strangeness and romance.

He walked farther afield, too, north or south along the river, west into the woods and fields that lay beyond the last house in town. Usually, though, when he wanted to venture past the city walls, he would rent a bicycle for the afternoon from a little shop by the post office that smelled wonderfully of oil. Then he could set off out of town down whatever road he chose.

He rode north, along the same road his bus had taken the day he arrived in Cluny. Then, it had been as new as the first day of Creation. Now, it was his, familiar. The little river was at his side, the animals were his friends, the leaves and weeds his to finger and feel. Yielding to an aimless curiosity, he wheeled down unmarked side roads that led into the green hills.

Or he rode south, to the château and chapel of Berzé, to Milly-Lamartine, to Pouilly and Fuissé, to the caves of Solutré. He sought out the little romanesque churches of every village, the ruined ones in particular, to study and sketch. He walked up and down the few streets of each hamlet, peered into cafés and shops and the doorways of old houses. Then back on his bicycle, wheeling downhill and away, sailing around curves, happy to be free and in France.

The air was fresh and blue, full of birdsong and greenery and fine French smells. The people he met were civil and kind, not at all like the French he remembered. His work was going well. Solitude could be oppressive, sometimes, in a town full of lean and ardent young bodies. But when it bothered him, he just worked that much harder, cycled that much faster, screwed himself that much deeper into the dense and appealing past. The Beaujolais tasted of new grapes. The apricots were perfect. Sensual satisfaction came in many and unexpected forms, and he tried not to long too much for laughter and dark arms.

There were other things, good things. Perhaps better things. The sun changing old stone walls from rose to old gold to a yellow-going-gray. Croissants, and pastries, and snails, and fresh local trout, and *poulet de Bresse*, and goat cheeses, and wine. The thin ink curves of fine eighteenth-century script. Trees flickering past, as one coasted down country roads. Coasting free, being free. It was worth being alone to be here, here in Burgundy and not in Berkeley (or in Paris), where people threw stink bombs and rioted in the streets.

Early mornings were difficult. Wrinkled sheets in new morning light, the sounds and smells of the innyard; the thought of other people, in other rooms, doing other things.

But he had his own body, when self-restraint became impossible, and his work and his freedom. And if sleep did not always come easily, when it came it was dream filled and deep.

Halfway through his stay in Cluny, something happened that broke into this agreeable routine. It occurred the first day of his fourth week in the town. Not that it spoiled his new pleasures — far from it. It complicated them, all right; it muddled them up. But for a while Ronald thought it the happiest accident of his life.

He had finished a good morning's work in his tower room in what used to be the palace of Jacques d'Amboise, thirty-second abbot of Cluny. He was sitting outside the Café du Nord, as usual, sipping his before-lunch aperitif.

Students in lab coats (or in bright-colored T-shirts) came out in twos and threes from the abbey, then drifted off into town. Every minute or two, a car would drive in one corner of the square, then drive out the other. A few stopped and parked. Couples or families got out, with their cameras and sunglasses, then clustered about the sign at the abbey door, where they learned (it happened every day) that the next tour of the abbey wouldn't be until two. Usually they went back to their cars and drove away. Sometimes they came over to the café, where they sat down to drink out the two hours. Exactly the same, every summer day.

This day, though, a fat *coach* lumbered into the square as well, laden with tourists. It pulled into one of the spaces reserved for tour buses alongside the café. Ronald watched with amusement, wondering what a busload of foreigners would do when they discovered they had two hours to wait.

The tourists were disgorged from their bus, hot and expectant. By the time the last were emerging, the first had already read the sign. Already they were beginning to harass their guide, a short, red-faced Frenchman with a moustache. He begged for order, reviled someone else somewhere else for his mistake, and went inside to argue with the porter. Like all French porters, this one enjoyed nothing so much as telling people they couldn't get in: noon to two was the high point of his day.

The tour guide came back after a few minutes, waved his arms, shrugged his shoulders, raised his voice. The foreigners protested this way and that, reasoned, commiserated, sighed; then one by one gave in and started to climb back into the bus. What else was there to do? No one could expect him to wait until two. On to Autun.

But one of their number, a young woman in a short daffodil-colored skirt, continued to insist, in loud, bad French, that *she* was going to stay and see the abbey, even if it meant waiting until two. That was what she had paid for, that was what she had been promised. In louder, better, very rapid French, the guide replied that they were leaving. She could go or stay as she pleased. They could not wait. They were far behind schedule.

Could she get her money back?

No she could not. *Hélas.*

She would write to the agency in Paris.

That was mademoiselle's privilege.

She would mention his rudeness and incompetence.

As she liked. He had been a guide since before she was born. The agency in Paris did not comprehend his problems.

Could she meet the tour later on somewhere else?

Naturally, if she could find them. But he could not be expected to guarantee the preciseness of their itinerary from now on, after this unfortunate occurrence.

"Et maintenant, mademoiselle, il nous faut partir. Est-ce que vous desirez continuer avec la groupe ou non?"

"No I don't!" she burst out in English. "I've had bloody well enough of you, *and* your stupid tour!" She stormed back into the bus and emerged seconds later with her raincoat and bags. She said something rude to the guide, then strode over towards the Café du Nord, long legs flashing, long hair flying. Faces like fat-faced aquarium fish gaped at her through the windows of the coach.

"Having trouble?"

She looked at him abruptly, eyes hidden behind dark glasses.

"Oh! oh, these *wretched* French!"

She put down her things, sat down on the chair opposite him, and crossed her legs.

"I am *so glad* to see the last of that stupid bus." At that moment it was backing noisily out of its place. From every window they stared in her direction, faces wonderstruck at the arrogance, the defection.

"And those stupid, stupid people!" She took off her glasses, shook out her hair, and turned back to Ronald with a liberated air.

"What's that purple stuff you're drinking?"

"Vermouth cassis. Would you like one?"

"I don't know. Never tried it."

"Black currant juice with dry vermouth, over ice."

"Sounds divine. I *adore* black currant juice."

And so he ordered her one, and so Ronald Alan Harrington met Gillian Catherine ("Call me Jill") Purley, who was from London ("Well, near London"), and twenty-three, and had just last month quit her job at Harrod's because she couldn't stand her boss. She had come to Paris with a girl friend, but they quarreled over something, so she decided to go south by herself. On the train she met a lovely man who told her to look him up at Lyon on her way back, so she did, but when he answered the phone he pretended he'd never heard of her, if you can imagine such cheek. So she went back to Paris, and fell for this stupid tour, stupid, stupid, stupid: Versailles and Chartres, the Loire Valley and Burgundy, all in one week, 750 francs.

This much he learned over one vermouth cassis. Jill talked rather freely when excited, even to strangers if she liked them, and she had already decided she liked this Ron. What a funny scar.

"It's been hell. Sheer and absolute hell. I hope they run off a bloody cliff. Autun!"

"Did you really want to see the abbey?"

"Oh, I don't care. I thought I did. But maybe I was just using it as an excuse to get away. I was so fed up with him, and his lies. Do you know they tell you lies about every place you go? You should have heard the nonsense he was feeding them at Chenonceaux! They make you feel such sheep. If I have to be herded through Cluny in twelve minutes by another lying guide, I say skip it."

"If you'd like, we can go and look at the abbey now, before the tourists come. For as long as you like. I have permission. Sort of a pass."

"I'd love it." She smiled at once, like new sunshine. "Thanks very much."

So he paid for their drinks, and left her luggage with the girl behind the counter. As they walked across the square, Ronald explained what he was doing in Cluny. Jill pretended to be fascinated.

At the window, Ronald crafted a clumsy tale to explain the

girl's presence to the porter, at the same time pressing a silver piece into his palm. *Ah oui, M'sieu Arring-Tone, entendu, entendu; nous nous entendons, nous les hommes, eh-heh?* He was surprised at Ronald's success: such fine legs. These two men of the world then exchanged a few pleasantries about the tour guide, and shook hands again. As she walked down the steps the concierge watched Jill's excellent swing.

"What was that about?"

"Your guide was insolent and uncultured, which means he didn't give him a tip. Otherwise you'd probably be here right now, along with all your fine friends."

"Thank God for small mercies. But I mean how did you explain me?"

"By giving him five francs. You're the Honorable Miss Purley, my research assistant from the British Museum and the Oxford University. If anybody comes in, look archaeological and wise."

"I'll do that," she said, and laughed. "I rather like this game." I think I may even like you. She tossed her hair, took his arm in two of hers, smiled at him easily. Don't think, Ronald told himself. Don't think anything.

"Have you found out what you came to find?"

He refilled her glass, then his, glanced around. They were almost the only ones left.

"Oh, I can't do that till my money runs out. It would be a terrible waste of a vacation."

"No, seriously."

"It all seems to come down to money, speaking of money. Good old twentieth-century greed.

"At first I thought it was the work of revolutionary vandals, angry mobs getting back at the rich monks, you know, like in all the history books. Atheists and radicals attacking superstition. But that doesn't seem to be the case." What incredible eyes. "At least not here."

"But you told me it was revoltuionary soldiers who dug up the abbots' bones." And then I kissed you. Remember?

"Well they did, but that wasn't the really serious damage."

Yes. Yes, I do. "I mean you can always get new bones. The last monks here were chased out in seventeen ninety, when the government took over all Church property. With nobody left in charge, people started helping themselves first to the gold and silver, then the tapestries, then anything valuable that wasn't bolted down. Even things that were. Door handles. Window casings. The iron grilles from the side chapels. Even the bolts. I found that out just this morning.

"The first really serious damage, though, came during the Terror, in ninety-three. Fourteen thousand major artistic monuments in this country were destroyed or damaged, according to one professor; anything identified with the kings, the nobles — which is to say just about everything that mattered. Or the Church. Seventeen ninety-three was apparently a real orgy. Sacrilege, profanation, all that. Absolutely animal."

"Have you ever been to an orgy?"

"No."

"I have. Once." *Un ange passe. Peut-être un démon.*

"What did they do, do you think? Dance naked in the aisles? Urinate on the altars?"

"Well, I don't know about that." This may not be as easy as we thought. "Some places they turned the churches into cabarets, set up actresses on the altars. Wore church vestments for carnival costumes."

"I've always wanted to try on one of those golden copes, haven't you? the kind the archbishop wears at coronations and things? They're so impossibly gorgeous."

Tomato and onion salad, omelette *aux fines herbes*, baby chickens cooked in pastry cases, a bottle and a half (so far) of Mâcon blanc; gone. She peeled a tangerine: the fine orange skin curled like glove leather onto a saucer in a single piece. She popped the tiny segments in her mouth, one by one. The afternoon sun shone through windows and wineglasses, cast wobbling amber shadows on the cloth. Two other lingering diners, two silent young waiters standing guard.

"Some places they did destroy entirely — Moutiers-Saint-Jean, Saint Bénigne at Dijon. We could visit them, if you like." Overnight. "If you stay."

Free fall, now; no rules. "Most places, though, they just smashed up the sculptures, tore up books and vestments, broke the windows, pulled out anything they could sell — gold vessels, organ pipes, lead roofs, ironwork, bells, things like that. At Cluny the big thing was to pry open the tombs, the ones I was telling you about, and throw out all the abbots' skeletons and dust: saints, popes, whoever. Can you *imagine* people doing a thing like that? I mean, can you?"

"I can. Yes. I really can." Whoopee, another skull! Whee, there goes a shinbone. More wine; too much wine?

Different responses, different heads. Accept it, fellow. Don't fight it. That's what it's all about.

"A lot of the tombs were made of marble and jasper, so they carved them up for the stone. But the big expert on Cluny thinks most of the damage here was done by a small gang of revolutionary soldiers. The ones I was telling you . . . In just three days. They smashed the windows and pulled out the lead bits, carved up the altar, burned old manuscripts, tore up vestments, set fire to the wood carvings, hammered out some of the stone sculpture. Even took the crosses off the towers, which must have been tricky. They're very high for . . . for romanesque."

"But if that sort of thing went on everywhere, why are the other cathedrals all still standing? Rheims and Chartres and places like that?"

"Well, it . . . It's . . ." It's dumb. "It was different here. In fact, that's what fascinates me.

"First of all, it was an abbey, not a cathedral, and people in those days were especially down on the monks. They *totally* destroyed Citeaux and Clairvaux, for example, leveled them to the ground, and they were really sacred to the Benedictines.

"Most places, though, they just repaired the damage once the Terror was over, and turned the buildings back into parish churches, or at least state monuments. But at Cluny the city fathers *sold* the abbey lock stock and barrel to three sleazy businessmen from Mâcon. I'm on the track of one of them now, an ex-priest, in fact, named Vincent Genillon. Madame Chachuat at the museum thinks that his papers are still in an old château near here. She's trying to get me permission to go see them." Maybe: "Maybe we could both go." She looked sleepy. Maybe not.

"My theory is that this Genillon is the real evil genius of

Cluny. You know, the devoted priest who turns against his own church, wants to smash it all down, a man driven not so much by greed, like his partners, as by some perverse lust for destruction. Of course I may be wrong. And the local prefect at Mâcon was getting his cut too, I think. It's the only explanation I can come up with for his letting the explosions go on, even after he got *orders* from Paris to stop them. I could show you the letter."

Sure you could. She smiled, wanly. Do shut up, my darling.

"Just think, Jill: the second largest church in Christendom, right out there, blown to bits in our own time! Well almost our own time. That really gets to me."

"Did they just blow the whole place apart then? Kapoom, just like that?" Oh shit.

"Well, not all at once." He watched her spilled wine soaking into the cloth. "It was already something of a shambles when the three bought it, what with rain coming in through the broken windows, locks ripped off, looters coming and going, unsavory types renting rooms. Genillon and his friends obviously bought the church with the intention of tearing it down and selling the stones for whatever they could get. But I can't believe there wasn't some other, larger obsession behind all that."

She touched his hand, fingered a finger. I don't . . . Another bottle? A half bottle?

The young waiter caught his eye.

"*Vous désirez?*"

"Would you like a cognac? Jill?"

"I'd adore an apricot brandy, if they have any. But if I drink one more drop I simply must have a nap after lunch." Zap. "If you can find me a place."

He smiled, she smiled back; fingers squeezed. I can.

"Ah, *un liqueur des abricots, s'il vous plaît, et un Grand Marnier. Et, ah . . .*" They smiled again. "*Et ça sera tout.*"

The body of another. He looked at it, illumined in the moonlight, and he suffered.

Suffered from what? From the very fact of it, from her presence, her tender sleeping presence. Why was the one thing

two hundred and ten

every normal person on earth most longed for to him such a searing source of anguish? How could anyone be at ease alongside the body of another? He could scarcely bear his own, so retrograde to his will were the chance and animal workings of his flesh. He could be made physically and morally ill simply by thinking too long or too closely about the hard cartilage of his ear, the hairs in his nose, the soft, moist lining of his rectum.

But another's body: *her* body, lying there in the light of moon, under the sheet, in all its appealing warmth and weight, hard inside, soft without, pliable, breathing, rounded, asleep but still so frighteningly alive. She moved as if to his thought. She shifted, twisted her limbs sensuously, a plump, white, undivided snake, breathed a little moan, the hair fallen across her face, wet against her lips. She reached towards him the interlaced fingers of two hands.

FROM RONALD HARRINGTON'S *Cluny Notes*:*
27 July 1790. Mayor Dumolin to the National Assembly.
"C'est l'enfance de la Ville de Cluny . . . son tempérament est fort et robuste. *We are desperate without the support of the monks and their abbey, and cannot afford to keep it up ourselves. If the Directoire wants to save the buildings, let us at least evacuate them and lock them up. I realize the problems of the national debt. We revere you, citizens, we want to help; but let us try to prosper first. Please use it for something* — a factory, un école digne de ce siècle. The few reformed clergy in the abbey are on the verge of leaving, and we shall be left with nothing but a worthless pile of ruins to tear down."

6 *Fructidor, An IV de la République. Prefect to Mayor.*
"*We must conserve and use this National Treasure. We have no power to go after these vandals, to punish them and demand reparations; under our very eyes they are doing these things, and we are without the power to arrest them! It is the*

* See also *Le Journal de Vincent Genillon*, ed. Walter Ackerman (Lyons: Presses Universitaires de France, 1971).

city's fault for letting in these tenants, these thieves and de-stroyers*, une foule des malheureux dont la probité est plus que douteuse."

21 April 1798. Greater part of abbey sold to Jean-Claude Bâtonnard and Philibert-François-Marie Vachier, contractors of Mâcon; and to their agent, the ex-curé Vincent Genillon, for 2,040,000 francs of the assignats of 1790, of an estimated value of 50,000 gold francs. Demolitions begin.

1 Nivôse IX. Minister of Finances to Prefect of Saône-et-Loire.

"It appears, Citoyen Préfet, that the purchasers of the church of the former abbey of Cluny propose to tear it down, and have already begun their demolitions.

"The Minister of the Interior wants if at all possible to preserve this monument of the early tenth century, insofar as it appears that the inhabitants of Cluny are willing to take on the burden of rebuilding the roof and converting the abbey into a school. Furthermore, I have been told that the purchasers have obtained for a mere 50,000 francs a property worth over four times as much.

"I ask you, Citoyen Préfet, to halt these demolitions at once, and to investigate the purchase to determine whether or not fraud was involved; and in any case, to obliged the three purchasers to defer a destruction they may very soon regret."

1801. Genillon drives his road through the main body of the church from north to south, cutting the nave in two after the fifth bay from the crossing, causing the vault to collapse.

1801. Genillon and partners demanded indemnity and satisfaction, after orders from Paris forbade them to tear down and sell their own property. Prefect of Saône-et-Loire allowed demolitions and sales to continue.

3 November 1808. Sale of remaining gardens and buildings by Sieur Vincent Genillon, priest at Chapaize, to Pierre Dojon of Cluny, along with "the cloister up to the fifth arcade."

two hundred and twelve

1808. Engineer Vaillant drew up plans for the expansion of the National Stables (Haras National) at Cluny onto the grounds of the existing abbey ruins.

1809. Bruys de Charly, President of the General Council of Saône-et-Loire, proposes an alternative plan for the Haras National, which would have utilized and thus saved the existing portions of the abbey church. "I realize that these destroyers, like true birds of prey, have but one idea, which we have been hearing for far too long: Tear it all down! . . . Mais enfin, our Emperor, the great Napoleon, is a man who builds, who preserves, not a man who destroys!"

1809. Bruys de Charly's plan is rejected by the Comte de Maille, Inspector General of the Haras National.

1809–1811. Major demolitions. Great transept; nave façade, piers, and vault; central and north towers blown up. Remaining south transept arm used as a warehouse.

26 March 1812. Letter of Bruys de Charly.
"I abstain, now, from any further reflections on the vandals who dared to tear it down. I spend my hours in this poor city, and the ruins of its once great church form the view from my apartments. The ravages of Time demolish buildings with a kind of artfulness, leaving on them the impress of nobility and majesty. But the hand of barbarians has attacked precisely what Time would have respected, century after century. If this edifice had been isolated in the country, or hidden away in a park, one might still come up with sufficient funds to preserve what is left: the choir of the church, one rank of pillars, fragments of several others. But M. Furtin assures me that total demolition has now become indispensable. Orders have been given.
"Remember us, my friend; be kind to us, I beg you. Our poor town is more to be pitied than condemned."

20 September 1814. The city of Cluny officially yields up the abbey church (i.e., everything north of the existing ruins) to

two hundred and thirteen

the Haras National. *Frères Jacquelot of Cluny bid to demolish the remaining apse and side aisles, to clear out 6500 square meters of land, and to preserve at least 2400 cubic meters of usable stone and other building materials for the stables.*

"If only we could have made better use of it," writes the new mayor. "Rid us of this ugly pile of ruins that so offends the eye. . . ."

10 June 1820. Foyatier, sculptor of Paris, to Mayor of Cluny.

"I learned from your assistant of your intention to tear down the ruins of your church, and that you would be selling the debris, such as columns and capitals. The English Ambassador would like some fragment of Gothic sculpture, and I write to ask details such as color, size, and price. He is leaving Paris soon, and I shall be seriously compromised if this sale is not effected."

18 October 1821. Prefect to Mayor.

"Monsieur, I beg you to be so good as to give the necessary orders to effect the demolition, as soon as possible, of the remainder of the side aisle of the abbey church. As long as it stands it is impossible for us to continue with the construction of the building designed to house the officers and employees of the Haras National. It is essential that this work be carried out without further delay, and I depend on your bending every effort at once to this end."

1823. Final demolition of the Apse.

That she could love me.

The double bells, the manic birds, the excess of light at 4 A.M. The blackbirds of Eau Bénite, huddled in against a rainstorm. Tens of thousands it must have seen. Clouds pass over, rain pounds down on cars, on tiles. Muddy rivers down the streets, water streaming into the Baraban *fouille*, the great hole by the narthex wall. Under shelter of the entry portal, they

two hundred and fourteen

imagined it looming up before their very eyes, taking its right-ful place. Look harder every day, he told her, and one day it will all reappear.

Blood on the sheet: his, not hers. A red, rubbed sore on the side of his cock. He held it gently in his fingers, tired wet little brother, fat and knotted, the veins dark, protruding, looking ill; wet, bleeding sore on the rim. Agony of spirit, and a numb, joyless pain. She slept. He tried not to wake her.

The *chattering* of birds, at 4 A.M. Will they never stop? Gray, heavy skies that close out hope and heaven, and promise only more rain, more mud. What now? What next? Longing. Shame. The hope of love.

This thing in my hand, the thing we have done. Oh my Jill! hold me. Don't ask, just hold me. *J'ai tel besoin.* Protect me against this alien appeal, against my desperate solitude, my terror of their foreignness: of my own foreignness, everywhere in the wide world. They don't want me, but I so terribly want them, even now that I have you. If I have you. Wrap your arms round me, hips against mine, twine our legs together. Close them out, close out my mind, my sense of homesickness: homesickness in this town, in this country, in this world.

It's not sex I want any more, our pitiful game of cocks and cunts: trying to forget all the rest, in the jolting and spurting of one tiny agitated part. All I do is get myself overheated, so pathetically supercharged with excess of blood that I *think* for a few moments all is different, all is well.

But it isn't.

Now dark in the morning, light in the night, it seems a dirty animal's game, like drugs or drink, and it leaves me more sick than before.

Can you understand that? *Ecoeuré.* The heart gone out.

I *am* sick. Sick to my stomach, sick in the groin, in the pores of my skin, the wet tunnels of my eaten-out brain. Nervous system totally out of whack. The pressure of the air, the racket of the birds, the smell of France have become all too much to bear.

Soothe me, if you can. *Le vent de nuit* (the juke box sang, awful juke box) *et ton doux corps* (awful place) *auprès du mien. Le vent de nuit.* Rub me, gently, in some safe and suffering place. Try if you can to trick me back to peace. *I cannot kill myself this way.*

4:30. Three hours of sleep is all I ask.

They walked all day, up steep narrow streets lined with shuttered houses, listening to the sounds of a French family Sunday. Through Notre Dame, masses over, looking up at all the corbel heads, some monsters, some fair faces; sculptor's hand at work. Uphill to the Promenade, crescenting around the rim of the town under fair fat bell-shaped trees on dry and ancient trunks. Sandy mud at their feet, the color of everything, walls, stonework, shutters. Past the Lycée, they stopped and leaned over the wall, watched nuns taking the air in their convent garden. Later two of them stopped to talk in the street. Their world, their walled garden, vegetables in neat rows.

"Have you ever thought of joining a convent? The peace, I mean?" The support. The simplicity.

"Good heavens no. Have you?"

"Yes. Yes I have. A monastery like this one must have been. Some days I would give the world to have been a simple monk of Cluny."

"Even last night?"

And they laughed.

Only an arm, a fine round arm. The transept she meant, but he remembered his poem of years ago. Worlds were given for less. Like the cut-off arm of some holy saint, Januarius's blood perfectly preserved, the rest of the body crushed, sold, disappeared.

They stopped to eat lunch in the little rose park, next to the convent school. Imagine away eight hundred years. Easy to do, from above, on a still Sunday in July: where do French people go?

They looked over the stone ledge of the little belvedere, down a wild-grown slope to the spire of St. Marcel, the pile of tile roofs, vegetable gardens, the Route Nationale, a junked car yard, piles of lumber. They lay, apart at first, then together, on the grass, under a roof of leaves held out by long stick-fingers.

two hundred and sixteen

Birds screamed from the leaves, millions of green leaves, millions of screaming birds.

(That night, a hot, sticky night, they went back to the belvedere after dinner, and lay down again to make love. Two motorbikes rode roaring into the path under the trees, twenty feet from where they lay. Dead in terror, he clutched her to him with white fingers shriveled with the shock. Loud laughter, indecipherable French slang. Weaving dangerously in and out the trees in their formal rows, two boys astride their *motos* tore off down the hill, racing into town. Had they seen them, had they not? Shaking, out of control, unable to do more. Jill kissed him gently, held him till the fit had passed.)

The walls of St. Marcel looked leprous with disease, moldy, stained, oozing damp, their decorations gone all faded under the rot of eight hundred years.

"How can you stand this place? Ugh. It gives me the creeps."

He had felt it home before he met her, loved it the more for its decay. Along the walls stood kitschy plaster statues of the standard French saints: Joan of Arc, the Little Flower, the Curé of Ars. A giant Christ crucified hung over the new turned-around altar. The apse vaults had been blue-painted once, but the blue was now stained with rot and peeling away.

He made her go with him over every inch of the rotting church. They sat down behind the altar steps and kissed for many minutes, till at last Jill pleaded the cold and begged to leave.

In the *grand-rue*, Sunday window-shoppers after church. Two patisseries open, the gift shops, the Syndicat d'Initiative. They climbed the Tour de Fromages, though she hated steep steps. Cafés were open all over town, but they looked too alien today, too Sunday-French to be inviting. Stares, minimal greetings. Time to leave? To go south, to the sea? A sudden fall of rain; they ran under a portal and kissed until it stopped, across from the house marked "1434," built from the top down.

Back to the Café du Nord, where they had first met, to watch the people, to try to guess one another's thoughts, until the rain fell in torrents, suddenly, and the place jammed with damp and chattering French.

They ran to the hotel, upstairs to his room — their room. Off the wet clothes, they toweled each other's hair, each other, fell happily onto the bed, and stayed there playing till dinnertime.

It *was* like a honeymoon, sometimes. Like what he imagined a honeymoon to be. So the abbey is gone, the statues hammered to bits: Let the small rain rain, let us love.

Nothing lasts, except the black birds that fly in and out of the arches, high up in the great tower he would one day make her climb. Nothing else lasts. That same small rain would one day wear away even the town, even the tower. As they were wearing away their own bodies by using them together, wearing out their love in the very act of loving.

Birds. Bells. Too many leaves, too much rain, too heavy smells. All the human world sleeps except me.

"Ron, what's the matter?"

"Nothing."

"No, tell me. Can't you tell me?"

"I did tell you. Nothing's the matter." He was lying on his stomach on the grass, his chin on his arms.

"Then why can't you look at me?"

So he turned his head sideways and looked at her, refusing to admit in so many words that all was not well, or that anything had changed. He raised his eyebrows and stared. *See,* said the eyebrows. *I'm looking,* said the eyes. *Make something of it.* Something the matter! he said, but not aloud. Everything's the matter! Can't you tell? Can't you feel it?

"Oh, if you want to be that way." She moved off, her shoulders sulking, and began to put their picnic things back on the bike.

Don't give up so easily.

"Shall we head back, then?"

Maybe I'll *tell* you what's the matter, if you ask me again.

"I don't care. Whatever you want."

"Oh, you are being a child, Ron!"

What? That was a perfectly reasonable, even a generous response: Whatever you want. He didn't *want* to stay sunk in this barren, gloomy mood, for heaven's sake. But he'd be damned if he was going to take the initiative in pulling himself out of it. If she wanted him to snap out of it, then let her show a little sympathy and cheeriness herself.

They packed up and left without speaking, and headed back the road to Cluny.

Then everything went wrong.

A blue car appeared out of nowhere on the long tree-lined lane, moving irresistibly, heading straight for Jill. Tootling its high-pitched horn, it grew in an instant present and large, but it did not swerve, and she could not, in time. She could not swerve, she could not scream, she could do nothing but sit there on her moving bicycle and be struck by a big blue French car, coming towards her like death, squawking over and over the three notes of its horn.

Ronald was alongside on his own bike by the time they hit. He had seen it happen, felt it happen. One spot of dust on a sunbeam ago, he was cycling home with Jill on a tree-lined country road. And now this.

He stopped, leaned his bike against a tree, and ran over to the scene, white and without breath. She could be dead, he thought.

On the tree, a torn poster flapped, yellow, wet, black,

JAMAIS, A DIT JOHNNY.
SHEILA EST DESOLÉE.

Two days later, he took the train back to Paris, and three days after that, the charter flight back to San Francisco. He spent a week at home with his mother, then, through the University Housing Office, found a "studio apartment" — a third-floor bedroom and bath with a hotplate and a fridge in the closet — in an old house on Derby Street for seventy dollars a month. He began typing up the notes he had taken in France, organizing them alphabetically by towns in four loose-leaf binders: Ameugny, Anzy-le-Duc, Autun, Auxerre, Avallon, Beaune, Berzé-la-Ville, Bissy-le-Mâçonnaise; Cluny had a binder of its own. Along with his descriptive and historical notes on the churches he had visited — the thirty-seven romanesque churches between Autun and Mâcon that had been damaged or destroyed by revolutionaries or speculators at the turn of the eighteenth century — he inserted his pencil sketches of their work: headless statues, hammered-out carvings, truncated towers, all the visual evidence he had been able to record of the destruction wrought by twenty years of enlightenment on a thousand years of superstition.

Many of the notes and sketches had nothing to do with revolutionary vandals or the *bande noire*. They were simply reflections, aesthetic or historical or purely personal, engendered by these old stones, or drawings made in the hope of seizing some fine and fleeting impression: the quality of light that penetrated some neglected church through a tiny triforium gallery; the silhouette of an old woman in black kneeling before a dark side altar; a trick of leaf carving; new green vineshoots on an eight-hundred-year-old wall. These he kept apart, in a separate folder, the drawings and the notes together, to page through when he had tired of more serious reading.

He checked in with Professor Ackerman soon after he arrived, and told him about the trip, about his discoveries and ideas: not about Jill. Ackerman was delighted, bright with the borrowed adventures of a younger man. He insisted on following every day of Ronald's travels and researches, and ended by borrowing the binders to read over himself, one weekend in September. Clearly, Ronald had made a major discovery in unearthing the Genillon papers, which was going to necessitate a rewriting of certain portions of Ackerman's own *History of Vandalism*, and of Cluniac studies in general. If only he could get them authenticated and in print before Conant found out!

Later, he invited Ronald to his home (it was the first time he had done so), a small authentic 1922 Maybeck in the Berkeley hills. Together they looked at old photographs and illustrated monographs of some of Ronald's churches, and finished off two bottles of good Gevrey-Chambertin.

Ackerman gave Ronald a number of clues where to begin his library work on the thesis, once his second go at the orals was over — histories and biographies, memoirs and letters, official papers, the monographs of his friends Aubert and Oursel and Virey, the work of the Medieval Academy and the Société Française d'Archéologie, even obscure passages in Balzac and Chateaubriand — everything that touched, in one way or another, on what the iconoclasts and vandals, the scrap dealers and stone sellers and city fathers and rebuilders had done to the great romanesque churches of France, and in particular, to those of Ronald's region. Most of them, naturally, concentrated on Cluny. But every church, even the smallest, had its angry defender. Each act of destruction was chronicled somewhere, in the memoirs of this abbé, the travel writings of that Victorian poet, in the academic ironies of some learned art historian.

The notes typed, the drawings filed, Professor Ackerman's suggested references copied down on 3 × 5 cards, Ronald forced himself to put away the precious binders. He kept them all in a special file drawer, which he neatly hand-labeled with the proposed title of his dissertation: *Les Églises romanes de Bourgogne 1793–1814: Un Bilan de leurs Pertes et Déprédations pendant la Période Post-Révolutionnaire.* Of course he would write it in English, but in French, the whole thing looked more serious, more *sérieux.* The title once contrived, in fact, the job seemed half done.

And now, *à nos moutons:* he had only one more chance at the Ph.D. oral exams, and he vowed not to blow it. He had important things to do in this world, and it would be wrong, it would be evil of him to collapse again. Many people, many places, in some ways a whole civilization depended on his passing — on his proving his right to the authority and power he required. It would mean discipline. It would mean, for a while, compromise, a kind of deceit; telling people what they wanted to hear, and masking his real intentions. But he could do that. Surely he could do that, for a little while longer.

Twenty-seven years old. He would pass the exam early next year, plunge right into the dissertation, pour into it all of his new faith and new fire, his burning, unanswerable case against Genillon and the barbarians — against those of 1969 as well as those of 1811.

What path he would follow afterwards was not yet clear.

The dissertation would be published, of course; the Genillon discoveries guaranteed that. That book would be a first stone, his shout of warning. At first, perhaps, only a select few would take notice, realize the unanswerable force of his case. The work would make its own way, that book and the ones to follow, as sacred texts in the war he was to lead — a kind of international holy war destined to bring his century out of its darkness and back into the clean light of faith, where everything cohered and all existence made sense.

Thus it was that Ronald talked to himself, and tried to keep his mind away from Jill, from a dead body on a country road. Fired by this desperate sense of mission, or something that felt like a mission, he settled in to work.

For two months he kept at it, working from nine to two at his job as cataloguer in the Art Seminar room, then reading in the library stacks for the rest of the day — until quarter to ten at night, in fact, five days a week. He brought apples and raisins and crackers to his tiny carrel in the library stacks, so as not to have to go out to eat. Saturdays he spent all day in the library reading, well out of earshot of football crowds and tourists. Sunday mornings he was there as well, one of very few. Sunday afternoons the library was closed, so he studied at home, after permitting himself a hike down University Avenue to the Marina, then a long walk along the docks — his week's one distinctive break. On the orange metal partition in front of his desk in the stacks, he had taped up a reproduction of an 1814 engraving of Cluny, made just after the explosions. In a corner of the desk he laid a small silver crucifix on a chain that his mother had given him, together with a religious medal from Taizé. At 10 P.M., when the library closed, he walked south across the silent campus, over a little footbridge, up the dark slope of Faculty Glade, between the ugly new Art and Architecture buildings. He crossed Bancroft and had — it was exactly the same, every night — cheeseburger, pie, and coffee for dinner at the brightly lit new Burger King on the corner of College. Afterwards, by walking down College to Derby, then down Derby to his apartment house, he managed to avoid altogether the unpleasant Telegraph Avenue scene.

At home, he tried to drown out the bass rumbles of other

tenants' rock music by playing records from his own collection, mostly old things from Josquin to Scarlatti, with a lot of Bach and Gregorian chant. He took off his shoes and lay down on the bed. Sometimes he just listened to the music. Other times, sitting in his armchair, he would read over his private notes from Burgundy, leaf through his sketches, look out over the Berkeley rooftops and try to wish himself back in France: sitting in cold little churches, looking through cemeteries, cycling down tree-lined roads between villages and vineyards. Talking with, living with, lying with Jill.

But Jill was gone. Through September he managed to keep to this regime, well into October, without a let. But on Sunday, October 26, he found himself falling into the first stages of a nervous crisis similar to the one he had undergone two years before, just after his father's death. Shivering, feeling bitter and empty, unable to read, he left the library at once as soon as he realized what was happening, and drove across to San Francisco. Almost without knowing he was doing it, he headed for Ocean Beach. Up and down the sand he walked, his shoes squishing in the wet, windswept and still shivering, feeling more, not less tense in the familiar presence of the waves. He curled up in a ball against the concrete seawall under the road, plunged his hands deep in his coat pockets, buried his head in his knees, and sat there for a long time, shaking, wishing himself gone. Then he climbed back up the steep steps, crossed the Great Highway, and stalked the joyless streets of Playland till nightfall.

Next day he called in sick to the library and spent the day driving through the old corners of San Francisco he used to haunt: Potrero Hill, the Embarcadero south of Market, the warehouses below Telegraph Hill. He drove out Broadway past the honky-tonks, though the tunnel, up to the Presidio wall; then along the winding drive through the woods. He stopped on the Lincoln Park Road just north of the Legion of Honor, and spent a long time waiting for a ship to come in under the bridge, but no ship came. Then the fog blocked it all out: the bridge towers, Marin, the bridge itself, the Golden Gate. He drove out of the park, stopped for a hamburger, then headed out Geary once more to the ocean, the beach, and the ghost of Whitney's Playland-at-the-Beach. There, as usual, he walked up and down, searching, waiting for something to happen. This time, something did. He was tripped, kicked in the face, and robbed of twenty-five dollars and a ring.

By Tuesday, he had pulled himself together well enough to go back to work. For four days he was able to force himself through his monkish routine, and keep away the foul fiend. But his nights were a shipwreck made of bits of pornography, bits of Burgundy, pieces of Jill, all swirling together in a scummy surf with the splintered timbers of an abandoned roller coaster. By Saturday, the first day of November, he gave in again. He had been working too hard, that was all: a week off was what he needed.

Air mattress, sleeping bag, Coleman stove and lantern were already in the trunk of the car. He took a couple of pans and some utensils, bought a bag of groceries, and drove out to the campground on top of Mount Diablo. For two days he hiked through the woods, or sat long hours on fallen logs, or lay back on his air mattress thinking, looking at patterns of leaves in the sky. For two nights he slept well and dreamlessly under the stars in the chill November sky. Then he came back down.

It was no good. Once back in Berkeley, he was taking long manic drives again, stalking compulsively through night streets, almost begging to be mugged or to drive off the road. He went into junk stores, dirty book stores, fifty-cent movies, East Oakland bars. To a late-night preview of a jagged ugly movie, at a theatre in San Francisco crowded with hippies. He dreamed of hellfire, burning ever and forever.

On Wednesday he walked all night. He walked the whole length of Telegraph Avenue, from the campus to downtown Oakland and back, looking into all-night laundromats and apartment windows, stopping at a MacDonald's to chew four thin hamburgers, exploring a supermarket late at night. Early in the morning a girl in overalls standing in front of Cody's offered him a seven-dollar ticket to the Rolling Stones concert in Oakland that Saturday for twenty dollars, a ticket downstairs, on the aisle, and he bought it, almost without thinking.

thirteen, and last.

It had never been part of Ronald Harrington's plan to hide out in the lower regions of the Arena between concerts. True enough, he hadn't wanted to leave. Not many people do, after a Rolling Stones show. But he stayed for reasons not entirely of his own volition, and certainly not to see more of Jagger.

He was already on his way out, in fact, along with everybody else, when he suddenly realized he had to go to the bathroom. He turned and tried to go back down the stairs, but people were making it difficult.

"Move, asshole!"

"Please."

"Who is this fat shit?"

"Please. I'm sorry. Please, I'm sorry." Damn!

It was silly, of course. No one had noticed. No one cared except him. But his whole mind was taken up now with the sole goal of getting back down, out of sight, washing himself off, being clean.

One-way lockstep homegoing traffic was packed tight up the stairs. Ushers were herding everyone out, so they could begin letting in the next lot, people who had been waiting outside in the cold for the second show. Ronald cut off into a row of seats and started clambering down over the backs of chairs.

"Other way, my friend. Everybody out." A large black usher was blocking his path.

"Please let me go back. I've got to . . . I've got to go to the bathroom."

"Plenty of bathrooms upstairs."

He darted around to one side of the man, and ran, ran as fast as he could.

At first Ronald thought the mess in the empty men's room was simply the debris left over from hundreds of sloppy users. A filthy, quarter-inch-deep puddle covered nearly the entire floor — no doubt a toilet plugged up and run over. Great piles of wrinkled brown paper towels stood along the walls — the bins must have overflowed — and more wadded up paper floated in the water.

But as he tiptoed cringing to the row of sinks, he realized with a jolt that the mess had been willfully and violently made. One sink had been pulled completely off the wall. It lay cracked in two pieces below its severed pipes. Another had been twisted around to a sick, crazy angle. The water in two others was still running, spilling over the edge of bowls

two hundred and twenty-six

clogged up with paper. As he turned them off, he looked up into a row of mirrors cracked in several places, painted over with red streaks and zigzags. One huge black swastika ran onto the wall. He stared at his own face in the shambles of a mirror, and saw behind him the reflection of a smashed-in toilet stall door with God knows what more damage behind it.

He quickly set about what he had come for. He unbuckled his belt, unzipped his pants, pulled them carefully off over the edge of his squishy shoes. He folded them and set them on the edge of the sink. Then he shucked off his wet shorts and kicked them over into a damp pile of debris in the corner. Next he pulled a handkerchief out of his pants pocket, soaked it with hot water, and standing naked from the waist down in front of the broken mirror, proceeded to clean himself off. He threw the handkerchief after the shorts, and reached for his trousers. As he did so, the reflection in the jagged, scrawled-over triangle of mirror before him moved, and he felt the blood drain from his face. Someone was sitting in one of the doorless toilet stalls behind him. Someone had been sitting there all this time. Someone who was now standing up in the half shadow, looking at his face in the mirror. For a full second he met its eye. Then he scrambled into his trousers, zipped, buttoned, buckled, splashed his way to the door, nearly slipping in his rush. Behind him he heard what sounded like a laugh, a phlegmy laugh; then, just as the door shut behind him, the words: "Wait up. Wait up."

He ran to the right, the direction a huge yellow arrow told him to take, then turned down another corridor. A stairway or hall must lead from here out to the parking lot level, since those big ramps outside ran only halfway up the building. But the corridor came abruptly to a dead end against two locked metal doors.

No: not locked. The one on the left gave way when he pushed it hard, and disclosed a wide, downward-sloping concrete ramp leading off to the left, bordered by a pipe railing and lit by orange overhead fixtures. Surely there would be someone downstairs here, some guard or janitor or stagehand who could point out to him the quickest way to an exit.

But when he got to the end of the ramp, he found that the

large concrete spaces below were uninhabited, except by rows and rows of vending machines, large soft drink, coffee, cigarette, and candy machines, and (lined up on the floor against one wall) small white gum machines, perfume dispensers, prophylactic and sanitary napkin dispensers — all of them empty and broken, some rusting, some smashed, some with missing glass or open sides. He walked up and down the rows of metal boxes, shining eerily under the yellow-orange fixtures above. They began to seem valuable, his for the taking, locked in a museum vault for the night. He began to catch a breath of that unearthly outlaw air of his nighttime prowls at Playland, and gradually he felt it gaining on him, the pull of the dark, the unknown, the illicit overtaking the impulse to find a way out and go home. He lingered in the storeroom, walking up and down the rows of broken machines, looking at his reflection in mirrors and sheets of glass. The Midnight Rambler.

A door at the end was unlocked, so he went through it into another space, which turned out to be some sort of engine or boiler room, dark and humming. He shut the door quietly behind him. To his formal self he pretended that he was still trying to find an exit, a way out to his car. But at the same time he was very near to admitting that he didn't care, that he was too drunk with this new adventure now to give it up: the simple fact of being where he was, and being there alone, just as he had once done in old underground sewer tunnels back in Fort Wayne.

The engine room was probably about the same size as the storeroom, but it was so dark that at first it seemed limitless in all directions. It was lighted only by small bulbs in cagelike enclosures, one on the corner of each large machine, and by a few illuminated dials and gauges, glowing circles of amber or red. Each boiler, or turbine, or whatever they were, emitted its own distinctive hum. The metal floor and railings around them then picked up the tune, so that the whole dark space seemed to vibrate, a ship under steam. Far off above, one could dimly make out girders and pipes, then a kind of catwalk that ran along two of the walls.

Ronald felt his way around the sides till he came to a ladder that led up to the catwalk. He climbed up carefully, so that he might look back down as he climbed on the whole assemblage of purring monsters below with their red and yellow eyes, so stable and so gentle. Only then did he realize that the center of the floor was cut into a square hole with a safety rail around it, through which he could distinguish a still lower level below. He quickly let himself back down the ladder, made his way to the railed opening, and descended a second metal ladder into the lower depths.

This space narrowed into a hallway extending for a long way underneath the engines, low ceilinged and similarly dark. It appeared to be nothing more than a corridor or tunnel for fat ducts and piping, snakelike white and gray and yellow tubes that ran along both walls and ceiling, occasionally branching out or crossing over one another or changing directions. Every thirty feet or so another caged bulb in the ceiling lit the way, and illuminated a set of dials and gauges on the wall. It was obviously some way of monitoring the flow and function of whatever it was inside the pipes.

After he had followed the duct corridor for the space of about five lights, Ronald realized that he was walking around the arc of a huge circle. Apparently this corridor, with its pythonlike pipes, went round the whole circumference of the arena. Big yellow letters were stenciled on the walls, walls that seemed to run on and on for hundreds of yards, with their pipes and their caged lights and their array of monitoring dials.

(You're in the bowels of a ship and tons of salt water are pressing against that bulkhead on your left; this curve is the line of the hull. The crew is gone, some freak accident, you're all alone looking for . . . what?

A slit of light: the mad doctor in his undersea lair. I must get to him before . . . something.) Ronald hurried his steps. The underground echo, a slight aftersound of his steps on the concrete, hurried too.

But no echo before.

Then another noise. Behind. Far away.

Very faint. "Hey, friend! Wait. Wait for me"

That man in the toilet.

Ronald ran towards the slit, which enlarged to a long thin rectangle of light: an open door. His mad doctor's lair was some kind of locker room, empty. He shut the door, punched the button in the center of the knob. Then he stood by the door, only breathing; listening. Waiting.

He waited a long minute, ninety seconds, more. Nothing happened. Then, before his fascinated eyes, the doorknob moved, all by itself, this way and that, back and forth. It stopped; moved again. Then silence. Silence, stillness, the air close with possibility. What, Ronald wondered, would a man like that do? What could he do?

He found that he wanted to reach out and turn his side of the knob, release the lock, confront the faceless creature from a vandalized latrine who had pursued him all this way, who wanted to call him "friend." Turn the handle, do it; leap into possibility. What else was life for?

NO: life was for holding on, for keeping steel doors locked *against* possibility.

But, oh my God, just once to risk, *really* to risk: not safe little schoolboy episodes, the eternal slumming of a frightened adolescent. *We are free.* Open the door, Ronald.

NO.

He could see right through the steel. A thin, pale face, red-ringed eyes and yellowish lips, a stubble of beard about the chin. Hair cut crudely and short above a long ropy neck. Fingers that clutched involuntarily (nicotine stained, nails bitten to the blood), clutching for *him* on the other side: young, untested, parts still virgin and soft. The invisible face smiled at his uncertainty; one thin wedge of curiosity was all that it needed.

NO NO NO Oh my sweet Christ, how is *that* brave, Harrington, how is that heroic, self-transcendant? To yield to some slavering old pig in an auditorium basement, just because you've never done it, just because you shouldn't, because you don't *want* to? Is it *better* to let yourself be violated and mauled than to go on forever feeling timid and incomplete? (Yes.) To let a filthy, drooling degenerate . . . he could feel the man's skin, smell his breath.

And yet the pressure inside him directing his fingers towards the knob was diabolical. Literally. He felt himself possessed by a demon of hell, a force greater than any self he had ever known, that *wanted* to see him spoiled, see him wasted and raped. Unable to believe this thing inside of him, he was still and ultimately more the self he had always known than this decadent and humiliating craving.

Throwing himself down on one of the chairs that stood around a wooden table, he pressed his face against his arms and wept; wept for his need, for his shame, for this awful force inside him whose existence he had never felt so keenly before. He seized hard the wrist that had come so near to turning that knob, and choked on his own tears to see it bleeding: Something, all along, had been pulling viciously hard at his hand.

But the whole business was so unreal that this discovery seemed no more strange than the rest. He felt for his handkerchief, to wipe his eyes and bind up his wrist; then remembered how he had used it and thrown it away. He took off his shoes, and used instead one of his socks to dry the tears, to stop the flow of blood from his wrist.

The crying had released some inner childishness, voluptuous and yet innocent. He decided to flow with it, yield to its course, be a child. He emptied his pockets on the locker-room table. Car keys, a pen, red ticket stub. Four ski-ball tickets from an Oakland gallery, left over from his all night walk forty-eight hours before. Eight cents. A small green stone. A bit-off nail.

He took off his jacket, felt in every one of its pockets: checkbook, wallet, library charge cards, laid them all on the table. A French railway voucher. He hung the jacket over the back of his chair and began to empty out the wallet. If he could put together correctly the pieces on the table he might be able to figure out who he was.

Money, pictures, an uncashed check. And cards. Lots of cards: driver's license, draft card, Social Security card, student I.D. card, library cards, business cards, credit cards. He laid them all out carefully in front of him, one lost man playing solitaire.

A picture of his parents, their heads squeezed together inside a take-your-own-picture booth. A picture of Hank as a sailor. He had kept it in his wallet for the past eleven years.

Little folded-up lists of phone numbers, addresses of places to go, books to read, records to buy. An old, old letter. A little note. He opened them up.

A money order would be best, since Hunter doesn't believe in checks. And soon, or else we'll have to leave before the end of the month.

Love to you all,
Billie Jean Dougherty.

P.S. It was nice to have met you. I wouldn't have thought Hank could have such a sweet brother. I really mean that. Play a record for me sometime at Hobie's.

It was the last anyone he knew had heard of Hank.

The little note was written in pencil on a piece of stationery imprinted in blue "Hotel de Bourgogne." Jill had left it on her pillow. On the back of it she had drawn a picture of a coy, smiling lady peeking out from behind a tower.

Sleep on, my precious baby. When you wake up meet me in the park, down by the little tower. I love you so much.

He sat there for a long time after the specter beyond the door had disappeared, bare feet on the cold floor, hands in his empty pockets, looking from his papers to the wall of lockers and thinking of many things, flowing on the stream released by his tears. At some point he realized that a low, rhythmic thumping was resonating through the room, through his chair even, on the walls and floor: something in the pipes, in the machinery down the hall? The air conditioning? No: though the rhythm was vaguely irregular, the beats seem to vary purposely in intensity. Thumpa thump thump. Thumpa thump thump. *Earthquake?* No.

Of course. The ten o'clock concert, finally under way. Two hours late.

His awareness of the faint, compulsive throbbing, of what it signified of life now and upstairs broke the flow of his reverie. The doors of each locker before him were vibrating ever so slightly in a shiver of stamped metal. He got up and tried a few doors. The first two were locked, but the next opened to his pull. A black uniform hung from a hanger, black shoes underneath. The same in the next locker; and the next; and the next. He took one of the jackets off its hanger and tried it on; then put it back. Behind each pair of shoes he found a long wooden club, a walkie-talkie, an aerosol can, and a first-aid kit attached to a web belt. He began to try all the doors, faster. Why had the room door been left open, the light left on? Why weren't these things locked up?

He found no weapons other than the clubs and the spray cans, but when he dumped out a fat laundry bag he discovered in a closet, a pile of bloodstained clothes tumbled out on the floor. He was about to feel through them, try to piece together the crime, when he heard the noise of other people in the corridor outside.

Security guards coming back. ("I'm lost, sir, I've been trying to find my way out.") But they'll see all my things there, my shoes, what of them? Quick. With his sock-bandaged arm he swept the lot, jacket shoes letters keys on top of the pile of bloody clothes, then kicked it all back into the closet with the laundry bag and shut the door.

"Fuck, it's locked."

"Light's still on."

"That's OK. I've got a key."

How many? Four, six? A gang of black security guards back from their shift. You see, sirs, I saw the door open, I was just looking for a way out, I went to the toilet and got lost down here, complicated place you got, ha ha, I just want to get to the parking lot, the one on the Berkeley side, I wonder if you could show me . . .

"Who the fuck are you?"

In the open doorway stood he couldn't tell how many black men, not guards, No, not guards, ha, pushing in front of them a teenaged white girl in a green dress, her mouth stuffed full with a dirty rag.

He looked at her. Choking, he felt as if his own mouth had

been stuffed with a rag of nausea and terror, to the very back of his throat.

"Hey look. He got bare feet."

"Wet his pants, too."

"Please, I was just looking for . . ."

"For what?"

They all laughed an evil threat of a laugh. The tall man in front put big brown hands over the girl's breasts.

"I just want to get out. I got lost. I don't care what you guys."

He tried not to look at the girl, tried to pretend she wasn't there. The tall man who held her was now rubbing himself back and forth tight against her rear, slowly. They were going to

"How you get lost in a room with the door locked way down here? Huh? And where's your shoes, white man? And what's that thing on your arm?"

"It's a sock. I cut myself."

"Come on, Goat, les get on with it."

The girl: the girl in green. The same one that Jagger had singled out onstage. Lookit that stoopid girl.

"What we do with him?"

"Sheeyit, I don't know. Lock him in the closet."

"Les pants him."

"Mebbe Little Billy can do him. What you say, Little Billy?"

"Sheeyit."

Minutes ago, in this very same room, he had argued with himself about unlocking the door to let in some unknown species of melodramatic evil, some faint breath of danger and risk; and here was evil more dark and incarnate, danger more present than he had ever known. Minutes ago he had teased himself with the possible thrill-adventure of physical violation; now he was *about* to be violated, he and the fat girl in green, who could not make a sound. By five tall black men, insolent and impatient.

"How bout we jes' lock him in the closet?"

"An' leave him?"

"Naaah," said the leader. "Let him watch. Fat white mans need their kicks." They all laughed. That same laugh.

"OK. Hold on to him, Little Billy. We'll learn him how it's done."

And so he sat there, Ronald Alan Harrington, twenty-seven, white, male, of Fort Wayne and Granger, Indiana, San Salvador and Berkeley, California, M.A. (Art History) and Ph.D. (cand.), from two to three in the morning on November 9, 1969, in a security guards' locker room in the lower level of the Oakland Coliseum Arena, and watched five black youths rape a teenaged white girl on a table. They had taken the rag out of her mouth — it turned out to be her own underpants — and pulled off most of the rest of her clothes. She cried helplessly but almost silently the whole time. One of them must have hurt her badly, because she bit him hard and tried to fight back, but when the leader — the one they called Goat — took out a long-bladed knife and held it near her ear, she stopped biting and fighting. As each unzipped and took his turn with her on the wooden table, the other four stood around and made jokes, giggled, shouted bawdy encouragements, and passed around a bottle. They pointedly ignored the girl's crying, ignored *her,* insofar as possible, altogether, except now and then to hold her legs and arms to make things more convenient or interesting for the man up.

After the first few minutes, they ignored Ronald too. The youth — the boy, really, no more than fourteen — who had been ordered to "hold onto" him sat beside him for a while, one dark hand on his arm. But curiosity, or lust, or the spirit of the sport got the better of his sense of duty, and he left Ronald on his own to join the others around the table until it was his turn. Ronald felt like throwing up, trying to wake up, making a break for the door. Something.

But instead he just sat there and listened and watched. Rape: all of his life it had never been more than a word. And yet people actually did it. He felt violated himself, and yet couldn't stop watching.

While the fourteen-year-old guard was at work, there was a

deal of laughter and cheering, a deal of razzing and slapping on the ass. He came, with (or despite) their assistance. They all applauded, helped him down. He did up his pants in mixed embarrassment and pride. The girl lay still, not even sobbing, rolled over crouched on one side.

The one called Goat came up to Ronald.

"Wha'bout you, fats? You wanna piece?"

"No, I . . . I don't."

"Can't do it, hey?"

They all crowded around, Ronald froze with a new kind of terror.

"C'mon. On your feet, fats. She's all nice and ready for you. Right? We jes' softened her up a li'l bit."

"Right!"

"Jes' your size."

"An' color."

The man called Goat still held his long-bladed knife. He moved it around till the point stood just in front of Ronald's navel, then slid the cold steel under his shirt and up his stomach, sending the touched skin into involuntary twitches as he broke open the buttons of his shirt. Another youth pulled his shirt off from behind, then held tight to his wrists. Ronald froze, in a dream, unable to act for himself.

Two of them hoisted him bodily onto the table. "Upsie-daisy." Two others rolled the girl onto her back. Ronald felt like a puppet, a limp doll, not himself. Red, wet eyes, a face like pounded dough, hair glued to fat cheeks in damp strings: she looked dreadful, nonhuman. Hands were yanking his trousers down his hips, *No*, down his legs, off over his feet.

"Hey. Ain't got no underpants either."

"Like yo mother, Li'l Billy."

"Hey fat man. A little action, hey."

"Whatcha waitin for?"

He buried his face in the girl's hair, so as not to see her, tried not to feel her, but she was warm and breathing and slippery-wet. She stunk of sweat and other men's sex. The whole room was pressing on him to move. He began to move.

"Attababy."

two hundred and thirty-six

"Les help him out."

Hands he could not see pushed against parts of his body from behind, began to coax it up and down.

"*Don't!*" he pleaded. "Please don't do that." He saw an image of himself from above, looked down on his own inept, unwilling heavings, his own fat flesh prodded by black hands.

"Faster, fats. You can do it."

The girl began to respond, to his drugged surprise, perhaps to ease the pain of his load. He felt anxious, even willing now. Blood ran faster, he felt warmer, everywhere — everywhere except there.

"Wassa madda?"

Someone stuck a hand underneath him, from the rear, reached along past his balls.

"He ain't even in."

"Sheeyit!"

He kept trying, tried to blot them all out and fix his mind on the one necessary thing.

"I gotta idear."

Ouch. A quick shock of pain ran through his body, then retracted to a tiny center of sharpness in his rear. *Oww.* Another, on the other side. *Ow.* Another. Another! *OOww!* What the *hell?* "Ow!"

They were jabbing him in the buttocks with something sharp. "*Stop it!*" He lifted himself up on his hands and knees to protest.

"You did it, Goat!"

"Look at that."

With a jolt, he redirected his attention, and realized that the shock waves of pain had filled and lifted his cock. One of the boys grabbed hold of it, and started to direct him in between the girl's legs. He let it be done for him, relaxed his arms and knees, and, once inside her, began to move again.

It was warm and pleasurable, it almost made sense. He moved now with a drugged, self-satisfied consciousness of the place he was in: the moist cave of another's flesh, flesh that responded to his thrust, molded itself about his. The pain in his buttocks, the terror along his nerves, the confusion in his brain were all concentrated now in this single intersection of sweetness and energy. There inside her cunt he lived, in the slippery used passages, and the whole world rocked to the rhythm of his probing.

She moved and moaned, and did something she had not done for any of the others. She clasped her arms tight around his back, her legs around his, the better to meet each of his thrusts with a *push* of her own, a deliciously arousing kick from the hips. She would open her thighs wide, then clamp them tight against his, and roll her body round under his fixed and pulsing prod. At first he was simply, sensually pleased; then shocked at her whorish compliance. Gradually, then faster, then in a heart-drowning rush, he felt himself flooding with tenderness for the girl on whom he lay. Fat and foolish and naked and ugly, she was, yes, but *so was he.* Inhumanly assaulted, degraded, insulted, injured she had been: so had he. He was no better for being on top, no freer for being bigger and harder. Love her, he thought to himself, help her. Be gentle. Be kind. Let her know, even here, that the world is not all animal and black.

The five behind had gone silent as she embraced and aided him, stung with envy perhaps, or finding pornographic relish in their more energetic coupling. But when he slowed to a stop, lifted his face to look into hers, they began shouting again.

"Come on, hey!"

"Ain't no love story, fats."

"You forget how?"

Someone slapped him hard on the ass, shoved him, tried to prod him back into an up-and-down rock. He did move again, slowly, but kept his head lifted this time, and found her eyes staring into his.

Who is rapist, who is raped? his eyes asked. There is room for love, a kind of love, even here in hell. *I'm with you,* he wanted her to read, and she seemed to. If I could I would know you, I would care about your life, I would help you. You would try to help me. They moved more gently together, kissed very softly. Her hands moved up to his neck, fingers digging into the muscles.

The insults increased. Ronald felt himself pricked again with the knife, manhandled about the legs and thighs. But he only controlled his speed and force all the more carefully, measured his movements to what he intuited of her needs, tried to build a stone cell of their two bodies that would wall out the evil and protect them with themselves. Whoever you are, wherever you've come from, wherever you'll go, I want you to know that, now at this minute, I want you, I will tell you things about gentleness and kindness and love.

She clutched his neck suddenly in an iron vise and began to shiver beneath him. He trebled his speed, plunged deeper in his thrust, blotted out reflection in a blind blaze of tightly closed teeth and eyes and mind, till he forced out a release deep inside her, drove out as many pulses as he could, and then swam on the waning ebb of both their energies. For a moment, he tried to believe, two had been one, and the world been made better.

Did she feel it? he wondered. Had he salvaged something for her, too? He lay with his lips against her cheek, penis already gone soft, scrotum squashed against her inside thigh. With the cold suddenness of death, he felt himself pulled down by the legs, *Ayy*, pulled out, off the girl, off the table, onto the floor. His legs would not support him, and he fell.

Someone kicked him.

"On your feet, lover boy."

Two of them lifted him by the arms, shoved him up against the door. The one they called Goat stood in front of him, inches away from his face.

"What the *hell* you think you're doing?"

"What you tryin'a pull, fat man? Huh? What you think you tryin'a pull?"

Ronald stared at him, eye to eye. The man slapped him in the face. He winced with shame and pain, but looked past him to the girl. Don't worry, he thought. I'll be all right. She smiled. She understood.

"You think you some big stud, huh? Big ass man?" Goat flicked his penis sharply with a snapped index finger. The others laughed; the girl too. Nervous she was; hysterical. Ronald tried in his pain to cover himself with his hands, but Goat knocked them away, flicked him again. *Don't* cry out, don't give in, don't acknowledge them, don't show fear. There is a better place. This will soon be all over.

"How you like that, huh fats? How you like *this*?" Grabbing Ronald's bare shoulder, he drove a knee with terrific force into his groin. Gasping for breath, Ronald collapsed against the door. But as he sank, he saw the long-bladed knife lying open on a chair alongside his arm. Quickly he snatched it by the handle and, still crouching in his pain, he faced the lot of them, gleaming knife held out before him.

"Let her go," he gasped out. "Give her back her clothes and let her go."

"You worry about yourself, fella." She was sitting up on the edge of the table. "I'm OK. Mind your own business maybe."

It was crazy. They were all crazy. He reached behind his back for the doorknob, turned it, yanked open the door, ran in red terror into the hall.

Then the girl laughed. A door slammed shut.

He kept running as fast as he could, doubled over, breathing hard, holding tight to a long-bladed knife, a naked man tormented in his gut running as fast as he could along a dark, concrete-floored underground tunnel, trying to escape. In his hand he held a power he had never held before.

He would kill them. He would go back and kill them all, the girl too. Yes, kill her too. He felt the force of the thrust he would use to stab them run along the muscles of his arm. Again and again, he stabbed at the air before him as he ran.

His bare feet ran suddenly into dampness, a wet puddle on concrete, and he stopped, tightened, cringed with the cold. Pulling his elbows close against his body, he clutched the knife against all comers, against all threats. Something fell plop into the water, and he jumped; it ran or swam away. He thought he could make out a small animal in the dark. Cat. Rat.

He explored the narrow space on tiptoe, trying to find the edge of the puddle, but it seemed to have no edges. As he walked on, it grew deeper. Up over his toes, to his ankles. Dimmer came the light: a sewer passage? No. But filth caught about his ankles and toes, wet paper, things. Perhaps something leaking, a broken pipe somewhere spilling out filthy water and things.

God for a flashlight. Not to get out, just to get on, find out where this ends. He would have stabbed the *wall*, but now the walls had receded; the hallway widened into a large unlit room, its floor awash in inches of dirty water.

A burst of noise crashed into his darkness, a great whiny throb from above. It kept up for several seconds, then degenerated into a muted knocking sound, and he felt himself lost inside someone else's mammoth headache, a miserable thought inside someone else's brain, pounded on by the other's pain. The space lit up in a flash, then darkened into absolute black, but in the flash he spied a ladder up the wall just across from him, across a long stretch of water and floor. To get to it; get up, find the one; kill. The noise kept pressing on.

Step by step he advanced, pushing the water and debris away with cold feet, waving the knife in a protective arc in front of him to ward off whatever might be there. The sound grew of a sudden louder, screamed right at his eyes; he screamed back, and in the sudden white flash he saw something standing, tall and huge, white and hairy, just in front of him. Again he screamed, but no noise came; plunged, tripped, was tripped, he fell headfirst into the water. He dropped his knife and began to panic, since *still* no noise would come from his throat! If the other were to turn the lights on and find it before he did? On his knees in the water he swept the damp and crud frantically with his hands, until he ran into the sharp blade itself and seized it hard, cutting the flesh of his fingers and palm. He rose to a crouch, protected again by his knife, and ran toward where he thought the ladder must be. The shape of the other was only inches away, though it made no noise inside The Noise, which was pounding on him now like the great iron clapper of a bell. The wall: where was the wall? So much farther than before.

He touched: ah: hard. Felt his way along, feet, yards, farther: NOTHING. Something ran across his foot, and he yelled. This time he heard his voice, and it reassured him. He scurried back in the opposite direction along the hard wall. Something touched his shoulder, felt down his back, buttocks, legs: another body was pressing against his. Then iron, an iron rail. The ladder. He held onto it with one hand, spun around, slashing out with his knife at whatever it was behind him, then turned back and began to climb up the grooved metal steps that were fitted into the concrete wall.

As he rose, the noise began at last to shape itself into music of a poisonous, seductive, evil kind, and he felt himself drawing nearer to, focusing more clearly on the thing he must do. Twenty, thirty steps he must have climbed, and when the steps ended and he stood again on a dry landing, the music was as sharp as his own blade, his own enlightened consciousness. It was exact, too exact, made up of pulled metallic strings and beaten drums and in the dark heart of it he could hear the cry of a goatish, bawling voice.

He was on another catwalk of some kind now, railed on both sides, and could hear under the throbbing racket the noise of water. He must be near the leak, the spilling water that had filled the area below. He listened to its soothing, voluptuous pour, the great splash down below. Then he saw a red light in the distance, and walked towards it. It grew larger, more red. Under it, a fine yellow-white line of light delineating a door, the closed door of a lighted room. Voices. He stood before the door, then pushed it open.

Four janitors seated around a table stared up, open mouthed. A wet, naked man with a knife was standing at the door.

He saw a row of hooks behind them, hung with clothes of various sorts.

"Those overalls. Give me those overalls."

He waved his long-bladed knife towards a pair of striped overalls hanging on the wall. The man nearest them reached up, took them down, and tossed them to Ronald. None of them had said a word. The din subsumed them all in its dream.

Ronald backed out of the room with his prize, slamming shut the door. He climbed into the overalls, slipping the straps over his shoulders. Too big for his body; the wrong size for anyone. Once clothed, he felt somehow more virgin wet and naked than before, inside this stiff and alien sheath. He shivered, damp and bare, white and vulnerable. Unprotected skin cringed against the touch of rough cloth.

My knife. He pressed it tight against his stomach, inside the overall bib. By now the noise was frantic, the goatish voice screaming out of its mind. He walked in the direction that made the sound louder, impelled towards the center and source of his grief. Yet another flight of stairs, yet another catwalk, a row of shut doors, a tangle of cables; people. Holding the knife tight to his stomach, he walked safely into their midst, through them, past them, unseen. Over ropes, around boxes, slipping by knots of men, protected by a long blade of steel held tight against bare skin. On he crept till the sound came up full, and an ungodly rainbow of orange hit him square in the skull.

He was on some kind of bridge above a stage. A narrow footway of steel tracked between giant cylinders shooting out light. A naked man in overalls. He grabbed for support with his free hand, not his knife-hand, the other, to the handle of one fat black tube. Below, a flame-red beam lurched free. Below, five: Charlie, Keith, Bill (*Brian Jones s'est suicidé*), Mick. And Mick. The Rolling Stones.

The knife they had used on him, down in the basement: even now the blood must be leaving tiny dots of red on the inside of his overalls. But the pain was as nothing inside the other pain, the one he called noise and identified with the noise made by five men now not more than ten yards away. Every vein, pore, hair, inch of thin nerve, each light dot of consciousness was as vividly present as if he were made of glass, and every fragile part, separate and illuminate, was about to be shattered by the noise.

It was more than mere noise, of course; more than *their* futile cawing and pounding down below. It was a malign force larger than anything he could do battle with or even understand. It had been there in the summer heat of a square tower room, at a stifling 4 A.M. in France. Two men in a car. A brother lost. Up on the cluttered catwalk he crouched wet with sweat, suffering, in great anxiousness and pain. Of him too had it been written: "He was exhausted with jealousy, worn out with the gaiety in which he had no part . . . Always with burning cheeks he had stood in his dark corner and suffered for you, you living, you happy ones."

On with the show.

Give it to them, my sad captains, play it hard, play it dirty, push till it clicks, till the juices run. Come on come on come on, *Down* now, Charlie, play me down, Kangaroo. 'At's it: bit o' ass; bit o' leg. Around now, around, have 'em with us, Ah, are they with us? Better'n last house: black bastahd: fuck up my show. Now up. NOW. *UP*. Slap and slap and *whip* it up. Whip! Whip! Oh my aching

> Shoot em dead brainball *jang*lah, yeah!
> Take-kit-teasy / *as* / *you* / *go*

good, good people, good boys and girls. Come to Micky. Come. Down, little Micky: kick, kick, kick, and *step*, feel it: mean it. Ass-to-side, ass-to-side. OK. Keith my love, scream 'er, rip 'er apart: GO!! Blood becomes sound and you GOT IT.

> All yer plate glass WIN-dows!
> Through yer stee-yel front DO-ah!

Oh-ow, am I hot: kiss me Hardy. Danca Pranca Donna Fixen, Donna? No. Marsha. That's all me, baby; right. Down the side, round the back, spread 'em, show 'em, have a LOOOOOOK now. Shattad shattad shattad shattad. Her party, 64, 65 it must have been; Christ what assholes coppers. My MAN Billyboy! Four hundred thou: pull it out, round it up. Going home. A wink to Keith, elbow to Charlie and   thatis

IT! Slooow it home.

Chickie with the tits. Purple nipples. It's for you, chickie-pie:

two hundred and forty-four

did   ja hear a   bout   the Mid night *Ram* Blah
foot print up and down your BALL

Yey-has, big smile for all the weensies with their cameras. How
I suffah. Good crowd you are, people. Feed me, I'll feed you.
Fuck 'em all. Tonight's a ball, tomorrow shit. Way to make a

    And if you evah catch the Midnight RAMBLAH
    Steal your mis tress   undah yoah NOSE

Buckle belts, happy people, here we go. Out: holes wide open,
lick 'em from below. *Right: you* I mean, chickie-chick, on me
'ands and knees for yer, can you dig it?

    Stick ma knife right down YOUR THROAT.

    High up in the shadows of the light-gantry, a man holds a
knife close by his side. He can look down and see light flashing back and forth along its blade as he turns it. A few inches
of flash. Silver, very sharp.
    He holds it tight against his hip, against the cloth of his
overalls, the fleshy ball of his thumb against its edge. Warm in
the palm, now sharp against thumb and side. He squeezes it
like an erection, like a last handhold on life.

    The old chord signal from Keith, five hundredth time, five
thousandth? Which way in. Foot hanging free, testing the air:
double twirl, slap, wee kiss for Littlemick, an'a bounce: a-one;
a-two: one more time, you sodden charlie, beat us in. One
more: beat. At's it. Beat. Evvabody: whump. whump. hump
and ZANG in the ear —

        I can't GET no
        Sat-tis-fack-shun

Oh you lovely people, eat me. Drink me. This is My Body;
This is My Blood.

        When I'm a driving in my *car*
        And that man comes on

                two hundred and forty-five

SCREEeeam blue bloody water. Where to be, millionth time, kick and kick and kick and NO WORDS, now

'Sposed to fire my 'magination

Step it *step* it *step* it round, almost home, kiss for Bill, light's all wrong, goddammit Chip

oh No no no,

Go, Charlie, go

Know *what* I say

Stars, wheels of stars overhead, a free high, pills and wine long gone, all mine, this one, mine and my music, fire from the groin, power from the people; the way it works.

Leap. *Leap.* JUMP!
NOW!

I can't GET no

Through the air and

Satis

Kill

faction